Howl for the Gargoyle

MONSTER SMASH AGENCY
BOOK TWO

KATHRYN MOON

Copyright @ 2023 Kathryn Moon

Howl for the Gargoyle, Monster Smash Agency Book Two

First publication: Dec 5th 2023

Cover Illustration by Sophie Zukerman

Editing by Bookish Dreams Editing and Jess Whetsel

Formatting by Kathryn Moon

All rights reserved. Except for use in any review, the reproduction or utilization of this work, in whole or in part, in any form by any electronic, mechanical or other means now known or hereafter invented, is forbidden without the written permission of the publisher.

Published by Kathryn Moon

ohkathrynmoon@gmail.com

Kathrynmoon.com

❦ Created with Vellum

The unauthorized reproduction or distribution of a copyrighted work is illegal. Criminal copyright infringement, including infringement without monetary gain, is investigated by the FBI and is punishable by fines and federal imprisonment.

Please purchase only authorized electronic editions and do not participate in, or encourage, the electronic piracy of copyrighted materials. Your support of the author's rights is appreciated.

This book is a work of fiction. Names, characters, places, brands, and incidents are the products of the author's imagination or used fictitiously. Any resemblance to actual events, locales or persons, living or dead, is entirely coincidental.

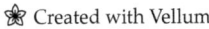 Created with Vellum

To my Patreon babes!

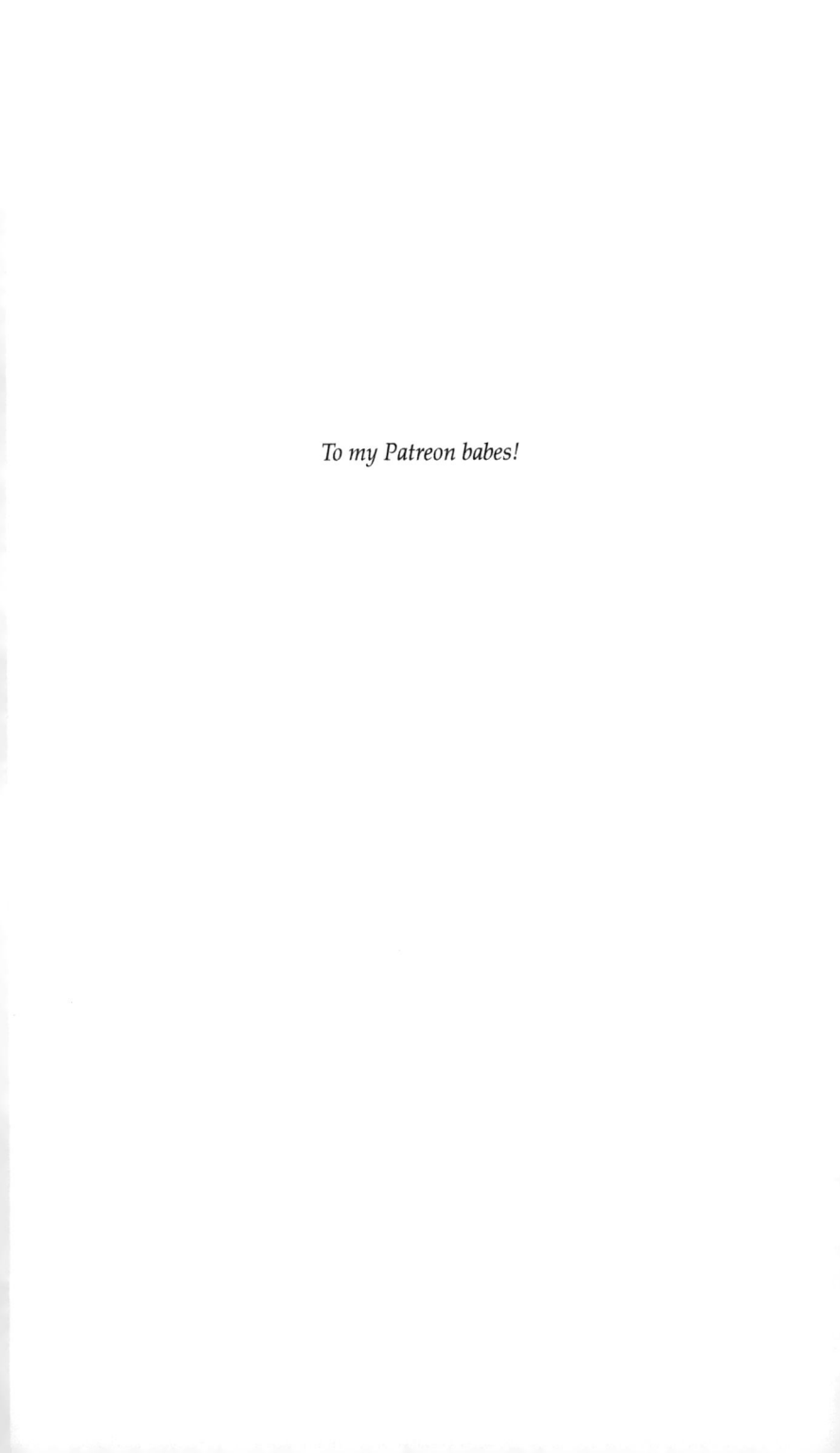

Contents

Content Information	ix
1. Hannah	1
2. Hannah	13
3. Rafe	21
4. Hannah	29
5. Rafe	37
6. Hannah	47
7. Rafe	59
8. Hannah	67
9. Rafe	81
10. Hannah	89
11. Rafe	99
12. Hannah	107
13. Rafe	117
14. Hannah	127
15. Rafe	135
16. Hannah	147
17. Rafe	159
18. Hannah	165
19. Rafe	175
20. Hannah	187
21. Rafe	197
22. Hannah	205
23. Rafe	217
24. Hannah	227
25. Rafe	239
26. Hannah	249
27. Hannah	263
28. Rafe	275
Epilogue	281
Afterword	287
Also by Kathryn Moon	289
Acknowledgments	291
About the Author	293

Content Information

This story was originally shared with chapter by chapter updates in rough draft form on my Patreon in starting in January of 2023.

The Monster Smash Agency series is sex positive and features sex workers as main characters. This does mean that the main male character has sex with other people during the timeline of this story, although it's more background information and there's no on screen scene of this.

Content includes some violence, past trauma, and consensual smut with light kink! You can find more information at kathrynmoon.com

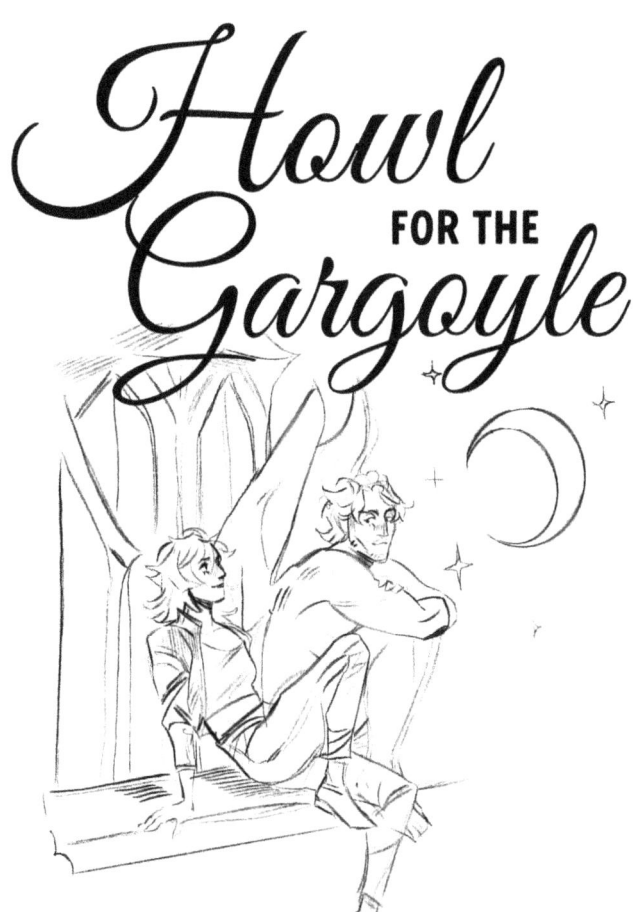

Howl for the Gargoyle

MONSTER SMASH AGENCY 2
BY KATHRYN MOON

CHAPTER 1
Hannah

"I WAS SO resistant in the first year. It was like everything that was new to me, every part of me that had changed, I hated. I drank too much. I considered…" Frank wet his lips, as he did every week at this part of his story. I tensed on the uncomfortable metal folding chair, bracing against a speech Frank never made.

I considered taking my own life. I was afraid I would hurt someone, or worse, turn them into a monster like me.

"I considered cheating on my wife. I thought I was an animal, that I wouldn't be able to control myself. But my wife found this group for me," he continued, chin lifting, eyes glittering with just enough red around the rims to believe it might've been with tears. "And it was here that I came to accept what I am. *Who* I am now. Regardless of how it happened. I am what I am."

"I am what I am," the circle echoed. I mouthed the words a beat too late.

Frank's cheeks pinked. "And there are good parts. The animal in me keeps my wife happy, that's for sure."

I ducked my head, letting my dark hair hide my cringe as the men all chuckled and the other women shifted and sighed and pretended amusement. *Every damn time, Frank.* I wondered if his wife knew how much he liked to brag about fucking her in our support group.

"Thank you for sharing, Frank," said Diane, our leader with the patience of a saint, the voice of a soothing grandmother, and vivid yellow-green eyes that made it obvious to anyone on the street what she was.

Werewolf.

"Thanks, Frank," the circle intoned.

Frank sat, sighing with relief, even after telling the same exact story he shared week after week. He did it for the new folks, he said. I thought he did it for the punchline about his wife.

"Hannah," Diane prompted, and my spine straightened as those glowing, cautionary, beautiful eyes caught mine. "Is there anything you'd like to share?"

I wake up, drenched in sweat, from the same nightmare memory four times a week now instead of five. I'm ruining all my personal relationships because I can't control my moods. I nearly bit a man in a bar who fucked me behind a dumpster before the last full moon.

I shook my head. "Not this week."

Diane's lips pursed, but she nodded, her gaze flicking briefly to Theo, my mentor. Theo was tall, gangly, broad-shouldered, and studious. His eyes remained a relaxed brown, even as we neared the full moon. He was mild-mannered, friendly, almost timid, and best of all, one of the only men in the circle who didn't boast about his werewolf libido or how happy his wife was. To be fair, I'd met Natalie a number of times, and she was far more likely to boast for him, so maybe that was why.

Theo ignored Diane's glance and the circle moved on smoothly. This was our routine. Someone would stand and talk about their life, the ways being bitten had changed their routines, relationships, body, and diet. Eventually, Diane would turn to me, invite me to speak. And every week, I would answer the same: "Not this week."

What could I say that hadn't already been said? I didn't choose this. I didn't want this.

Ian had been a vegetarian when he was bitten, but he'd given into the cravings for meat and was happier for it. Good for him. Nancy had grown up in purity culture and struggled with the sexual urges, but now she was carefully and consensually discovering sexual pleasure and open relationships. Good for her. Ben's ten-year relationship with a girlfriend dissolved when he realized he was experiencing mating urges for his best friend, and now he was proudly queer, happily mated, and thriving with his newly and voluntarily turned werewolf fiancé. Good for them.

I hated being a werewolf, hated the monster who turned me, hated that I was now like them. Good for me.

"I am what I am," the circle recited, and this time I didn't bother moving my lips.

"SORRY," I said the second Theo joined me at the fruit plate. The big crowd was surrounding the charcuterie board, and I had this smaller platter more or less to myself.

Theo shrugged. "You know it doesn't hurt me if you don't want to talk with the group." He took a breath, and we said the next words in unison. "It hurts you."

Theo snorted and shook his head. "I'm getting predictable."

"I'm not ready," I said.

Theo nodded. "Okay."

He was twitching, leaving the pause between us, waiting for me to bite.

"But?" I cued.

"But the premise of the group isn't that you wait until you're healed to share. It's that we heal together *by* sharing. You might find more benefit if you…participated." Theo laughed at whatever he saw on my face, and I fought to smooth my expression as he raised his hands in surrender. "Fine. End of lecture. Natalie would like you to please come over and work whatever magic you have on our son."

My shoulders softened, and I smiled in earnest. Theo and Natalie's home was like a fairy tale to me, idyllic and comforting in its simplicity, a cozy redstone in Albany Park. Before meeting Theo, it'd been a long time since I'd spent time with a family like theirs, a world away from my father and his legacy.

"The magic is that Emmett terrifies me," I admitted to Theo, who grinned and nodded.

"He takes after his mother. Natalie loves a captive audience too. So you'll come?"

I nodded. I was greedy for time in the busy, loud, narrow little house at the edge of the city. Perhaps Theo knew, because he'd invited me after every weekly meeting this past month.

"Come on. I'll drive," Theo said, eyes lifted over my shoulder to wave at the crowd behind us.

Our meetings took place in a Boystown community center, with bright glass windows facing busy Clark Street. I pulled the hood of my coat up out of habit, ignoring the glare of the bright autumn sun. I didn't get recognized very often, but it was never a comfortable experience when it did happen.

"How's the band?" Theo asked as I followed him around the corner to the side street where he'd parked his car.

"Shit," I admitted. "The label is still pushing the tour, and I'm not ready."

"And the others?" Theo asked, a gentle reminder that there were others involved, as if I could forget.

My bandmates were dealing with their own fallout to my becoming a werewolf, their careers on hold while I tried to keep my head above water.

"Their patience is running out too," I said softly. "I think even Kiernan has started looking for other gigs."

"It bothers you," Theo noted.

"He has to work. I understand that," I said.

"You can understand it and be bothered."

We stopped at Theo's old Jeep, a mellow shade of gold, prone to acting up in traffic jams on the Dan Ryan. I glared at Theo as he rounded the hood of his Jeep, and he flashed an undisturbed grin at me. My lips twitched.

"Fine. I am understanding and angry that he'd consider leaving the band," I said.

The doors unlocked, and we both slid inside.

"I should tell Diane how much better you are at her job," I muttered, pulling the seatbelt on.

"Diane was my mentor when I started attending the group."

I stilled, watching him turn the key over in the ignition three times before the Jeep finally roared to life. "You never mentioned that."

"I was really young. It's been... It'll be twenty years this New Year's," Theo said, gaze distant for a moment before he started to maneuver his beast of a car out of the tight spot.

It was Theo's story, offered shyly on my second visit to the support group, that had convinced me to keep attending.

Theo had been sixteen when he was bitten. It was New Year's Eve and he'd had too much to drink, so instead of calling his parents or risking driving, he'd decided to cut through the woods between his friend's subdivision and his. He hadn't remembered that it was the full moon, and by law, werewolves were required to seek secure locations for their transformations. But the one who'd bitten him had been loose in those woods, another teenager taking chances, an unfortunate circumstance between two people too young to feel the weight of consequences yet.

I wondered about the werewolf who bit me. Were they

young? Had they been newly turned, not understanding what would happen? Was it my fault for not noting the calendar better, for building a running habit that left me vulnerable on full moons, for trusting that werewolves would follow the law to find shelter and that those rare, unfortunate incidents of someone being bitten were too statistically low for me to worry about?

Or had my instinct that night been right—had I been hunted down in the cemetery, targeted, terrified, and turned intentionally? Had the shivers running down my spine been a warning from my subconscious? Had the barely audible snarls I'd heard under my own panting breaths been a teasing hint, meant to unsettle me?

Theo's thoughts seemed to turn with mine. "Any news from the police?"

I shook my head. "They're not really looking."

"They are," Theo said, glancing at me as he drove. "They are. Ray is looking."

I ducked my head. Ray was the single werewolf officer assigned to my case, a fifty-plus-year-old silver wolf all set for retirement until I'd landed in his case files, bloodied and bitten and baffled. Theo was right—Ray gave a shit about me, about my case. He'd scented my torn clothes and the bite marks on my shoulder and ribs and hip. The sheer quantity of wounds was stronger proof that I'd been turned intentionally. He'd spent weeks digging through files. There simply wasn't anything to find.

"He calls to check in more than my dad," I admitted, flashing Theo a half smile.

"My parents didn't adjust until I was living on my own, really," Theo said.

I wasn't sure that sounded like they had adjusted, or if they'd just had the burden of a werewolf living with them lifted from their shoulders.

"It's not that. It's just how...Virgil is," I said.

Virgil Darwood. Lead singer of The Knock 'Em Deads, one of the world's most enduringly popular rock bands—Dad said the *greatest* rock band—style icon, rebel to all things domestic, and somehow…my dad. In the ways he managed to be.

"But he calls too, and that's big for him," I continued before Theo might express concern or sympathy. Dad called to talk about the reunion tour, to let me know when he'd be passing through or stopping in Chicago, to ask me how it was going with the label I'd signed with—a small label, one that hadn't seemed curious about my father or our relationship or any potential collaboration. And at the end of the conversations, he would check in, in his small way.

"How's it going, howling at the moon?"

There was no view of the moon in the safety cubbies provided at the shelter.

We reached Theo's house, the drive passing in easy silence, and Natalie was already standing in the doorway, a sticky handed Emmett banging on the glass, sobbing.

"It's not too late to turn back. She's going to pass him to you the second you walk in," Theo warned me.

I laughed and slid out of the front seat, Emmett's wails audible from the sidewalk. "I signed up for it."

I knew Theo and Natalie both had siblings, but I was aiming for the role of Emmett's best auntie, and if that meant getting peanut butter in my hair, so be it.

"Hammah!" Emmett screamed as Natalie opened the front door, his short chubby arms straining for me.

"I made the mistake of trying to bribe him with the promise of you coming over," Natalie said. "He doesn't like waiting."

I managed to catch Emmett as he dove out of his mother's arms and latched his surprisingly strong arms around my neck, still weeping, as I followed Natalie inside.

"Sorry, buddy, your dad drives like an old man," I said.

Natalie snorted and shot me a grin over her shoulder. "I told Theo we were having mushroom risotto, but I didn't tell him he was making it for us. I need wine on the couch, and Emmett needs to show you every single one of his toys."

Emmett grunted in what might've been agreement, and Theo called to us from behind.

"Like I didn't know what your plan was all along!"

NATALIE GROANED as she stretched out on her couch, and upstairs something thumped heavily from Emmett's room. I glanced up at the ceiling when Theo came racing down the hall.

"I'm on it," he called.

Natalie opened one eye and smirked at me, her hand trailing down to the floor to find her wine glass. "He knows he's on duty, don't worry. And I've got the monitor on," she added, flashing her phone to show Emmett digging around in his trunk of toys.

"Long day?" I asked.

Natalie shrugged. "Actually, it's been this week. Toddlers have nothing on prima donna clients who don't know what they want but love to make demands. Theo's making me mute my emails until Monday morning. He's a good mate."

I stared at her, sipping my wine and chewing over a question I'd been wanting to ask. She stared back and raised her eyebrows, silently daring me.

"Do you want Theo to bite you?" I asked.

Natalie smiled. "Sometimes. But it's a big adjustment, and Emmett's still really young. And then if we had another baby, they'd be a werewolf by birth, and that might... I dunno, kids are never on equal footing anyway, but that just seems like it would complicate dynamics. Theo knows we're mated, so I know we're mated. I'm okay being human until the timing feels right."

I didn't know any other mated couples, not both parties, but it made sense with Natalie and Theo. They had a harmony I'd never seen in a relationship before, although I hadn't grown up around the best models. My parents had never been more than a brief fling, and my mom had decided that raising me was going to be her entire life until suddenly, in my teens, she died in a car crash. And then I'd been Dad's problem. He'd had plenty of marriages and relationships, but none of them remained harmonious for very long.

"Is it my turn to ask a personal question?" Natalie asked, a dangerous gleam in her brown eyes.

I laughed and reached for the wine bottle. "Wait, I need this first."

Natalie scooted back against the arm of the couch, pulling her black braids over her shoulder and staring at me like a predator who'd caught sight of prey.

With a full glass of wine in hand, I nodded for her to continue.

"Theo won't ask, but I will," she said, and I tensed. "How are you dealing with the full moon hornies?"

I blinked. "The what?"

"The full moon hornies," Natalie repeated, just as Theo thumped down the stairs.

He ran for the kitchen again, pausing to offer a quick "he's fine" through the open doorway.

"Thanks, babe," Natalie called back, then lowered her voice, leaning toward me with narrowed eyes. "You know, the days leading up to the full moon when the libido gets all spiky."

I knew it was normal—I'd found all the information I could possibly want on it online—but it wasn't something we talked much about in the group, aside from a few innuendos and carefully phrased mentions.

"I… Not great," I admitted, wincing.

Natalie frowned. "Cut me off if you want—I promise I respect boundaries—but I'm going to keep poking for now. You're gorgeous, so I'm sure it's not a lack of opportunity?"

I opened my mouth, closed it again, glanced up at the ceiling, waited for my buddy Emmett to create another distraction, and then decided that *if* I was going to get this off my chest, Natalie would be the friend to share it with. She was in a specific compartment in my life, a new one, but it was the one best prepared to help.

"I keep…getting too rough," I said slowly, not making eye contact. "I don't mean to, but the second I'm—"

"Invested in the moment," Natalie supplied, polite but blunt.

I shrugged. "Yeah. As soon as I stop thinking and just enjoy it, there's…scratching or biting, or I'm shoving some poor guy around—"

"If he's not into getting tossed around by a beautiful woman, that's on him," Natalie said with a dismissive sniff.

Theo appeared in the doorway, staring blankly at us. "I don't want to be here, do I?"

"No," Natalie and I said at the same time.

He nodded and disappeared again. "Working on the garlic bread now."

"I'm so glad werewolves don't have the garlic thing," Natalie mused before returning her focus to me. "So you're talking about human men, right?"

"Werewolves aren't… I'm not—"

Natalie waved her hand. "Fair enough. I was just thinking… You know, there are so *many* species, and a lot of them are more durable than humans."

I fell silent again. I knew she was right. I passed plenty of other species on the street every day. There was a ghoul in the garden apartment of my building. I just existed in a social circle made up of…almost entirely humans. I frowned at the realization. Until I'd been bitten, until I'd joined the group therapy circle, I'd really *only* known humans.

"I might know what you're thinking about now. Until Theo and I met, my social circle was pretty limited. Actually, before my friend Sunny mated an orc, Theo and my social circle was still kinda human and werewolf. It happens," Natalie said. "You just need to know where to hang out. Neighborhoods have some species oriented bars, but there's also places that are kind of free-for-alls."

I cleared my throat, and Natalie paused. "You've given this some thought?"

Natalie laughed, the sound warm. "It's not like I'm regularly worrying about all my friends' sex lives," she said.

"Lie," Theo shouted from the kitchen, destroying the illusion that this conversation was really private.

"Okay, fine, I occasionally worry about my friends' sex lives," Natalie huffed. "I'm very nosy."

I fought my smile, but it broke free, and Natalie sagged in her seat. "So what, I go to a bar and I ask people...how durable they are?"

Natalie laughed and shrugged. "Honestly, that's a really good pickup line for some species, I bet. Sure. You do that, or...you hire a professional. My friend worked with the Monster Smash Agency, and she had an amazing experience" —Theo's steps drummed down the hall as he approached— "and said it was super safe and super specific to her needs."

"Just to clarify, those needs were very different," Theo said, staring hard at his wife, eyebrows raised up above the rim of his glasses.

"Go back to the kitchen," Natalie and I said in unison.

Theo sighed and marched away.

"Isn't that kind of for, like...if you have a species specific interest?" I asked.

Natalie shook her head. "I may or may not have run this

scenario by a former employee, and he said it's totally normal for werewolves to book with them for exactly this purpose."

It was a little odd to hear the phrase 'totally normal' applied to the idea of booking a 'monster' sex worker to help me get through my werewolf libido issues around the full moon, but maybe it made a kind of sense.

Natalie clapped her hands together and threw her feet down to the floor. "There, I made my pitch. Theo's definitely going to pretend he didn't hear a word of this. Now you just get to think it over, and if you wanna ask questions or pretend this never happened, that's fine."

"I'll think it over," I said, rising with her. "And maybe also pretend this never happened."

"Someone come and taste test this risotto," Theo said.

"You go. I'll go get Emmy," I offered. I could use a moment before facing Theo after that conversation. I didn't have a frame of reference—somehow, for all his indiscretions, I'd managed to be the only kid Virgil ended up with—but I was pretty sure Theo was like a brother to me, and we were both going to be embarrassed.

Hire a sex worker. Hire a sex worker who was…durable. My nose wrinkled as I considered the idea, taking the stairs up and following the notes of some kind of musical toy running low on its batteries.

I didn't mind Natalie overstepping to suggest the idea, but I wasn't convinced it was for me. Still, I needed a solution. Maybe it was time to really consider my options.

CHAPTER 2
Hannah

THE CITY GLIMMERED outside of the tall glass windows of my new gym. I'd joined a couple months after being bitten, when I'd finally accepted that I was too paranoid to go running outside again. The scents were too strong inside, and the sounds buzzing out of headphones and television screens mounted in every corner were too busy in my head, but at least I could get back to running—although running on a treadmill made me feel like a hamster on a wheel.

Behind me, reflected on the windows, I watched a young man lifting weights, our eyes occasionally meeting in the glass. He looked like he might be in college, or a little older. His body was big, with thick muscles clearly built by the many hours I'd seen him here. He was not my type at all—too young, too physical, too smug as he stared at my ass while I ran.

But today, he smelled fucking fantastic.

The full moon was tomorrow.

He grunted as he hefted the weights from the floor, and my feet stumbled as the sound seemed to stir through me. The sound he'd make thrusting into me. The sound he'd make as his back hit the ground. The sound he'd make as my nails raked down his chest and my sharp canines nipped at his throat.

I closed my eyes and tried to ignore the heat in my core, the ache in my breasts, the slow pound of my blood in my ears.

Being an animal was humiliating. The fact that a grunt or a whiff of good sweat would turn me into a panting, dripping mess of need was galling. He was just some guy, cocky and unfamiliar. I used to grow aroused over coffee conversations, over slow kisses and whispered words, and, at my basest, over really high-quality porn. Now one *ungh* and a little pheromone magic, and I was going to—

I hit the stop button on the treadmill, bracing my feet on the edges, catching my breath as the room seemed to keep running past me, my brain tricked by the hour of stationary momentum. I was growing slick and ready, blood rushing to my sex, and my hands tightened painfully on the bars on either side as I watched the young man's reflection in the mirror, flexing and posing, his gaze holding mine.

Animals. Understanding what came next on an unspoken level.

I turned slowly, searching the gym. I was the only woman here at the moment. Women traveled in packs for their own safety, usually. But I was the predator. I'd learned how to sniff out other werewolves, and there were only humans here. Humans and me.

The younger man set his weights down, combed his fingers through bright gold strands of hair, tensed his arm for show. He thought he was catching me, snaring me, and maybe he was. Maybe it was mutual.

I walked toward him, my chin high as his eyes narrowed and his thin lips curved up. He opened his mouth for small talk.

"Come on," I murmured, grabbing his wrist, tugging gently.

It was his turn to stumble, to gasp, to follow. He let out a brief laugh.

"Yes, ma'am. Where are we—"

I walked faster, and he fell silent. *Good boy. Just shut up and get fucked. Don't ask questions.*

The women's locker room was just there in the hall. A few of the other men shot my victim a wink, a grin, but no one said anything. There was some kind of universal boys' club for gym bros getting laid.

"What if someone comes in?" he whispered as I threw the door open.

"They won't," I answered. They hadn't two months ago, the last time I'd pulled this stunt.

He reached for me then, hands grabbing at my hips as the door clicked shut. I tensed as my back hit his chest, humidity and heat from our fevered skin making the air around us muggy and thick with our scents.

"You want this?" he asked, kicking his hips forward, grinding his crotch into my ass.

My chest rumbled, even as I rolled my eyes. *Unfortunately, yes*, I thought, my body rocking back into his. I reached back, grabbing onto his T-shirt collar and pulling hard. He grunted and followed the yank as I twisted out of his hands, turning us to face one another. Pain pricked at my fingertips, claws wanting to burst out and dig into this man's flesh. I pushed at his chest with the heels of my hands, ignoring the human part of me that bristled at his smug laugh. He stumbled back, bumping into the benches between the rows of lockers.

I stepped forward, ready to push him to sit, to step out of my tight leggings, to shove his shorts out of the way, but he shook his head.

"Nuh-uh, you're not in charge, babe," he said, his voice crackling as it lowered.

We reached for each other at the same time, and this time

he had the upper hand, spinning me to the lockers. The metal doors rattled as my palms hit them, bracing.

"This'll be easier," he said, more to himself than me.

And then his fingers were hooking into the back of my leggings, pulling them down over my ass, his body crowding around me to push me closer to the lockers. A handle ground into my hipbone, and I snarled as he wrestled with his shorts, fumbled between my legs. He was right, this would be easier. Quick and simple, and we could redress faster if we were caught. But I didn't like having this stranger at my back.

I bucked as he tried to guide his cock into me from behind, and he laughed again.

"Jesus, you're so fucking wet. Horny little bitch, aren't you?"

"Fuck off," I growled, throwing my elbow back into his chest, needing to take control of the moment again.

He grunted, and I knew at the moment of impact I'd used too much strength. It was too close to the full moon. I was reckless. This was stupid and dangerous. He fell back, and I heard the shout, the bang, the slap of flesh on tile as I turned. I'd shoved this poor guy into the benches and sent him toppling back.

"What the fuck?!"

His pants were down, cock out, and his legs were sticking up, his shoulders and head against the lockers. He'd tripped backwards over the bench and crashed down to the floor.

"What is your problem?" he shouted, groaning as he tried to sit up.

"I'm" —*a monster*— "sorry," I gasped out.

I didn't wait for him to get back up. I was still throbbing, and the wolf in me wanted to climb over the bench and hold him there, ignore his protests, and take what I needed.

But the full moon was tomorrow, not tonight. I used the fragile fraction of control over myself I did still have. I pulled my leggings up and ran, grabbing my coat from the locker I'd stashed it in, and rushed out of the gym before he'd gotten himself up off the floor.

It was late, and pure luck to see a cab approaching the corner of the block. Salvation. I leapt off the sidewalk into its path, heart clapping in my chest as the tires screeched to a stop. There was no sign of the gym security or the man I'd essentially attacked coming from the building, but I tore the door of the cab open and clamored inside. I was more afraid of myself than I was of the consequences.

"Sheffield and Roscoe."

The cabbie's eyes flicked up, widening slightly. He knew where we were headed, and I wondered if he might throw me out. I wouldn't blame him. I could run there, but the cab would be faster, especially when the driver wanted me out of his backseat as soon as possible.

The light turned green, and he was rough on the gas pedal. I collapsed with a sigh, my eyes falling shut.

"Full moon's tomorrow," he said, as if to reassure himself.

"It is," I said quickly.

The rest of the ride was silent. My hands slid into my coat's pockets, finding my wallet and phone with a faint and absent sense of relief. I'd find a new gym. I'd stop going out before full moons at all.

I would…

I had put Natalie's suggestion out of my mind, blaming it on the wine and Natalie's enjoyment of throwing people off their guard. But what if…?

The cab pulled to a stop outside of the shelter, an old hotel that'd been reinforced and refurbished to suit werewolves on a full moon. I paid with a generous tip and slid out the back of the cab.

"Be safe," the driver called, and I'd already shut the door before I could answer.

The lobby of the Lakeview shelter was deceptively cozy, like it was trying to fool those of us who visited that we might just curl up in one of their plush green wingback armchairs and sleep through our transformations.

"Checking in early?" the young woman behind the counter asked as I stepped inside. I nodded, and she offered a sympathetic smile. "You're not alone. Seems like a rough one."

I pulled my pass card out of my wallet, pressing it to the scanner.

"Welcome back, Hannah," she said. "Room 1630 is ready for you. Need anything before the morning meal?"

"No, thank you."

"Have a nice night."

I pressed my lips together to keep from screaming, and breathed the carefully balanced sterile air of the shelter to help cleanse my lungs of the lingering tickle of that man's scent. The elevators were silent, waiting on the ground floor. No one who checked in early would be out of their rooms for at least a couple days. I rode up, listening to the jangle of machinery, the steady beep of passing floors.

I'd stayed in the shelter for my first month after being turned, adjusting to my newly heightened senses in an environment built for them. There was a comfort to returning every month, and also heartache. I was this creature now, not Hannah.

The sixteenth floor was quiet, and I used my card again at the door to my room. I paused on the threshold, door open. The room smelled like me, my beast. Sweat and blood, but something warm and familiar too, comforting at this time of the month. I stepped inside and didn't bother turning on the light, the beam from the hall growing narrow as the door swung shut.

Open closet to the right, bathroom to the left, my nest of cushions and blankets around the corner, the rest of the room open, room to pace and growl and howl. I left my coat on and walked to the nest, sinking down to my knees, sucking in lungfuls of my own scent. It was safe here, but barren too, more like a jail cell than a shelter.

There had to be something better than this.

CHAPTER 3
Rafe

I STRETCHED MY WINGS SLOWLY, grimacing at the ache in the joint on the right wing. I was getting too old for being thrown around. I'd be healed in the next couple of days, as long as I didn't have another appointment like last night's, but it seemed like more often than not, I was walking out of work with a wing sprain.

I twisted in front of the MSA bathroom, checking the scratches on my back from the chimera I'd just partnered. She'd left her mark for sure, but the red welts were already shrinking. I'd be fresh and ready for whomever came next. No one wanted a punching bag who looked like he'd already had a few too many turns.

The locker room door opened, and I lowered my wings, folding them close to cover my back as Edgar, one of the vampire partners at the agency, walked in. He was pink-cheeked, freshly fed, and walking a little bowlegged.

"You look like you had fun," he said.

"My client had fun," I allowed, reaching for my shirt, ignoring the pull of sore muscles as I twisted my arms back to fasten the clasps around my wing roots.

"That's right. You get the rough ones," Edgar recalled.

I grunted. "I can take it."

"Astraeya's looking for you," he said, reaching into his locker as he unfastened the campy black cloak from around his shoulders.

I paused with the buttons down the front of my shirt. Astraeya only needed us when we had complaints or new clients.

They can't define it, but they know something's off. What can we change?

I'd tried to play my part. I'd been hyperaware of my behavior ever since the comments had started coming in. I'd lost two clients in the past five months. If I lost another one, got another mild remark about my lack of commitment to the experience, MSA was bound to consider letting me go.

"Thanks, I'll find her," I said, nodding to Edgar as I grabbed my bag and headed for the door.

Weekends at the agency were busy, the back halls—the ones for staff, not clients—full of various species running from one appointment to the next. I reached Astraeya's door and found it hanging open, filled with a fluffy golden and brown figure.

Elias—moth fae, part-time partner at MSA, vague and occasionally a snob—stood leaning against the doorframe.

"Don't you have a business to run?" I asked as I reached the door.

"Nightlight's doing great, Rafe, thanks for asking," Elias answered, his glittering antennae twitching in my direction before his head followed, slowly turning. "I'm bored. Trying to get Astraeya to find me someone."

"I've found you several someones, you just turned them down," the succubus said, her chair turned to face the door, bare feet wiggling against the floor, black high heels abandoned to the side.

"Someone more interesting," Elias said, shrugging.

I leaned back, some of the dust in the ruff of fur around his throat puffing into the air. It was an aphrodisiac, and it tended to accumulate on the moth fae when they neared their quarterly mating cycles every few months.

Astraeya didn't bother disguising her eye roll. "I'll see what I can do. Have you considered maybe *you* ought to be the one hiring the service?"

Elias's nose wrinkled, and his antennae drooped. "I can find my own sex. I want work, a fun puzzle."

Elias was the only partner at MSA who picked his own clients. I didn't know what he meant by *puzzle*, but Astraeya must have, because she nodded and started to turn back to her desk.

"I'll watch the intake forms for you. Come in, Rafe."

Elias huffed at the dismissal, but he moved out of my way and left without another word. I rounded Astraeya's desk, helping myself to a seat.

"Good news or bad news?" I asked.

"Good, I think," Astraeya said, glancing up from a folder, not pretending to miss the meaning of the question. "You got good scores on your last appointment, and I have a new client for you."

It *was* good news—a relief, actually. *Be excited*, I reminded myself, but the words rising to my lips weren't thankful.

"What kind of client?" I asked.

Gargoyles and humans were technically compatible, but it required a lot of control on the gargoyle's part to keep from hurting the human. I wasn't interested in holding myself back, so I skipped the human clients who flocked to MSA.

"Fairly new werewolf," Astraeya said.

I reached a hand up to cover the frown that fought its way onto my lips. "Full moon?" I asked.

"Before, yes."

I nodded. I'd had werewolf clients in the past who needed to burn off libido and aggression before a full moon. Sometimes during. They were rough and dominant, and seemed to enjoy the freedom that came with an impervious partner—

claws, fangs, and all. I'd just had one werewolf client cancel with me recently because they'd mated. It made sense for MSA to find me a new one. And with recent cancellations, I couldn't really justify turning this one down.

"Less than a year into her transformations. She's...she's interesting," Astraeya said, flipping through her file. "In the initial interview, she was primarily concerned with not being able to hurt her partner. We did an early arousal response test, and it's definitely not typical werewolf stimuli, although we are a couple weeks out from the full moon, so maybe that's not so present at the moment."

My hand slid from my mouth. "What do you mean?"

Astraeya's mouth hitched in a half smile, and she shrugged. "See for yourself."

I leaned forward, accepting the tablet from her and turning it to face me. MSA tested arousal in clients by giving them visuals and text scenarios, asking for them to be rated on a scale of one to five.

"Conversation," I said, eyebrows bouncing up. "She's rating higher in mental stimulation than visual?"

"She made us some notes about what seems to trigger her libido near the full moon, but her normal scores are definitely more intellectual than physical. Romantic too. Intimate. I'll make sure she does a second stimuli response test the day of the appointment, but I figured I'd show you these since they're outside your usual wheelhouse."

I smirked. "Ast, are you saying I'm not intellectual?"

"I'm saying your clients don't usually give you a lot of opportunity to make conversation," Astraeya pointed out, clicking sharp black painted nails against her desktop. "What do you think?"

"Think?" I asked, and then scoffed at myself. Maybe I *wasn't* very intellectual. "About the client?"

"Do you want to work with her, or should I ask someone else?"

I pulled up the file of the images she responded most positively to. Muscular and veined forearms, lush interiors, a full window of plants, a throat exposed by an undone collar. I paused on one image. It was a plate of food, fancy like in some kind of five-star advertisement or cookbook, roasted carrots and a dribble of sauce, puffs of puree dotted around the edge.

"I want to work with her," I said.

This was what Elias was talking about when he said he wanted a puzzle, I realized. A woman booking a sex worker to help her deal with new aggression and hormones, but one who got turned on by fine dining, luxury, and small physical details. If her werewolf urges weren't leading the way for our appointment, I would have to…seduce her. I couldn't remember the last time I'd had to put much effort into prepping a client.

My eyes narrowed as I flipped through the images again.

Shit. I might need to ask Elias for advice. He'd be so smug.

NIGHTLIGHT WAS PACKED. Elias was right, it was doing great. I wondered why he bothered even looking for work with MSA when it was obvious he could survive on his businesses alone.

I squirmed on the outrageously comfortable bar stool, keeping my wings tucked close so they didn't take up too much room in the crowded bar, and tried to fight down the jealousy burning through me as I watched Elias scoot past the bartenders and head in my direction. His bar offered more room for the employees, I noted. For his wings. Even my own would fit behind the massive bar top our friend Khell had built.

"Repeat the question," Elias said, setting down the tray of pub food I'd ordered and a drink I definitely hadn't.

"How do *you* go about…making your clients, uh…aroused?" I asked, and it wasn't any easier to get out for being the second time he'd made me ask.

Maybe the drink would help. I grabbed the glass and took a quick and full swallow, my eyes widening as I trapped a cough in my chest, the alcohol scorching its way down into my belly.

I gasped as the alcohol settled. "What the hell was that? Gasoline?"

"Ghost Pepper moonshine," Elias answered, lips twitching. "You passed the challenge. Your tab is on the house."

I narrowed my eyes at him, but the alcohol did have a curious reaction in me. I didn't get drunk without a lot of effort, but the burn of the pepper mimicked the warmth most people might feel from a good whiskey.

"How have you been at MSA for almost a decade without taking a course in seduction?" Elias asked.

I rolled my eyes. "I have taken them…years ago. But mostly I have to focus on stunt work, self-defense, and role playing." Elias blinked, and I shrugged, helping myself to a fried spicy pork egg roll. "You have your work, and I have mine."

"Right. Well, make conversation, but not too much. You should mainly be listening," Elias said, eyes tipping up in thought. "Compliments are good if she responds positively to them, but you want to invite touch. Initiate it slowly or casually at first."

I thought of the image of the forearms and flexed my own on the bar top, studying myself in a way I hadn't in years. Were my arms and hands attractive? Or too big?

"Make eye contact. If she's uncomfortable, back off. If she's enjoying herself, move forward." Elias shrugged. "There's a higher art to seduction, but I can't imagine Astraeya would match you with someone who would pose that much of a challenge."

"She's a new werewolf," I admitted, and Elias scoffed.

"There you have it then. Your clothes will be shredded within minutes. What are you worried about?"

I nodded along, saving myself the trouble of speaking by eating the feast Elias had left in front of me. He was probably right. Astraeya liked us to be prepared and cautious, and it was her job to be thoughtfully protective of the clients. But I'd worked with werewolves before, especially around the full moon, and seduction hadn't played much of a factor. Even if it did now, I wasn't a complete amateur. I was a trained professional. Everything would be fine.

I WINCED into the icy bite of Chicago's night, flying toward downtown instead of home. Night flying in Chicago could be treacherous, the wind brutal and surprising, but I liked the challenge, and I'd only ever slightly damaged a piece of architecture, with no one the wiser about the chipped facade. I swept my wings out, coasting well above the halting traffic on Kinzie Street toward the high clock tower of the Wrigley Building.

Gargoyles liked good architecture—it was in our slow-moving blood—and Chicago had some of the best in the country. I'd grown up in New York in the highest apartment my parents could afford in Queens, but I hadn't caught my breath in a city until I'd moved to Chicago. I didn't know if it was the ever present weight of the lake to the east, or the sly and deceptively friendly energy of the city, or the diverse range of rich architecture, but I'd known the first day that I'd found my home.

My wing hooks caught onto the ledge of the clock tower, and I climbed up, pausing to catch my breath and give the sore joint of the right wing a moment of rest. I could see my destination from here, facing northeast, glaring down glittering Michigan Avenue to my favorite building in the world.

Tribune Tower, crowned golden against the dark rust sky, winter clouds stained with the light of the city at night. The building knew its best feature, lit it up like a beacon at night, calling to a creature like me. I rolled my shoulders and my neck, stretching and contracting my wings. I wasn't allowed up here, but the city had better things to do than chase down winged species who helped themselves to the best views of the city without paying the tourist fees. I just needed to make sure I didn't linger.

I bent my knees, leaping hard into the air, snapping my wings wide. Chicago didn't disappoint, wind catching and thrusting me backwards. I grinned at the force. It was hard to budge a gargoyle, but the lake's weather always made a good effort. I beat my wings, and then the Windy City and I were in cooperation, harmony in flight. Five minutes in the peaks of the Tribune Tower—one of the condos that faced the lake that was almost always unoccupied, neglected by its owner—and then I'd be on my way again. Maybe ten minutes.

Maybe fifteen.

CHAPTER 4
Hannah

THE WOMAN SITTING in the velvet armchair across from me was exceptionally pretty, with moon-pale skin and pink hair and wild violet eyes. She had petite horns and exquisite bone structure and a pair of lips women would pay a great deal of money for. I'd never met a succubus before, and this one was doing her best to put me at ease, but I found myself fighting the urge to unleash my claws and scratch them over that pristine skin.

I wasn't sure if it was sexual interest raging through me, or an aggressive response to a threat, but I wanted to escape her presence *immediately*. If this was any indication of how my "appointment" was going to go, it might be time to cancel.

"Your partner today is a gargoyle. He might look vulnerable in his flesh form, but it will put you on even footing with him. You can scratch, but you can't do any harm, and he's worked with werewolves before," Astraeya said.

I nodded and glanced at the vast windows to my right. The downtown MSA location was a cross between an upscale hotel and an apartment building. Astraeya and I sat together in an unoccupied lobby bar on street level, and the Chicago work denizens were pouring out of their offices and marching down the sidewalks just feet away from us. But the windows were mirrored—we couldn't be seen.

"I've updated your file, but do you have any questions for me?" Astraeya asked.

My head was scattered. The full moon was only two days away, and I wasn't sure if it was because I was nervous or this moon was going to be worse than the last, but all my instincts and cravings were running wild.

"Can he get away, if he needs to?" I asked.

"He can. Gargoyles are nearly impenetrable, and they're exceptionally strong, although he won't use that strength unless you ask him to. Trust me, your partner is prepared, trustworthy, and skilled. You are safe with him," she said.

I glanced down at the pretty marble table between us.

"And he is perfectly safe with you," she added, softly.

My shoulders drooped slightly. I was torn between racing to the elevators to take them up to the apartment where I'd meet this gargoyle, and curling up on this silly velvet settee for a cry and a nap.

"Here's your monitor," Astraeya said, setting a small wristband down on the table between us.

I'd been assigned an alert word if I needed to contact an outside agent and interrupt the appointment. There'd be every security measure and precaution that left the control of the appointment in my hands. She'd described them to me several times.

It just wasn't my own safety I was worried about.

Gargoyles are made of stone. MSA knows what it's doing, I reminded myself. *That's why you're here.*

I reached for the wristband and slid it into place.

"I can take you up now, or if you'd like a drink first—"

I shook my head. "Is it… Can I…go up on my own?" I didn't dislike this woman, but I wasn't sure how I'd fare stuck in an elevator with her. I wanted to be calm as I approached my appointment, not simmering with irrational aggression.

Astraeya paused, pressing her lips shut and considering. She glanced down at her tablet, eyes narrowing slightly. Maybe it was a rule that guests had to be escorted, so they didn't interrupt anyone else, or find themselves in a place they didn't belong.

"I think that would be fine," she said at last, pulling a thin plastic card out of her pocket, with a glossy back and a hint of metallic glimmer. "Room 1603."

I flinched as I reached for the key card. 1630. 1603. Did they... No, it was just an ugly coincidence. The card was cold against my fingertips.

"I'll send the number to your wristband so you don't forget," Astraeya said, mustering a smile for me.

I bit my tongue against the urge to answer. I wasn't likely to forget.

Succubi could sense arousal in others, but I wondered if the same was true about other emotions. Could she taste my anger, my desire to lash out or to run? I lifted my bag from the floor as Astraeya rose from her seat.

"I hope you have a wonderful time, Hannah. MSA is on hand at any time if you need anything."

"Thank you," I forced out, and she nodded, backing out of the way, giving me plenty of room to walk past her.

My spine was painfully stiff as I moved, the vulnerability of having someone at my back scratching at all my overstimulated instincts.

"You'll have fun," she called as I marched toward the hall with the tidy line of elevators.

The words were confident, and there was a friendly glitter in those gemstone violet eyes as I glanced back. She was petite and beautiful, wearing sky-high heels and a silky wrap dress. My brain couldn't make up its mind on whether she was friend or foe. I nodded once and made my escape.

The tiled walls of the hallways reflected a darker version of myself back at me, flecked with copper and brass. The interior of this not-quite hotel was luxurious, a blend of dark art deco and mid-century modern, with crisp metal details and a romantically deep color palette—a clear message of glamor and class to reassure clients or oppose any negative stereotypes. If I'd been less full of nerves, less wound up by the half-hour meeting with the succubus, I might've appreciated it more. Instead, what I appreciated was the readily available and blessedly empty elevator on the ground floor.

Polished brass doors slid shut behind me, and I closed my eyes before I could get a look at myself. I knew what I would see: a haggard and pale woman, clothes slightly askew from fussing with fabrics that felt all wrong on my skin today, long dark hair in tangles from the Chicago wind.

At least that I could fix. I combed my fingers through the strands, taking grateful breaths of the clean, still air.

Be calm. Breathe.

The ride was smooth and over too soon, a gentle chime rousing me before the purring mechanics of the doors opening. I stared at the empty hall, its wallpaper a shade of wine or black cherry, and nearly let the doors shut again before lunging forward, dragging my bag along with me. I'd brought a change of clothes and a bottle of wine, although I wasn't entirely sure why. Was it a gift for my 'partner,' or potential consolation for me if this went awry?

A discreet plaque on the wall offered directions between the four apartments on this floor, guiding me down a brief hall. I stood in front of the door, allowing my heightened hearing to eavesdrop. Nothing. Quiet. I had the key card in my hand, now slightly sweaty, but I was resisting the urge to knock on the black door in front of me.

Then there was a *clink* from inside, like porcelain or metal, and a quietly muttered "Shit!"

My lips twitched, and my shoulders softened. I hefted my bag higher and tapped the card to the door handle before I could talk myself out of it.

Beep.

A sudden inhale.

The door opened silently, and I paused on the threshold. The walls were eggplant purple, and the fat glossy leaves of a happy rubber plant stretched around a corner. The room ahead glittered with pretty decorative objects, and broad windows showcased Chicago's bright blue and orange evening sparkle. There was even a promising glimpse of a massive round cushion or stool of some sort, and then—

"Hello."

Gargoyle. *Handsome* gargoyle. The figure standing before me was as tall as I was—no, taller, I realized as he approached. He had dark curls, nearly hiding a pair of small horns above his temples, and a large, ever-so-slightly crooked nose. His eyes were dark and his lips were full and his shoulders were broad. And a pair of purple-black wings, darker than the shade of the walls, hid the rest of the apartment from me.

The distinct Adam's apple in his incredibly defined throat bobbed, and my mouth watered. I didn't know what to expect from a gargoyle, and I'm not sure I would've known the difference between him like this—with warm tan skin and a stretching smile—and a demon or imp or some other winged species.

Except that he was so remarkably beautiful. Not perfectly so, which was better, but with artistic details. As if he *had* been carved out of stone by a thoughtful hand, one who wanted beauty in character and vice versa.

"I—"

I was saved by whatever might've come out of my mouth when he reached me, a large hand outstretched toward my shoulder.

"Can I help with that?"

He was clean shaven, skin so flawless I was jealous for a moment. I hadn't recovered from my surprise, still busy studying him, and his fingers hooked under the strap of my bag. My hand snapped up, grabbing his wrist, and we froze for a moment, gazes locked. His skin was cool to the touch, smooth, and incredibly firm. My fingers squeezed, but there wasn't any give, and I turned my head to see it for myself.

"Sor—" He started to pull away, but my grip was enough to hold him in place.

"Thank you," I said, shrugging out of the bag and releasing his wrist. The bag dropped for a moment, the awkward exchange leaving us both off-balance it seemed, but then it was caught, the leather twisting around his hands.

"Heavy," he noted, eyebrows bouncing. "Did you bring toys?"

Could I have? "Wine," I answered, covering for the drop of my jaw.

The gargoyle helped himself to flipping open the bag. *Impertinent*, I thought. The wine bottle stuck out of the top, and he didn't dig further, pulling it free and reading the label. His lips curved, and his eyes flicked to their corners, glancing at me. "Better than the stuff the agency leaves for us. I'll show you around. I've been...*investigating*."

I blinked as he turned around, those massive gray wings folded against his back. The skin was leathery, spines darker, and there were sharp hooks at the top of the bent joint. They were the most *non*-human part of him, and I was fascinated by the sight of them. Were they as inflexible as his skin? Cool like stone?

I followed after a beat of staring, a little too absorbed in him to take in the space. He paused by a door and set my bag inside, and I watched his forearm flex, muscles and veins so clearly defined they were like outlines, a sketch filled in with muted colors.

"Investigating? You haven't been here before?" I asked, peeking inside of the room. It was the bedroom, the mattress huge and elegant and promising. But the ceiling was mirrored with antique glass, and I flinched and turned away.

The gargoyle laughed. "No. Well, to this building, yes, but not a suite like this. They really decked it out for us. To be honest, I'm a little nervous."

My eyebrows rose higher. "Nervous?"

He flashed me a grin, temporarily halting my steps. The living room of the apartment was open and wide, full of art and plants, one of which was a fern that was brushing against this man's wings.

"Lots of trinkets," he said, nodding toward a side table where a glass vase and a brass statue sat next to one another. "I know the agency doesn't mind if we break things, but they're usually more careful about the potential for us to get…rowdy."

I was standing next to a huge round platform of a stool that rose and curved and fell like waves. It was big enough for me to spread out across and share. That was almost certainly the intention behind an otherwise ridiculous piece of furniture. All around me were fine details and little works of art and vibrant greenery. The room was spacious, but designed and decorated to feel decadent and informal.

The gargoyle waggled his eyebrows and then his wings spread, briefly and not even to their full breadth. He slapped into a plant with one wing and knocked against a painting with the other.

I let out a strange sound, a laugh and a sigh and something like panic in the mix. "I see," I said, and I did. If I was pushing this gargoyle around like I had with the man at the gym, we'd make a mess of this place. My muscles started to tighten again, worry setting back in, and I forced myself to speak, to find a distraction. "What's your name?"

"Raphael," he answered, wings rustling as he started to turn. One hand was clutched around the neck of the wine bottle, and he waved it between us. "Now? Or after?"

After...? Oh.

He trailed into the next room, and I paused, sliding out of my coat, draping it over a vintage chair that was clearly meant for style more than a function we could offer it.

"Now," I said, a little too breathless.

CHAPTER 5
Rafe

SHE WAS NERVOUS, quiet. I'd filled the pauses with chatter at first, talking mindlessly, probably making things worse, but I'd managed to slow myself down since then.

Mostly listen, Elias's voice reminded me.

But there was nothing to listen to. She followed, watching me, and I waited for her to strike, to stop staring at my throat and my arms and to lunge, to help herself to what she'd paid for. Instead, she propped up the wall at the entrance to the glossy, overly decorated kitchen, and watched my arm flex as I cranked the corkscrew. She was attracted to me, at least. Subtleties may not have been my strong suit, but I knew how to read that much from a person.

The silence was starting to grow awkward, her eyes drifting down to study her own feet—never a good sign. I couldn't listen if we were both mute.

I considered a dozen things to say. Tell her she was beautiful—she was, all androgynous elegance and sly features. Ask her how she was feeling. Talk about the damn furniture again. None of the sensible options were what came out.

"What are you most nervous about?"

She looked up in a rush. *Hannah*. A breathy name, suited to whispered secrets.

And I went and bluntly spat out the most awkward thing I could think of.

"I...I've hurt men in the past. Not seriously, and it was always an accident," she hurried out. Her voice was warm, husky. "But I just...don't want to try this and find out I still can't control myself."

My clients booked me because they didn't want to control themselves. They wanted to be rough and merciless, without the guilt. And the secret of my work was that it *did* hurt. They couldn't break my skin, and it took a great deal of effort to bruise me or sprain my muscles. But there was no magical guard against the sensation. I could be hurt, but not harmed.

Her cheeks were pinking, high cheekbones turning away.

"Would you feel like it's safe to say that I know more about werewolves than you know about gargoyles?" I asked.

She startled, and I caught her attention again, her eyes narrowing and brow creasing slightly. "Ye-yes? Probably."

I poured us each a glass of wine, but she was out of reach and I was forming a plan. The glasses remained on the counter as I crossed the stone kitchen floor. She straightened against the doorframe as I neared, stiffening as I crowded closer, her eyes starting to glare. I stopped just inches away from her.

"Shove me," I said.

"What?"

She had a slight underbite that would suit her werewolf form and was more noticeable as she jutted her jaw out in defiance.

"Shove me," I repeated, more gently. She'd taken off her coat, revealing a sleeveless blouse and long, muscular, slim arms.

Test touch, retreat if she responds poorly.

I circled my hands around her arms loosely, stroked down their length, and watched her pupils bloom. A shiver rolled through her as I reached her wrists and drew them up to my chest, planting her palms there and then letting go.

"It's okay," I said, but I barely got the words out before her hands were pushing at my chest.

She grunted, but it was her back against the wall, not mine, and I didn't budge. She gasped and stared up at me, lips parted.

"Harder," I said, trying not to tease or to smile.

She frowned and shifted, planting her feet, palms incidentally stroking against my chest through my shirt. I liked the splay of her fingers on me, and it was a rare kind of power to watch one of my partners struggling against me, cheeks burning red with effort, body tense and strong yet unable to gain ground. I was supposed to let them win, not prove my own strength.

I covered the backs of her hands again and then slowly, tiny fractions of pressure at a time, allowed myself to be guided backwards. She was sagging by the time I stumbled into the wall at my back, glare dissolving into confusion as I let her shove me with hardly any effort on her part.

We stopped, my wings and back pressed to the mirror-tiled kitchen wall, her breaths panting and body crowded up against mine, eyes blinking as she studied me.

"You didn't come here to learn control," I said, holding those warm hands over my chest, fighting the urge to laugh as her eyes narrowed again. "You came to let go of it. You can push me around as much or as little as you want to. Just let me know."

She pushed once more and stared as my head thunked back, the sound of stone against glass muffled by my thick hair.

"And you play along?" she asked.

I shrugged. "Whatever you want, Hannah."

Was I imagining the pressure of her leaning in, or was it

there, a brush of her hips against mine? She was tall, and the fit of us was easy, tempting.

Her lips pursed and her gaze trailed over my shoulder as she thought. I circled the backs of her hands with the tips of my index fingers. She frowned, and I wondered if I'd miscalculated, failed in seduction and lost myself another client.

"Whatever I want," she repeated, the words low and silky.

Sharp pricks nicked at my chest, and I glanced down from her face to her hands, watching black claws extend from under her close clipped nails. I laughed as they caught in the fabric of my shirt, scratching through to my skin, and the sound was a warning whistle of friction. There was a challenge in her stare when I looked back up, but only because she didn't understand. She thought I'd draw a line here?

I arched an eyebrow, and then my breath caught as those claws ran down my chest, through my shirt, shredding it open. The sound of her scratch was awful and exciting at the same time, abrasive and electrifying. She didn't even know yet how *gentle* she was with me.

Her gaze tried to fall to my chest, to assess the damage, and I caught her chin, holding it high, admiring the natural defiance in her stare.

"Let me look," she growled.

"You didn't hurt me."

"That's not why I want to look," she said, and her smile was crooked.

I laughed and released her, and those claws were more gentle as she pushed the ruined fabric out of her way and off my shoulders, yanking free the snaps around my wings. MSA had a special budget for my clothes because of how frequently they were torn off. She could shred as much as she wanted. Her claws had retracted, hands returned to human, and her fingers tickled against my skin, my stomach jumping and clenching under her touch. Her eyes hooded as she stared at me, at my chest. I had the strangest urge to stretch and pose for her.

I was used to playing the part of prey for my clients, but I'd never really felt cornered before, not like this. Not studied, as if this woman was planning a detailed attack rather than giving into uncontrollable lust.

"You're very beautiful."

The words stunned me. They were observational, quiet, and wholly unexpected. I opened my mouth—maybe to thank her or reply the same—but then her stare caught mine, brown eyes glowing with intent.

I braced myself, but her attack was slow, a liquid rise of her body, leaning into mine, silk fabric rubbing against my bare chest. She paused, nose to nose, but it wasn't hesitation. She was thinking, considering, watching me still. Who was seducing whom exactly? Because I was trapped, waiting for her to strike.

Anticipating the moment.

Caught off guard when it came, arrived just as I was at the edge of impatience.

Her lips pressed openly against mine, but it wasn't a kiss. I was glad I was made of stone and could hold my breath, could hide the stutter of my heartbeat in the solid cage of my chest. Our eyes slashed back and forth against one another, fencing gazes.

She's waiting? She's teasing, I thought.

And then dark lashes shuttered her stare. The brush of her mouth was a caress, and I opened my lips to her at the faintest urging. Warm hands stroked up to my shoulders in time with the hot tongue sliding in. She growled and retreated at the first touch of my cooler mouth, and then she was back, forceful and hungry, slick and searching.

Kisses were rare in my work, usually served up as apologies, afterthoughts to a rough session. Requested from me as proof of absolution. Almost never the precursors to sex.

This woman tasted good, my own tongue growing brave and needy too. Her arms were strong as they wrapped around my neck, stealing me closer. My shirt was tangled around my arms, buttons still holding at my waistband, and her fingers slipped under cotton to grip at my back, to stroke and explore.

She moaned, and the sound was rough, her hips pushing against mine, rocking slightly, begging. I grabbed her ass through thin pants, and then her legs were around my waist. She was slender and tight with muscle, and I stepped away from the wall, holding her wrapped around me as the kiss raged on.

I scratched my teeth over her bottom lip, and she gasped, pulling away, her face now above mine. I grinned up at her, her pupils blown black and irises now a brighter shade of amber. Her canines were slightly larger and sharper now, a little slip from woman to werewolf showing in her arousal. She glared, one hand reaching for my jaw, grip commanding and pushing my head back further. My cock stirred in my pants, and my eyes widened slightly.

"You're right," she said, words rasping. "I came to fuck."

Yes, ma'am!

Her mouth slanted over mine, still holding me in place for the kiss, and she shivered as she tested a drag of sharp teeth against my firm lips, the friction surprising her. I realized I was waiting for her to shove me to the floor, or to throw me against the wall, and the moment wouldn't come.

She came to fuck, Rafe. Get to it.

I recalled the layout of the apartment we'd barely explored and headed for the closest destination. My fingers tightened on her ass as I carried her out of the kitchen and into the living room, and she bucked in my arms.

My shins hit the edge of the huge cushioned whatever-the-fuck-it-was in the center of the living room. Sex ottoman, probably, and one specifically designed for exactly this moment. I bent, and she released me, falling back into the cushions, hands immediately flying to the waist of her pants.

"Undress," she gasped, focusing on her own clothes.

But I wanted to watch. I wanted to tease her until she tore more of my clothes off. She was dressed like one of the downtown business crowd, all in well-tailored black, but I caught a glimpse of vivid raspberry lace as she shoved her underwear down, kicking the tangle of clothes off with her short boots. Her pussy was on display for me, a tidy trim of dark hair at the peak of mile-long lithe legs.

She paused as the heel of her boot thunked against the floor, huffing and sweeping her hair back.

"It's my turn to look," I said, knowing it would antagonize her, wanting to draw her out.

Discovering I was wrong, once more.

Her eyes rolled, and she leaned back against the upward wave of a cushion, spreading her knees apart. "Fine. Look."

The lips of her pussy were dark rose and slightly swollen, stretched just enough to give me a glimpse of darker, sweeter fruit. Would she let me…

One slender foot stroked the outside of my thigh as I stared, and I chuckled, reaching for my own belt. She reached for the buttons of her blouse as I stripped, peeling away her shirt to reveal a lace bra in that same shade of rosy red. Her breasts were small, dark nipples full and round behind the lace. There was a flush staining her chest, matching the twin spots high on her cheeks, but there was no proof of embarrassment in her expression otherwise.

I stood before her, naked, and let her look her fill. Her head tipped, resting on the knuckles of her hand.

"Are all gargoyles so perfect?" she asked, but she was reaching for me, and I wasn't inclined to tell her that I was on the shabbier end of the gargoyle scale.

Her claws were back, scratching against my hip, dragging me down to kneel between those long legs. I braced one hand above her shoulder, and here in the center of the room my wings were able to relax and stretch for the first time. Her eyes watched them over my shoulder and I used her distraction, poising myself at her entrance.

Her breath hitched at the brief kiss of cold stone, eyes widening and flicking to mine. I pushed, and her eyes fell shut on a moan. Her nails dug against my hips, and she guided as I let my weight sink me in, hissing against the heat of her.

A soft snarl vibrated in her throat as her hips lifted to meet mine, her head falling back.

"Fuck," she breathed out.

She was slick and scorching and already starting to squeeze around me.

I watched from above, slowing the forward drive of my hips to savor the moment. The taut and stretched shape of her, back cresting over the rise of the cushion, breasts now displaying tight tips pressing into the bright lace of her bra, long arms and legs splayed and tense, muscles coiling. It wasn't a view I'd often get of my clients and I held my breath, afraid to break the moment, knowing she'd steal the reins back from me.

Wet, hot lips kissed the base of my cock, my body nestled against hers, and her head lifted again, eyes bright and wild.

"What the *fuck* is with your magic cock?" she gasped.

I barked out a laugh, not expecting the question, and drew out a few inches, her gaze dropping and then growing huge, staring at the textured flesh, raised and swollen scars drawing vines around my length.

"We carve our stone when we come of age," I explained. "It's tradition."

Her mouth hung open, and a cry of pleasure fell loose as I thrust in again.

"I'm glad you like it," I said, and the words were true.

She huffed, licking her lips, and I tensed, knowing what came next. Her smile was fanged and feral.

"'Like' is an understatement," she said before she snapped her arms around me and threw me sideways.

CHAPTER 6
Hannah

I WAS MAKING a mental list of what MSA hadn't prepared me for.

No one had told me a gargoyle would be so damn pretty, the sight of a smile would make my brain dry up. No one mentioned *carved dicks* that teased you from the inside out. No one mentioned my partner would laugh and grin as I threw him to the side and rolled us until he was flat on his back with his wings spread. That I would sit on that delicious cock and find myself breathless and torn between trying to see how hard I had to scratch this perfect chest before I made marks, or licking every inch of flesh beneath me.

The city glowed outside, night settling in and leaving the world a dark glitter, the cut gem of illuminated windows. Raphael looked even better in this light, shadows highlighting all the heavy definition of his muscles. I planted my hands on the chest I literally *could not* stop touching, and glared down at that cheerful grin.

He was stupidly beautiful and so at ease in this moment that I'd found so terrifying and vulnerable. Did I want to erase that smile or take a photo of it like a souvenir?

"Does this hurt your wings?" I asked. I had too many

questions, and I was too impatient to ask most of them. But this one mattered to me.

He shook his head, smooth hands stroking my sides. His hands were huge, wrapping around my hips until his thumbs pressed over my pubic bone, just shy of slipping down to my clit. I hoped they would.

"This is fine," he said, just a hint of mocking in his tone. He lifted me up with too much ease, and the rub of his cock inside of me made me shudder. "Take what you came for."

My face heated at the words, the blatant invitation, the obvious reminder that this was an appointment for *fucking* and I didn't need to worry about his feelings.

You can't harm him.

I didn't want to. I wouldn't. I just—

We both groaned as I sank down again. Stone curls. Stone *fucking* curls on his pubic bone. I ground in place, and he hummed and sighed, chest rising and falling under my palms. It felt good to him, or he was good at pretending. Either way, it felt fucking fantastic to me. His skin was smooth, and the curls were dense and resistant without being painful, more like silicone than stone. I stayed in place for a selfishly long time, and he didn't grab at me and force me into motion.

Finally, it clicked.

This was for me. He was here, *willingly* for me. I didn't know if it was part of the act but he even seemed to be enjoying himself.

Take what you want.

So I did. I bounced on his length, gasping with every stroke inside of me, with every circle of my clit over those thick and heavy pubic curls at his base, that had just enough give to keep from bruising my tenderest flesh. His hands helped me make a rough rhythm of the movement. Up, down, grind. Up, down, grind. Our breaths chorused with the motion, his grin ever present. I scratched at his chest with every rub of friction between our bodies, my eyes growing heavy, my entire focus on the burn of my thighs and the heat where we met.

The piece of furniture we were on started to move. It was subtle at first, a little shift, a squeak of a leg against the floor, and then more obvious the harder I fell into this gargoyle, the more determined I got as I thrust against his hips. We were scooting across the floor, the thump and scratch laughable if not for the urgency.

Knees braced behind my back, and then Raphael was bucking up to meet me, the impact heavy, shooting out to my toes and up into my head.

"Fuck!" I grabbed his shoulder and drew him in, gasping as his mouth found my breast through lace, sucking roughly with lips firm enough to pinch.

He released me, and I closed my eyes against the stare he offered up. "That's it. That's it, fucking take it."

I clapped a hand over his mouth, and he laughed but fell silent. I didn't need encouragement, I just needed this—this motion and pressure and the rough and almost stinging clap of skin to skin where we met at our cores. His mouth was cool and wet against my palm, tongue licking in a circle that had a curious and incredible effect on my insides. I slid two fingers into his mouth and we both groaned as he sucked them eagerly.

I almost fell still, staring at him, marveling. He was so pretty like this, eyes half-lidded and mouth pursed obediently around my fingers. He took over the work of our fucking, and I let my breaths hiccup and gasp, the cord stretch between his tongue teasing me and his cock filling me.

My free hand slid into his hair, curious and testing, and his curls were thick and hard to comb through, heavy in my touch. He groaned as I pulled on them, eyes slipping shut, and the sound slid through me, a warning flutter in my core.

I drew my fingers from his lips and then slipped them

between us, working my clit and falling forward into Raphael's chest as the first shudder of pleasure crumpled my strength. His mouth found mine, tongue stroking in, a soothing contrast to the fever of the rising release. I clutched the back of his head, and one of his hands joined mine between us, picking up my work when the wave hit, making it suspend and carry me as I cried out. My legs and arms tangled around him, my body surging, fighting the pleasure at the same moment I tried to grab it tighter, make it permanent.

Lips trailed over my jaw and down my throat as the strength bled away with the storm, leaving only a drowsy and soft relief behind, tickling warmth racing through my veins. Leathery wings blocked out the light of the city, blanketing me as the room turned, as soft fabric brushed against my back. Raphael was still thrusting, shallowly and slowly, and I bit my lip when his touch grew to be too much, pulling his hand away.

He stilled, above me again, and my head cleared slowly. He wasn't grinning now, but I thought there was still a hint of humor in those eyes.

"Feel better?" he asked.

I grunted, but I wasn't going to deny that he was right. All the simmering irritation from less than an hour ago was now brushed away. I hadn't been this relaxed since…since before I'd been bitten.

I ignored the surprise on his face as I pulled him down, kissing that absurdly perfect mouth, brushing my nose against his.

"Bring me the wine," I said.

THE BEDROOM WAS full of candles, and Raphael took the time to light them all as I settled on the bed and drank my glass of Cabernet Franc and enjoyed the view. He hadn't dressed, his cock was still mostly erect, and his ass was a goddamn masterpiece, only slightly curtained by his folded wings. I'd been a little turned off by the idea of a mirrored ceiling at first glance, but now I was considering the advantage of being able to watch that ass as Raphael thrust into me, and the concept was promising.

I stirred, shifting against the bed, letting the embroidered coverlet brush against sensitive skin.

"You said you know more about werewolves than I know about gargoyles," I said as he blew out the match between his fingertips—burnt down farther than any human might be able to stand.

He turned to face me, and I reminded myself to get it together and quit gawking at his magnificence like a teenage girl in front of her celebrity crush.

"Werewolves and vampires are…set apart from other species. Gargoyles are gargoyles. We were never human. Same with orcs and fae and all sorts of others. We're raised navigating the diplomacy between species, and it helps to know as much as you can. Humans…haven't quite gotten there yet," he said, shrugging before crossing to the bed. "So yeah, I know a fair amount about werewolves—strengths, weaknesses, how the full moon affects you."

He didn't point out the obvious; that I knew nothing about gargoyles.

I twisted, setting my glass down on a side table, and then rolled to my side. He stretched out next to me, long and perfect and new all over again. I tried not to stare at his dick, but I couldn't resist a glance.

"I always thought werewolves got a raw deal. Strength, sure. But then you only get to shift once a month, and it comes with all sorts of other bullshit," he said, waving a hand in the air. My eyebrows rose, and he froze. "I mean, I'm sure it's—"

"Fucking awful, you're right," I said softly, relieved to say so, to not be in a group therapy sharing circle where everyone always seemed to try and find some sort of positive. Before he could answer, I changed the subject. "I scratched you."

I reached out to the spot on his chest, a slightly raised and pink mark.

"It'll fade soon," he said, catching my hand in his, his thumb digging into the center of my palm and creating a surprisingly erotic warmth in my core.

"You're made of stone, but your skin responds to scratches?"

"Gargoyles are made as dense as stone, and when we shift our skin hardens to a similar texture as stone. But no. Obviously, if we were really made of stone, we wouldn't be walking, talking creatures," he said, shrugging and planting my palm over the scratch mark. "We wouldn't feel sensation. Which I do, of course."

I recalled his groan as I'd pulled on his hair and smiled, sliding my hand down his chest, over the stern cut of his muscles, to the perfect nest of tidy dark curls around the base of his cock. Raphael hummed as I pushed my fingers through, the heavy spirals resisting me harder than the waves on his head. His breath hitched, and his unflagging cock twitched.

"How do you cut your hair?" I asked, the idea popping unbidden into my head.

His eyes crinkled in the corners as he laughed. "Um, chisel. But like pretty much all things gargoyle, it grows really slowly. I haven't cut my hair in four years."

My eyebrows bounced. His hair hung a little long around his ears, that was all. My fingers circled his cock and I thought about his words, searching absently over the decorative design etched into rigid flesh.

"You didn't come, did you?"

He blinked at me, then shook his head. "Don't take it

personally. Like I said, gargoyle physiology doesn't do anything quickly."

I nodded. It would be an advantage in his work too.

"Refractory period's not bad, though. We got lucky with that," he continued, eyelids growing lazy and tongue flicking out to wet his lips. I was still stroking him, his chest rising and falling at a slightly quicker place. I wasn't touching very firmly, just exploring, which meant he was sensitive.

Which meant I *could* hurt him. But sensation and damage were different, I supposed.

"Hannah," he whispered, flexing his hips forward into my grip.

I smiled and tightened my grip enough to be intentional, listening to the catch of his breath, finding my footing in the moment at last. I was still relaxed, sated for the moment, but it'd been such a long time since I'd had sex for more than necessity. Once was not enough.

I released Raphael, holding his stare as I stretched out on my back, and he followed in a liquid motion, a wave following my body onto shore. His wings stretched slightly, the sound of them like heavy vellum pages unfolding, and his face hovered over mine. Above him, our reflections glowed on the bed. I lifted my knees to frame his hips, watched the glide of my hands up his ribs and under his wings to map his back.

"I like the view," I admitted, aware of my own smile and surprised by the sight of it.

"So do I," Raphael murmured. "Grab a wing hook if I get too heavy."

And then he lowered down on top of me, stealing my breath with his cool weight, catching my bottom lip with his teeth, and reclaiming my attention from the mirrors above. His tongue traced my mouth, slipped in and out, teasing.

"I like the wine," he breathed.

I lifted my chin for another kiss and pulled his waist closer until he was just shy of crushing me. My mind went blank to everything but the feel of him, the bite of his hip bones in my thighs, the prick of his hard nipples against my breasts, the outrageous ridges of his back under my hands.

He barely moved at first, one arm sliding under my ass to position me for the gentle nuzzle of his cock against the lips of my sex. He was stunningly heavy on top of me, kissing me with nips and licks and delicate presses until my head was dizzy trying to predict what came next. When he started to glide between my thighs in earnest, rocking us together for pretty friction, I realized I didn't care. He could do what he wanted with me, as long as he didn't stop. My werewolf approved of all his methods.

"You should come this time," I gasped, pulling away from the kiss, finally setting my eyes on that view above again.

His ass dimpled as he thrusted gently, teasing my clit and getting those perfect carvings on his dick wet. I slid my hands down to memorize that clench with touch too.

"You might regret saying that," he said, pausing and kissing my jaw.

A challenge. My claws appeared and I dug them into his ass, learning how much force it took until I pressed tiny dents into his flesh.

"Do it," I ordered, turning my head to find his stare. "Fuck me until you come."

His moan was a full body vibration on top of me, hips bucking in my grip just enough to find my entrance. My own cry joined his as he slid into me. I was going to write an entire *album* about that cock.

A HALF-DOZEN POSITIONS LATER—BECAUSE I kept finding new places to be sore—the tapered candles had burnt down several inches, and I was at the edge of my sanity.

I whined and clawed at the bedding as Raphael grunted and gasped over my back. His wing hooks were rooted in the mattress, his hands searching and soothing under my stomach. The sheets were soiled with sweat and release—mine, not his—and pulled up from all but one of the mattress corners.

But the gargoyle was starting to crack.

Not literally.

I snorted into the pillow at the idea of his stone form cracking—if anyone was cracking up, it was me—and Raphael shuddered and wrapped his arms around me, hips moving in a sudden storm.

"I'm—I'm close," he rasped.

Thank god, I thought, giggling mindlessly again. I didn't *regret* inviting this insane marathon—I'd never come so much in my life—but if he would just *stop moving* I was sure I would fall right to sleep.

I arched my back, and he let out a long and beautiful moan to echo in my ear.

"Can I—Fuck, Hannah—"

His shattered voice was *so* gratifying. I wondered how often gargoyles came. I couldn't imagine masturbating for hours just for one orgasm.

"Can I shift?" he asked, voice cracking into a whine.

I answered, not thinking or understanding what the words might mean. "Of course."

He gasped and pulled out of me abruptly. I sighed, sagging on the bed, eyes falling shut, brain long since evaporated, and deliriously imagined for a moment that the night was over.

Then frantic hands rolled my limp body onto my back. My eyes opened as I grunted in protest, and then my breath caught.

Raphael was a *gargoyle*.

I mean, he had been from the start, but—

"Oh my god," I whispered, taking in the (not really) stone form kneeling between my legs.

He makes more sense like this, I thought blearily, stunned by the sight of his perfect form now set in shades of gray, his arms darker and weathered compared to his chest. And then any thought was wiped away as he scooped my hips from the bed and plunged back inside of me.

We shouted together, my hands finding the strength to grab onto his forearms as he pulled me onto his cock, then pushed me away. He was moving my body rather than his own, I realized, careful not to slam me onto his length, his grip tight but not painful. I couldn't catch my breath and I didn't care. He was so beautiful, head thrown back on a melody of moans, throat flexing, candlelight painting the polish of his hard skin gold.

"*Fuck*, Hannah, oh god, I—"

He bowed forward and I braced for the crash of him, but he landed gently, cool lips kissing over my ribs and breasts, suckling briefly on my nipple. I gasped at the strong pull, the purse of stone around tender skin. Raphael's head turned and he rested his cheek on my chest as he groaned.

"So good. Fuck, fuck, I'm going to—"

I was exhausted, wrung out, boneless, but triumph burned through me as Raphael fell apart. I reached up and tested his hair, harder to grab onto than before but not impossible. I pulled, and he bellowed and stiffened, eyes wide and startled. His wings beat, huge gusts of air blowing out half the candles, and he finally bucked into me, grinding those dense curls into my weary clit.

I came anyway, a shadow of pleasure, the last dregs my body could manage. Just enough to squeeze on his length, making him choke and shudder, as ravaged and ruined by one orgasm as I had been by handfuls.

"Hannah!"

Somehow, my name on his lips, desperate and stunned and grateful, made me blush. Luckily, his eyes were squeezed shut and it was my secret to keep.

CHAPTER 7
Rafe

"NO TOUCH."

I paused, my mouth hovering over Hannah's still swollen sex, sunlight hidden behind heavy blackout curtains, one final candle still burning near the door.

"Not even a little morning thank you?" I asked, grinning.

She hadn't so much as budged in the night, although she'd let out a few fairly adorable growls in her sleep.

She didn't respond, and I bent my head again, pressing my lips to her clit in a chaste kiss. She grumbled but didn't move, and I continued, slipping my tongue out to stroke her folds. I'd been wanting to taste her since she spread her legs and gave me that look on the sex ottoman in the living room, and I hummed thoughtfully as I finally got my chance. There was a bit of mineral bitterness from me, but something musky and feminine and animal too. I opened my mouth wider, staring up the length of her. I circled my tongue around her opening and fought my smile as one dark eye opened just enough to glare at me.

"You don't have to do any work," I said against her pussy.

"I don't know if I have it in me to come again," she said, and I tried not to feel too smug about how rough her voice was this morning. "But that does feel nice."

Aware that my cooler temperature would probably be soothing, I kept my licks and kisses light, cleaning away the taste of me until she was rich and thick on my tongue.

Last night had been…different.

Fucking awesome, I corrected myself. It wasn't as though I'd never come with a client before, but it'd been more about lucky timing than the actual goal. And there weren't many species aside from gargoyles who wanted to be fucked nonstop for hours. I burrowed my tongue into Hannah's core in gratitude for her patience last night, and this time I managed to draw out a gasp, her hand clenching on the pillow behind her.

This was different too. The opportunity to be gentle, to please sweetly, while my client rested. Enjoying myself this much was different.

I paused and Hannah sighed, falling still again.

"If you…" I hesitated, aware of the agency faux pas waiting on my tongue.

"Hmm?"

"If you book again, you should include the full moon," I said, stumbling quickly over the words. I dove back down, closing my eyes and focusing on my work, licking and kissing.

"Is that—" Hannah gasped, and her hips rolled into my mouth. "Is that possible?"

I hummed and nodded, wrapping my lips around her clit and suckling. She shouted, back arching, and we skipped conversation for a few necessary minutes, her fingers diving into my hair and her body rocking.

I slid two fingers into her cunt and stayed the course of sucking her clit until her thighs clamped around my ears, muffling her cries as she came.

She was hot on my tongue, sweeter now, and I cleaned her until she growled and pushed me away. I sat up, ignoring my own arousal and bending a knee to hide it from her—not that she was ready to open her eyes anyway.

"It's possible," I answered finally. "It'd be fun, actually. They'd put us out in a secure section of the woods. I don't know what kind of setup you have at home—"

"I stay at a full moon hotel."

I blinked at that. Full moon hotels were…pretty dismal. If her tastes ran along the vibes MSA had brought out for this apartment, then she had to be miserable in one of those sterile rooms, packed in the building like a sardine with dozens of other werewolves.

"Well, then the MSA housing will definitely be an upgrade," I said.

Her eyes opened at that, staring up at the ceiling and then wincing away. I glanced up at the mirrors, but I didn't look away. She was splayed out, all elegant and wiry and *satisfied*. I smiled at the sight and then realized she was looking at me.

"I've never…shifted in front of anyone else," she said.

My last werewolf client, Sarah, hadn't shown any signs of shyness in shifting around me. Her werewolf form had been about as aggressive as, if not stronger than her human self, and just as libidinous. The other werewolves I'd worked with had been more or less the same. But from one night, I knew Hannah was nothing like Sarah or any of the others. My experience with a werewolf was starting over from scratch.

Hannah was nervous about shifting around me. Noted.

"Think about it," I said, shrugging, and then I risked adding, "I'm told I'm really fun to hunt. Hard to catch me when I can fly."

Her eyes widened and she paled slightly, and I thought for a moment I might've misstepped, but her lips curved up. "I'll think about it."

I nodded and slid from the bed, already aware of the way she watched me. I stretched on purpose, studying her in the mirrors above us as she gawked. I felt good. Relaxed and well rested. She hadn't really touched my wings at all, and the ache had healed at last.

"We have a couple hours. I'll start you a bath, and you can put a breakfast order in on the wristband," I said, heading for the double doors of the glitzy dark bathroom.

She rustled and groaned in the bed behind me and I grinned, resisting the urge to look over my shoulder at her. That was a good sound, shocked and pleased at the same time. It was a shame she hadn't booked more than one night. I wanted to earn that sound again.

GRIVENS, a cervitaur staff member of the agency, hummed and glared at his tablet, one hand reaching up to pull on his antlers. I fidgeted in my seat across from his desk, awaiting my verdict.

I'd been confident all morning, prepping Hannah a bath surrounded by crystals, filled with blossoms and oils and salts. I'd even hand-fed her the fruit plate and chocolate croissant she'd ordered for breakfast. She had a sweet tooth, apparently, and I was surprised she wasn't craving meat before a full moon.

I'd been the exemplary MSA partner.

And yet for some reason, my damn knee wouldn't stop jiggling and the minutes seemed to crawl by as I waited for Grivens to finish reading the report.

"You haven't had great ratings recently."

My jaw clenched. "I know." Obviously, because I had to sit through one of these debriefs after every appointment.

"Clients seem to feel a certain lack of commitment on your end."

My lips pressed to a flat line. Hannah and I had been rutting in that bed for hours last night. What part of that lacked—

"What was different about this appointment?" Grivens asked me, finally looking up from the screen, brow furrowing so tightly it made his antlers twitch.

Different.

I released a sigh. "Umm…a lot was different, actually," I said, shrugging. Grivens's head tilted, and I cleared my throat, considering my words. "The client's needs were different. The environment too. It was a different kind of appointment. And I've been working on getting my ratings back up with *all* my clients."

"Are you no longer interested in providing the services—"

"No, I am," I rushed to say, sitting up straighter. I couldn't afford to lose my entire client base just from one slip of the tongue. "This was just…a refreshing change. And a reminder of how much I enjoy my work with the agency."

Grivens's attention returned to the tablet, reading whatever notes were there.

"Can I…see her comments?" I asked, itching to know what the cervitaur was studying.

"There isn't much," he said.

There had to have been *something*. Grivens wouldn't be quizzing me on the appointment if there wasn't some kind of positive feedback.

"She was only estimated at a forty-three percent likelihood to return," Grivens said.

My eyebrows lifted at that announcement. Forty-three was pretty decent odds. Most clients were estimated a bit lower because it was a once-in-a-lifetime experience for some, or a special occasion, or a personal experiment. The one exception was werewolves, who had a monthly need for the relief.

"She booked me for next month?"

"She booked you for five months in advance," Grivens said.

A sharp, shocked laugh burst out of me and I choked as I tried to swallow it, Grivens rustling and stamping his hooves across from me. Skittish cervitaurs took after their deer brethren a little too much.

"Sorry, just…" I shook my head and fought my grin. Even Sarah had only ever booked month to month. "With full moons?" I asked, curious if Hannah had taken my suggestion.

"Not next month's, but she put a hold on the others," Grivens said.

Considering, but not yet convinced. That would be my job next month.

"This is promising and a relief to the agency, but may I recommend you strive to create a similar loyalty with your other clients?" Grivens said.

I nodded, slapping the arms of the chair I was seated in. "Of course. Yes, that is absolutely the plan."

And as a reward, I would have regular appointments with Hannah, a welcome change in my otherwise exhausting routine.

"HOW WENT THE SEDUCTION?"

Elias may have been a smug, pretentious moth fae—pretty typical traits for his kind—but he did have a great bar. With a great menu of snacks. And decent taste in liquor.

"She pre-booked me for five months."

Elias's golden eyebrows jumped. "Well. Either you performed even more admirably than anyone could have expected—"

"Thank you."

"—or she really likes to be prepared with a routine." I scowled at the mothman, and he smiled gamely back at me. "Hopefully, it's a routine you'll enjoy."

Recalling the thunderous, shivering, shocking relief I'd found in bed with my newest client, I brightened. "Think I could stand to repeat the events, yeah," I said, shoving a loaded potato boat into my mouth.

Suddenly, someone decided to swing an entire tree trunk square into the middle of my back. I choked on my potato as a massive green figure helped himself to the seat next to me. Ah, not a tree trunk. Just a friendly greeting from Khell'ar, an orc friend.

"Where's your mate?" Elias asked, turning to the door.

Khell'ar had previously been an MSA employee as well, until he'd met his future mate in a week-long fuck-a-thon that had turned his world upside down. Sunny, the petite and endearing human mate in question, was generally found attached to Khell's side.

"She's getting sick of having me in her hair," Khell said, surprisingly chipper about the declaration considering how much he seemed to *enjoy* constantly pawing at the woman. "Wanted to work in her studio and told me to come here."

"You don't seem disappointed," Elias pointed out.

Khell's smile widened, and his eyes glinted coal orange. "She'll miss me. We'll fuck outrageously tonight."

I snorted. By Khell and Sunny's mutual accounting, they fucked outrageously every night.

"What are you doing here?" Khell asked me.

"Eating my entire kitchen," Elias said.

"Celebrating booking a client for five monthly appointments," I answered, reaching for a soft pretzel, and slapping Khell's hand away from my spinach artichoke dip. "Order your own."

"I'll put your entire bill on my credit," Khell bargained with me.

Elias's wings rustled in irritation. Khell had built Elias his bar top, as well as a number of the more unique and rustic tables in the bar, partially in exchange for bar credit. And I *had* ordered a lot of food.

"Deal," I said, retreating.

Elias scowled and turned on his heel. "Fine. Use it all up. You can't eat free forever."

Khell chuckled and waited for Elias to be distracted before reaching over the bar and grabbing himself a bottle of stashed whiskey.

"Do you like her?" Khell asked.

"Who?"

He shrugged. "The new client."

"Oh." I frowned. "I don't know her, really."

Khell snorted. "Fine. Do you like fucking her?"

It probably wasn't appropriate for us to discuss, not by agency standards. Then again, Khell wasn't with the agency any longer. He'd committed the ultimate error: developing a real relationship with a client. *Mating* one.

"I do. It's different with her," I said. Khell's eyes widened, and I scoffed. "Not like that! It's just new. I haven't done anything new in a long time."

Gargoyles weren't usually creatures of change, the phrase 'set in stone' applying to our lives a little too well. But I'd moved cities. Found my own work. Made friends. I liked change.

So sure, maybe I did like Hannah. I'd have time to decide that more over the next few months.

CHAPTER 8
Hannah

"MEETING IS IN FIFTEEN," Kiernan called to the others as I pulled the foam earplugs from my ears.

I watched my two departing bandmates, Lawrence and Mikey, out of the corner of my eye, their backs disappearing down the stairs that would lead to the bar on the ground floor. We'd started renting the empty space above the bar years ago, just when the indie scene in Chicago began to recognize our name. Back when our debut album was downloaded directly from our own website and our songs streamed online just enough to make us a little cash on the side. Back when we'd piled into a converted van and toured the midwest together.

Before the record deal.

Before I was attacked.

"Dunno why we bother to rehearse if we can't tour," Lawrence muttered at the door.

I froze while wrapping the black cable, and behind me Kiernan sighed. Lawrence's timing was intentional. He wanted me to hear.

"Ignore him," Kiernan murmured.

Kiernan and I had been a team for years. He'd been my

guitarist, my co-writer, my lover for the first half of our tenure together, and my best friend for the rest.

I finished wrapping the cable, elbow to wrist, and shook my head. "He's not wrong."

"We've got Milwaukee, Detroit, St. Louis," Kiernan listed off. Easy trips. Easily planned inside of the windows of a full moon.

"Not New York," I said, glancing over my shoulder, leaving the rest unspoken.

Not London. Not Tokyo or Sydney or Mexico City.

"We'll see what the label has to say," Kiernan said. He was tall and lanky, ginger red hair in a riot of curls, too outrageously huge for his slim frame. He sat down on a speaker, long legs crossed in front of him, and stared at me as I finished packing up.

We used to pack up together, order pitchers of beer together, drink too late and unwind together. Now Kiernan and I let the others go, get their frustration with me out of their system, safely away from my earshot and my unpredictable temper.

"You seem…a little lighter," Kiernan said, words laid out with careful precision.

It was probably wishful thinking on his part. I hadn't been the easiest creative partner in recent months, except…

"A little," I admitted, offering him a smile.

I'd managed to sleep through most of the full moon, worn out from my night with the gargoyle, and I'd been less tense in the week since. I owed Natalie a discreet thank you for her suggestion.

"You honestly don't know how relieved I am to hear you say that."

I rolled my eyes. "Look, I know I haven't been—I know the touring thing is—"

"I'm relieved because I've been worried about you,

Hannah," Kiernan said, eyes wide. "I'm not saying I don't know why. I can't relate, but I can…imagine."

No, you can't.

"I'm just saying, as your friend, I'm glad to see any improvement. For your sake."

"It doesn't mean everything's better," I said, fighting past the heavy rock that had lodged itself into my throat.

Kiernan's mouth flattened briefly. "I know that."

"Or that I'm comfortable with the tour the label laid out for us."

"Hannah—"

"But thank you," I finished. Kiernan fell silent and nodded, his shoulders relaxing. "I'm relieved too."

"Any news from Ray?" Kiernan asked.

"We're grabbing a bite to eat after this, if you want to come. No news though. He just likes to check in," I said.

Kiernan's gaze dropped. "I've got…an audition after this."

I blinked. "An audition."

"Just a local studio gig. Nothing permanent."

Footsteps hit the stairs and I stiffened, backing away from the conversation, the news. A position as a studio guitarist would be a good way to fill the gap, it was true. It would create conflict with our band's schedule, but that was irregular now anyway. Mikey, our drummer, had already started taking gigs with a local wedding band who needed a regular stand-in. The studio might also put Kiernan in a position to join another band.

You're supposed to be happy for him, I told myself. He deserved to make a living with his talent. That had been the goal for us all along.

Us. As a team.

"Catch, Han."

Werewolves were meant to have good reflexes, or so I'd been told, but my head was stewing in Kiernan's news, the ache of a betrayal I was meant to forgive easily but couldn't. I didn't really hear Mikey's call to me, and I didn't see the water bottle spinning in the air.

"Hannah, shit!" Kiernan said, startled and urgent.

I stiffened and turned only in time to get smacked in the face by a pound of water contained in flimsy plastic.

"Ow!"

The bottle fell to the floor, and the lid cracked against the wood, a sudden splash and flood of water sending us all into a chaotic dance to gather up guitar cases and amps. Ice cold water soaked through my jeans into my skin, and the past brief minute caught up to me, a sudden snarl escaping my lips.

The room froze, but the sound rumbled on.

"Sorry, Han. That was…stupid."

Mikey was short and stout, and had the kind of ubiquitously manic energy typical of all the drummers I'd met in life. It was pretty standard character for him to "helpfully" toss something in my direction without warning. He was eternally well-meaning and frustratingly impulsive. Once upon a time, when I'd found his chaos amusing, one spilled water bottle would've been par for the course and barely worth noticing.

I didn't know what bothered me more now. Getting smacked in the face, the fact that I was no longer laid back about it, or that Mikey had realized the change in my temperament too and was prepared for me to snap.

"Here," Lawrence said, digging into his bag and pulling out what I was pretty sure was a used gym towel.

I shook my head and tried to ignore the growl in my voice. "It's just water. I'm fine."

Mikey's mouth opened, and I wondered how far and fast I had to run to keep myself from snapping at him if he apologized again. Thankfully, my phone rang in my back pocket.

"That'll be the label. I'll meet you guys on the couch," I said.

Lawrence dropped the towel on the spill, doing a shitty job of mopping it up with his foot, and Kiernan crossed to me.

"I'm good," I said before he could ask. "Couch."

He held his hands up and retreated, and a shiver of frustration raised predatory hairs on the back of my neck. I wanted to rewind time and go back to that moment in the apartment living room, where the city was blocked out by dark wings and I was unraveled and calm. My next appointment with Raphael was still weeks away, and I wondered how unreasonable it would be to book him outside of the full moon too.

I pulled my tablet from my bag and answered the video call on the larger screen. George Daniels' face stared back at me, and I choked on the growl in my throat. The last thing I needed was to lose my shit with Daniels too.

I'd liked the man when I'd met him, but perhaps in the face of a record deal that didn't come attached with my father's name I was bound to like him. He reminded me of some of the musicians I'd met through my dad and his band, but he didn't show the same wear and tear of drugs and alcohol. I'd respected his even keel and strictly business approach to our band to start with. He stayed out of our music for the most part, and focused mainly on how to market us.

Namely, booking us as openers for a half-dozen major acts, putting us on tour for the majority of a year.

"Hannah, good to see you. You're looking better!"

George had said the same to me at the start of every phone call. And compared to the one when I'd been freshly attacked, pale from blood loss and haggard from terror, I was looking better.

"Hello, George," I answered, helping myself to the open spot at the center of the couch, turning the tablet to get all of us in the picture together. Kiernan, Mikey, and Lawrence echoed the same after me.

"I'm going to start with the bad news," George said

abruptly. "The Jamesons have cut us from the tour quarter slot we were offered. We sat on it too long. Which is why it's more important than ever to sign with the others."

"Fuck," Lawrence hissed behind me, pacing in and out of frame.

"What about the dates?" I asked. "With Benson Fame?"

George sighed and sat back in his chair. He had a humble office for a record executive. He had good rapport with all of the bands we'd met through him. I *wanted* to like this man.

"We cut two full moon dates with him, Hannah. Asking for the days around is too much. It's easier to replace you," George said, shrugging, holding up his hands at his sides.

Had he even fought for me, tried to find a compromise? Traded us for local smaller acts that wouldn't require contracts securing them for weeks?

"There's no reason why you can't perform."

"There's dozens of reasons," I snapped. "I'm not myself for days before a full moon, I—"

I cleared my throat and shook my head. There'd be men around, groupies. Backstage environments were always tense and wired anyways, and there was always too much energy to burn at the end of the night. Add in my lack of control, my instinct and urges, and I'd meet disaster.

"Hannah, if we can't put you on tour, we're shelving the record release."

There was a brief and painful silence, a sudden shot through both of my ears before the words collided in my thoughts.

"You're canceling the record?" Kiernan asked, making sense of the sound in my throat, putting words to my growl.

"Postponing," George corrected, but there wasn't much optimism in the word. "Until Hannah is ready for a tour. We'll just have to start from scratch on finding the right acts."

"Jesus," Lawrence muttered, leaving his spot behind the couch and marching toward the door.

He was there, beyond the screen in my hands that I wanted to throw at the wall, staring at me. Lawrence wanted to be a rockstar more than any of us. He was beautiful, charming, and he made his role as our bassist engaging and performative for the audience. He'd tempered his ego while working with me for years, but ever since I'd been bitten and resisted the idea of a tour, the cracks between us were crumbling wider. He'd also wanted us to sign with a larger label that had been interested in me for my father's sake.

I was Virgil Darwood's daughter. I was his ticket to fame, and if I was suddenly faulty, incapable of serving him, then I was useless.

"How long do we have now to make a final decision about this tour?" Kiernan asked.

George's stare was fixed to me too, cutting through the screen. Was he thinking the same thing as Lawrence? Was it time for all of these men to cut me loose? Would even Kiernan give up on me?

"I made a final decision," I said, and out of the corner of my eye I saw Kiernan glance at me. There was an edge in the air, a warning from the men around me, and it made the hairs on the back of my neck rise with irritation.

"If I do some sweet-talking, make arrangements *sooner* rather than later, I could probably move The Huberts dates to the end, just push your start date back another month. But if I don't have a firm yes by the start of December, that's it," George said.

My head shook, and Kiernan took the tablet from my hands, standing up so I was no longer in frame. Lawrence was glaring at me from across the room, his stare flicking up to Kiernan and then back down again.

"That's really generous. Thank you, George. Any time you can buy us would be appreciated. We want this tour."

"And we want the album to be a success," George

answered, his and Kiernan's conversation carrying on without me with carefully balanced words.

The label needed us to take the tour in order to sell the album. They'd already put the money in to produce it, but they wouldn't bother to put it out without us there to market it. We'd be a loss, but a controlled one.

"I can't do it," I breathed, imagining the tension of this room trapped inside of a bus for weeks on end. I imagined my wolf's cravings and hunger turning on my bandmates, on charming Lawrence or hapless Mikey or…

Would I fight with Kiernan? Try and fuck him for the sake of long-lost chemistry? Or would it be a blur of starvation and strangers that would get me through the stretch of stressful and intoxicating months?

Kiernan only moved farther away from the couch, finishing the conversation with George. A warm hand settled on my shoulder, and I jerked out of its grip.

"Sorry," Mikey rushed out, moving out from behind me so I could see him at the side of the couch. "It's just… It's gonna be okay, Han."

I didn't know what he meant. It would be okay that we lost our record release? That we didn't go on tour? That he and Lawrence and Kiernan cut their losses and quit the band? Or that it would be okay if I was somehow dragged along, feral and frightened and out of control?

"Hannah, we have—" Lawrence started, his voice too loud and drawing out another growl from me.

"No," Kiernan said as I stood up from the couch. "Not today. We meet up on Tuesday night, bring some new ideas, music. We can all talk then."

Lawrence had always listened to Kiernan in a way he hadn't to me. Asshole.

"Fine," Lawrence muttered, but he took his time stomping around the room and gathering up his things.

"Been a while since we worked on anything new. I'll bring

something funky," Mikey said, too brightly, trying to make up for Lawrence's temper.

Kiernan was out of reach, a fact my hands noted as they tightened on my own knees, claws itching and burning in my fingertips. He faced forward—faced *away* from me—with his arms crossed over his chest, tablet dangling from his fingers.

I watched him as he waited for Mikey and Lawrence to leave, the whole band actively aware of the atmosphere about to boil over, waiting for half of us to leave so there'd be the least amount of casualties in the aftermath.

"What are you doing?" I asked as the door clicked shut.

Kiernan's breath gusted out of him and he turned, eyes down as he tossed the tablet onto the couch cushion. He crossed to stand in front of me and then immediately fell into a crouch, the sudden meeting of our gazes startling me.

"This isn't just about you, Hannah," Kiernan said.

I stiffened and my mouth fell open, but he continued without me.

"This is my band too, my music too. My *life* and the career I've built too. I love you, you know that. I love our music. And I've worked *really* hard, at your side, with you, to get the band to this point. So have Mikey and Lawrence. We need you to find a solution to this problem."

"What do you think I've *been* doing?" I snapped. "I *am* the problem, Kiernan!"

"You've been sulking," Kiernan said, eyebrows rising. "You can afford to. If this record falls through, if this band falls apart, *you are going to be okay*. This is our job, and we both love it—we've both put the work into it, the time and the money and the love. But you don't need it the way I do. I only mean that in the most concrete financial terms."

"Fuck you," I said, the most useless response I could give, the most petulant. As if I was proving his point. The truth tore through me as effectively as the werewolf's claws had that night, months ago. "You know what music is to me, you *know* that it's not just about money or—"

"Hannah, you've been holding back." I gaped at him and his mouth grew flat and pale before he spoke in a rush, "You give half effort in rehearsals, there's no energy. I know what music *was* for you, but are you sure you still feel the same way?"

I couldn't feel the couch beneath me. My entire body was buzzing. "You don't understand," I breathed out. He wasn't wrong. I didn't find the release in singing that I had before the attack. My body wasn't *mine* anymore. My voice had new textures that didn't belong to me. I no longer trusted any part of myself.

Even my music.

Kiernan stood and turned to the side, nodding. "I know I don't. I'm sorry. But it's true. I'll see you on Tuesday."

"That's it?"

Kiernan paused with his back to me, looking at me over his shoulder, a wince in his gaze.

"You tell me that I…it's just my fault and I—" The words curdled in my throat, and I lost track of what I wanted to say, what accusation I could throw.

"Of course it's not your fault," Kiernan said, almost shouted. "But how much of your life, of our work together, are you going to let it destroy?"

I bent forward, doubled over with a queasy blend of guilt, shame, and anger. Kiernan's footsteps clapped across the floorboards, pausing at the door. But I couldn't bring myself to look up, and he didn't wait for me to recover.

RAY STOOD outside of the Chicago Diner—a stalwart vegetarian landmark, filled with remixed greasy spoon classics—tall and broad and grizzled, with thinning salt and pepper hair that hung shaggy around his ears, his hand cupped around his cigarette to shield it from the gusts of wind barrelling up the street. From the start, he reminded me of a detective out of a noir novel, and a little of my mother's father too, smelling of stale cigarettes and of the candy peppermints always available from a pocket.

My jittering nerves and turning stomach bounced through me as I crossed the street to meet him. I was late, having sat in the wreckage of the rehearsal space for too long after Kiernan's departure, holding arguments in my own head.

Most of the arguments were with myself, with the truth I tried not to remember more often than I had to and that Kiernan had forced between us. I hadn't grown up wealthy, and when my father's accountant went about the matter-of-fact arrangements laid out for me after high school, the relief had been too great to refuse. I was taken care of, financially at least, for life. I did my best to let the money sit, lived a balance between style, comfort, and modest usage of the money. The appointments with MSA were my most extravagant purchase to date.

But the money was there. An undeniable privilege. A safety net to catch me in this freefall moment.

Ray ground out his cigarette on the concrete ledge of the diner and then pocketed the waste. I'd never seen him drop a cigarette to the ground once in all the months and meetings.

"Hey kiddo," he greeted—another grandfatherly detail that made my chest ache. He was younger than my father, but I couldn't shake the familiarity, the sense that Ray was the indulgent elderly figure in my life who would spoil me with peppermint candies and forgive me for all my worst behavior. "How's it going?"

I blamed that familiarity on why I burst suddenly into tears on the sidewalk in front of the investigator in charge of my case, in front of the rush hour traffic and the bus full of commuters, and the diner with its dinner rush crowd.

"Shit," Ray sighed.

And then heavy arms pulled me into a comfortingly rounded stomach and a steady chest and the scent of stale cigarettes and peppermint candies.

I cried like a child on the corner of the street, in front of a window full of gawking college students, until the world blended into a dreary collection of colors. Ray hugged me tightly, offering only a brief grunt of discomfort, and waited for me to go through the passing storm of emotion. No one had held me like this since I was a little girl, and a small part of me was strangely delighted by this horrible and uncomfortable moment. There was nothing like a good hug, especially one offered with an unconditional resolve while you wept. I didn't want it to end, didn't want the inevitable awkwardness that came afterwards, and I suspected a lesser man would've rushed me.

Not Ray.

He waited until I settled, until the embarrassment forced me to pull reluctantly away. His arms squeezed once more, a reassurance, and then he slid to my side, one arm still over my shoulder.

"Come on, we need some good soup."

Ray led the way as I kept my head ducked, aware my face was probably a swollen red mess and that anyone who hadn't watched me break down through the window would be able to tell I'd just been crying. But we were given a corner booth, and Ray set me down gently into my seat, my back to the room.

He sat across from me, the menu open even though Ray always ordered the same thing from here—a heavy bowl of chili that best replicated the meat he really craved and that I refused to eat. He waited in a silence that made me squirm, flipping through the pages, waiting for me to speak. Detectives were patient, and I held out until after we'd ordered our usuals.

"The label is threatening to cancel the record release if I won't go on tour," I said.

Ray scowled but didn't speak, and the quiet worked its usual magic over me, the past hour spilling out. I didn't tell him everything, about my fears of my own cravings, certainly not about my current attempts to curb or sate the pre-full moon hormones. I didn't tell him about my father or my money, or my history with Kiernan. I didn't have to—Ray was good at inferring and drawing conclusions. I just talked until our food showed up, falling silent on a simple truth.

"My band is going to fall apart, and it'll be because I can't control myself."

Ray leaned forward and started to eat his chili. My cheeks heated, and I shifted on the torn and taped back together vinyl bench seat, scooting forward and following suit, eating my vegan reuben.

"Your introduction to our kind was to meet the absolute worst of us," Ray said, resting his spoon back in his bowl, his elbows on the tabletop and chin in his hands. "It's going to take you time to realize that doesn't mean *you* are the worst of us too. If you keep fighting against your werewolf, you'll never really get to know yourself."

I wanted to flinch back against the words, even as gentle a chastisement as it was, but I was too weary to move at all. So I watched Ray return to his chili instead.

"I'll keep looking for the one responsible," he said, head nodding once, as if making the promise to himself too.

CHAPTER 9
Rafe

I TWISTED THE PEPPER GRINDER, my gaze scanning the apartment once more. I wasn't sure if Hannah had requested a more open layout for us this time or if MSA had adjusted for my wings, but the lack of clutter in this new space was a relief. Especially considering my wings wouldn't stop *fidgeting*, stretching and flapping, hooks searching for a grip. I rolled my shoulders, settling them back into a tidy fold, and then tapped my finger against the skillet. I hissed at the heat, the butter sizzling up around my impervious digit, and then retreated, sucking on my fingertip and lifting the filets I'd been preparing, resting them in the pan.

The apartment door beeped at the same moment the sizzle and pop of the skillet intensified, and I stumbled back, a sudden burst of electric energy rushing through me. Hannah's footsteps were softer than mine as I jogged out of the kitchen and toward the entrance hall.

Recently, in the month since I'd last seen her, I'd wondered if I was recalling her correctly. Had she really been that tall? That lithe? All muscle and sinew and the hard amber stare above sharp cheekbones? But my memory had been vividly accurate.

She's fucking sexy, I decided. We paused on opposite ends of the hall. She was in a dress this time, tied shut with a single bow at her hip, and I knew immediately that it would take two string tugs to strip her. Her jacket was already off, one arm raised to hang it on a hook. Her jaw was clenched, dark circles underneath glowing eyes.

"Fast," she bit out, and I didn't bother fighting my grin, even as she growled.

Her bag dropped to the floor as I reached her, her free hand already at her hip, black silk whispering as it sagged open. I found the other tie, staring down briefly to appreciate the sight of her. Her stomach was already tensing, thighs braced wide, and she hadn't bothered with lingerie of any kind. The dark curls hiding her pussy were a little damp already.

"Raph—" she started in a snarl.

I hunched, and she gasped as my cooler mouth clasped one pert nipple, fingers delving between her legs. The snarl turned into a cracked moan, and I pulled away from her breast to watch her as I stroked inside of her slick opening, stretching and teasing her. Her brow was furrowed, jaw still tight with frustration, but she panted as I pressed in deeper.

I grunted, somehow surprised as her own hands found me, gripped me through loose pants. Our feet tripped and guided us to the door, the closest place to rest against, and Hannah let out a soft whine as I started to fuck my fingers into her in earnest. Her hips rolled into my hand, brow untangling slightly. Up close, her eyes looked a little bloodshot, and her lips were slightly chapped and bitten, like she'd been chewing on them. Something was wrong. No. Something *had been* wrong. It was a bad moon coming, or a bad month, and she needed…

This. Me. *Relief*.

Her head tilted to the side as I dipped mine down, and I

nosed past her long thick hair to suck on her throat. She shuddered, shrinking into the door, and I noted that the spot responded but it wasn't entirely positive. I moved my mouth up to her earlobe and she softened, driving down onto my fingers, stroking me through my pants. Much better. Her dress was still resting on her shoulders, hanging open and trailing against the floor. She smelled freshly washed, and her hair was cool and slightly damp from a recent shower.

The taste of her skin reminded me of cloves.

Hannah's head turned, nose bumping mine, our lips sliding together. Her hands pushed the pants down my hips, and any temptation to tease her slid away as I considered that tight, almost pained expression on her face. I reached behind the curtain of cool black silk and lifted her by the backs of her thighs, her legs bracketing my bare hips. She drew away from the kiss, head resting against the door, and her eyes fell shut on a sigh as I rocked my length into her. The tension loosened, her lips parting and jaw unclenching.

She could've rushed at me, tackled me to the floor, fucked me there like the tool I was meant to serve her as, as I'd served so many others. She hadn't, not even when I seemed to be the solution to whatever was troubling her.

Her eyes blinked open as the dense curls over my pubic bone pressed against her.

"Fuck me," she murmured. A frown etched into her face, a slight purse of her lips, and she added, "Please."

As if it were even necessary to be polite.

I obeyed, hypnotized by her reactions—the gasp and groan as I ground against her, the absent gaze that slid over my shoulder and then up to the ceiling as I thrust in and out of her, the clutch of her fingers at the base of my wing roots, and the ache that spiked down to my balls in response. She sagged into me, my arms sliding around her waist to hold her close, her tension diffusing into a soft and supple relaxation.

Her lips started to curve up, sighs catching and eyes widening as friction and relief turned to pleasure.

Would she let me fuck her until I came too, this time? I wondered, speeding up slightly at the idea. I hadn't come since our last appointment, and while that was normal for me, the potential was too exciting not to anticipate. Would she flutter and flood on my cock again as I came? Let me turn into hard and impossibly sensitive stone?

"You're close," I said as she started to clutch my length inside of her, marveling at the way she didn't tense and scratch toward her release, but melted into the process.

"Yes, Raphael…there!"

"Rafe," I whispered, leaning in to suck at the corner of her jaw again.

She purred in my arms, arched her back, and scraped firm nipples against mine, gasping as the tight beaded flesh on my chest scratched her skin. "Mmm…Rafe!"

It was a breathy exclamation, a private plea, and then she moaned for me, unable now to stay relaxed as she rode my length, soaking and squeezing on it as she came. A pride I hadn't felt in my work in months, or longer, shone through me, and I hitched her against me, shifting the angle, remembering exactly how to drag inside of her, extending her shivers and cries into a second wave to crash over the first.

Her chest went still, breath stolen, eyes unseeing and pointed up toward the ceiling so she couldn't see my triumphant grin. There. *That* was not a utilitarian orgasm. She stiffened and tightened on me, her hands echoing the grip around my wings hard enough to make me grunt.

Hannah liked to kiss in the aftermath of an orgasm, a detail I remembered from our last appointment. Her tongue licked and stroked against mine as she relaxed and drooped in my arms again, and I answered the touch, adding in little nibbles to her lips. I'd take her to the cushioned sex bench in the living room—I was glad they'd kept that detail in this apartment—and wind her up all over again. We'd finished our last appointment together with tired bodies and lazy smiles. I wanted to finish this one with her all but crawling out the door, unable to return to whatever had left her so tight and stressed again.

Except when we pulled away to catch our breath, I found not a slow and sated smile on her lips but a wrinkling of her nose.

"Something's burning."

"Fuck," I muttered, not thinking straight as I drew out of her, a sudden clumsy scramble of grunts, hisses, and flailing limbs as I rushed for the kitchen. "Sorry, sorry, sorry," I called back to her, running for the thin trail of smoke.

She huffed, but it sounded more like amusement than anger, and her own footsteps were following soon too.

"I...forgot I was making you dinner," I said, scowling at the ruined filets in the pan.

My attention was briefly diverted as Hannah appeared, tying her dress closed, one breast still visible for a moment. I yelped as my hand grabbed the hot handle of the pan, and it rattled on the burner.

"I'll send up for new filets," I said as Hannah frowned at the sight. "It won't take long."

Except she didn't look amused or relieved, just tense again, rearing back slightly. Her gaze flicked to mine, oddly wary, and I wanted to explain that I really *was* a good cook, but I was just distracted by...her, and anyway she'd needed fast—

"I'm a vegetarian," she said softly.

I blinked at her for a moment, and then I ignored the scalding heat of the pan handle as I lifted it from the burner, yanking open the drawer for the garbage and dumping the scorched meat into the bag without a word.

Hannah barked out a sound of surprise, and we both jumped as I tossed the pan back onto the stove.

Fuck. I should've *known* she didn't eat meat. MSA would know, and if I'd even thought to look at her file before calling in for the food—

"I've never met a werewolf who was a vegetarian."

"Neither have I," Hannah said, a slight bitter note in her voice. Or maybe it was defeat.

MSA hadn't corrected my error, and they'd know my mistake with my second request, but I was already coordinating a new menu in my head—lentils, beans, and kale for protein, with a curried cauliflower steak. The roasted potatoes in the oven would be fine, and the berry crumble I'd prepped for dessert, after we'd unwound, worked too. Maybe I could convince the agents the pair of filets were for me, rather than fess up that I'd been the idiot who hadn't finished his client research.

I shut the garbage more gently than I'd dropped the pan and took a breath, finding Hannah's stare on me. "Sorry," I said, wincing slightly.

She shook her head. "It's fine."

But the soft, close mood from moments ago—when I was still buried inside of her and planning seven more ways to fuck her before morning—was gone now.

"Give me a five minute restart," I said, forcing a smile to my lips. "I have a plan."

Hannah's head tilted, glow brightening in her gaze. The tie of her dress was barely closed, just a simple single knot of the strings. She nodded, finally slipping out of the kitchen and into the living room.

"I'm going to stretch out for a bit."

There was a window through this kitchen, which meant I had a perfect view of her long-legged pace to the couch, the elegant flop of her body onto the generous cushions. Her groan carried to me as she stretched, hands reaching back behind her to brace against the arm of the couch, shoes sliding off to the floor, and toes curling as she arched.

Dinner, I reminded myself, tearing my stare off of her and reaching for the tablet to call down to the kitchen. A dinner that was delicious enough to make up for ruining the mood. And then I could draw another one of those groans from her lips.

CHAPTER 10
Hannah

RAPHAEL—*RAFE*, which suited him better—was watching me eat. It would've been annoying, or it was annoying, but not enough to distract me from the food in front of me. I hummed softly as I bit into another buttery, crispy potato, and my mouth watered as salt and rosemary filled my palate. Rafe was a *very* good cook, and aside from the initial scramble over the burnt steaks, he hadn't hesitated to whip together a stunning replacement for a meal. A meal I didn't really need, because I'd thrown together a peanut spring roll before I'd left for the appointment, but one I was devouring enthusiastically all the same.

Because it was fucking *delicious*. I sighed over the perfect balance of salt against heat, acid against fat, and then stared lovingly down at my plate, deciding on my next bite.

"I really am sorry about earlier," Rafe said, the wobble and panic in his voice vanished now, and that dark resonant tone my skin loved to goosebump for returned.

I scooped up more sautéed beans and lentils and shrugged, glancing up at him. "I understand the mistake. Like you said, we don't know any other vegetarian werewolves."

And even burnt to a crisp, my mouth had watered and my stomach had clawed itself alive at the smell of the meat. It'd also made me queasy at the thought of eating it, and not because of the poor preparation.

Rafe opened his mouth to answer, closed it, and then paused. He had a curl standing upright right at the front of his hairline, a comically sweet touch to his outrageously handsome face, and I briefly considered abandoning my meal to go plant myself in his lap and study the leaden and silky texture of his hair in my hands again. But no, the food was too good.

"You have more self-control than any other werewolf I've met."

I stilled, a loaded fork halfway to my mouth hanging open, and stared back at Rafe. The statement was too absurd, jangling through my head, to say anything but "No."

He laughed, sagging back into his chair—designed with one narrow line down the spine that accommodated his wings to hang over the back—and it delivered a mild protesting creak. "Yeah."

I set down my fork, taking a consolatory lick of my lips and wanting to sigh again at the lingering flavors. "Not around the full moon."

Rafe shrugged and rolled his eyes. "No werewolf has self-control around the full moon. That's part of the package. But to get through months without changing your diet takes a massive amount of self-control."

I winced. "Then maybe that's where it's all getting spent," I said, finally returning to my plate.

"I doubt it," Rafe continued. "You have yet to barrel-roll me flat on my back the second you walk in the door."

I snorted. "Is my ability to stand upright upon entry all it takes to prove control?"

Rafe sat up, picking up his wine. "Yeah, kinda."

I hummed around a bite of *perfectly crispy and tender* cauliflower, and considered the words. "I have a friend…a mentor, actually, from a support group. He is the most mild-mannered werewolf you'll ever meet."

Rafe tipped his head. "You've spent the full moon with him?"

I shuddered at the idea of being around another werewolf when we were both shifted and shook my head. "No, he spends it with his mate."

"Probably fucking like animals," Rafe said, nodding.

"She's human," I pointed out. "But he doesn't hurt her."

Except Natalie mentioned something about liking Theo in chains, so...

I tried not to think too hard about my friends together in a full moon frenzy—there was an involuntary arousal to the picture this close to my own frenzy—but it did make me wonder if I'd been ignoring a few puzzle pieces I could've put together.

"How long ago was he turned?" Rafe asked.

"I don't have a decade to get my shit together," I said, thinking of the band.

"Do you have a human boyfriend you're afraid of hurting?" Rafe asked, the question so painfully neutral in tone it was impossible not to read into it.

"God, no," I said, and he only blinked in response. "But I... Sometimes, if I'm not careful...with a stranger around the full moon..."

Rafe's lips pursed, and his eyes flicked back and forth. "You can't force yourself to fast and then not expect to be starving, Hannah." My fork clicked against the plate, my breath tight in my chest. "Your friend has a partner he's presumably regularly fucking. You don't have a higher libido just around the full moon."

That was true. I'd invested in a whole new arsenal of vibrators and toys when it became clear my basics weren't up to the job. But it was like trying to dull a knife against cotton

—utterly useless. The beast in me wanted the wrestle and strain and contact of another body.

I glanced at my plate, which was mostly scraped clean by now. I'd had less satisfying meals in five-star restaurants, and I wondered what made Rafe choose MSA over a career as a chef. Unless he just loved this work more than cooking. Which made me smile. I rose from my seat, and Rafe's eyebrows jumped. He smiled too as I approached, helpfully scooting back from the table. When he made to stand, I pushed him back into the chair, and he laughed as I set his dish and glass aside.

"When was the last time?" he asked as I perched at the edge of the table.

"Don't you remember? Just an hour ago at the door," I said, lifting my bare feet up from the floor and setting them on his shoulders. My dress parted and slid back like a curtain. Rafe's cool hands clasped around my ankles as his gaze focused down to my core.

My answer was easier and lighter than the truth. I hadn't had sex with anyone since my last appointment. I'd barely had *contact*. So yes, I'd been starving—starving for any touch at all. The hug from Ray popped up in my head, but it vanished quickly as Rafe lifted my feet from his shoulder and then pulled them back to his wings, tucking them into the gentle hooks at the top of a joint.

"At the door was just an appetizer," Rafe said, smiling at me.

"Well, we've had dinner now, so…"

I gasped as his wings flashed open from their fold, yelping as the motion stretched my legs wide. My hands clapped against the table behind me, and Rafe grinned wickedly, bending forward. I panted and followed the push from his wings, bending my knees, brazenly positioned and exposed.

"Time for dessert," Rafe said, turning his head to place a kiss against the inside of my thigh.

I lifted one hand, helping myself to that unruly curl, teasing my fingertips into the dense locks around one of his petite horns. He groaned and leaned into the touch. Apparently, the raised flesh around his horns was as sensitive as the spot around his wings. Which made me curious...

I rubbed my feet at the base of his wing hooks and smiled as his eyes fell shut and the broad wings shivered. Gargoyles were curious with their erogenous zones, so unexpectedly sensitive for beings everyone considered made of stone.

Rafe's eyes flashed open, lovely and dark, and I wondered what his thick eyelashes felt like, if they were sharp and heavy, or feathery-soft like a human's. But his gaze was heated and his next kiss on my thigh came with a swirling tongue and dragging teeth, drawing a harsh breath from my chest. I tugged on his hair, trying to draw his mouth to my cunt, but it didn't do more than make him hum, the sound vibrating against my skin.

"Relax," he murmured against my tense thigh, quivering as I waited for him to reach a better destination. "We have all night."

Except I'd had one night with him, and it'd been exhausting and satisfying and bone melting, and it hadn't been enough to get me through the month. The thought might've left me bitter, but Rafe chose that moment to slide a cool, firm, wet tongue along the crease of my thigh, and there was nothing to do but tighten my grip in the curls at the back of his head and let sensation soothe the restless clawing in my chest.

IT TOOK a great deal of effort to turn my head away from the growing foggy blue light outside the bedroom window. It would take even more effort in a few hours to get up out of this bed and leave the appointment. I didn't want to think about that. I just wanted to enjoy—

I gasped as Rafe's lips ran over my shoulder as I lay on my belly, his hips tilting and the rub of his cock aimed faultlessly inside of me.

I was vaguely aware of his goal for the night. He'd been wringing one orgasm after another out of me from dinner to dawn, but he'd been using mouth and hands and even one beautiful hour of just grinding his cock against my clit without penetration. He'd fuck me between each break, until his own breath was rough and his hands grew almost bruising. He was dragging out his own orgasm for both our sakes.

"Is this okay?" he rasped.

And now he was kissing over the scratched scars on my shoulders and back, licking them. And a teeny-tiny wounded part of me wanted to scramble away. It made my heart beat a little faster in my chest, the hairs on the back of my neck lift in warning. But mostly, I was exactly the kind of exhausted I'd come to Rafe for, and it was shockingly nice to be a useless sack of bones on the sweaty sheets and let him explore the most vulnerable, still healing, part of me.

"Yes," I whispered, my lips numb from the night's kisses.

His tongue stroked up and down my right shoulder blade, over the spot that had been the last to heal, the deepest scratch. He was grinding into the sweetest place inside of me —a ruthless and impossible to refuse orgasm rising up in me —and licking and kissing that scar. I was going to cry as I came, but there was something nice about that too. I buried my face in my pillow, sobbing out pleasure and a worn out sorrow I'd been nursing too long, and Rafe's hand slid around my hip to stroke one fingertip up and down over my clit. As if I needed that.

He drew out of me, mouth trailing down to the scars on my hip, and then paused, lifting away. If I'd been less delirious, I would've avoided this position, avoided letting him really get a look at the wreckage on my back. One hand ran from my shoulder, swirling over my shoulder blade, tracing down my spine, arching back to my hip. The path of the violence. There was no mistaking the intent behind those marks, no assuming I'd been a volunteer.

Ray had seen them in the crime scene photographs. My doctors and nurses and the trauma team that had passed me from one pair of hands to the next that night. No one else.

I licked my lips, leaving any tears on the pillow, and lifted my head.

"Fuck me until you come," I said, hoping it would dissuade him from asking any questions.

Or maybe he wouldn't have asked. He wasn't my lover or my friend. He was the gargoyle I'd hired, who rolled me over to my back in the sheets we'd ruined and then tried to lift me up, as if I had any strength left.

"No, like this," I said, pulling on his absurdly firm and lovely biceps, managing just enough effort to slide beneath and spread my legs in offering.

If he'd had any opinion about my scars, there was no sign of it now. "I don't know if I'll crush you."

"So crush me," I said, because I thought that sounded nice in my fuck-drunk state.

Rafe laughed, but then he was stretching out above me, elbows braced on either side of my shoulders, hands cupping my face. His thumbs stroked my cheeks, and there was a pinch of pain where he had some of my hair caught beneath him, but he was already correcting the issue.

"You really don't have to let me do this," he whispered, grazing his mouth over mine.

"I want it," I said, which was the lazy version of *There's something incredibly beautiful and satisfying about watching a man who doesn't get to take his own pleasure selfishly and quickly, finally find it because you offered him that.*

I bit his upper lip as he found his way unerringly back

inside of me, the path slick and open and just swollen enough for me to enjoy the beautiful designs on his cock.

"Carved for her pleasure," I murmured, and Rafe's laugh was tense, his body already in motion, his tongue searching hungrily for mine. He was close to the edge; he'd probably been holding himself there for the latter half of the night.

I wrapped my arms around his back, and his wings beat, a force of motion that made us and the bed rock.

"Wrap your legs around me," Rafe said, and I would've protested, but there was a hint of a whine in the words.

I strained into position, rewarded with the musical groan, the lift of his head and squeeze of his eyes shut. His lips were damp from kissing, parted with heavy breaths, and our chests glided against one another. Stone didn't sweat, but it did seem to become...polished, moving smoothly over me.

"Fuck, you feel so good," he muttered, barely forcing the words out, so I wondered if he really meant to say them at all.

This was...illicit. Well, of course it was—it was sweaty, desperate sex. But even more so, because there was a guilty eagerness to Rafe that made me think he wasn't really supposed to do this, to close his eyes and tell a woman to wrap herself around him because *he* liked how it felt. So I slid my hands up his back and grabbed onto the roots of his wings.

Rafe bellowed, eyes flying open, and his wings beat harder, the muscle pulsing in my grip.

"Hannah!" he moaned, eyes glancing down at me in thrilled panic.

"Stone," I said, a simple encouragement.

He let out another broken sound and then shuddered and transformed. He *did* crush me, but he braced his hands in the mattress to ease the weight just enough for it to be dangerously good, tempting me to tell him to let go and really steal my breath. And *fuck*, he felt so good inside of me, so achingly solid that it made me into something almost unreal. I was smoke compared to him, liquid for him to sink into. If he wanted to drive right through me, he could, and I would be a ghost in the wake.

"Hannah," he said again, weak and grateful, and I met him in the kiss, tightening myself around him and swallowing his cry as he bucked and bowed and came in a long frenzy of beating wings and messy kisses.

Any of his clients who *didn't* offer him this were idiots, I decided. I didn't need or want control in this moment, because I was *everything* this man needed to survive for just a few exceptional minutes.

MY SCARS ACHED and burned as I shivered and snapped back into my human body a day later. There was a fresh scratch on my calf, my own impatient claws punishing me during the moon hours as I'd paced my cell at the shelter.

I was cold, having long since shredded and cast aside my blanket. I lay naked on the mattress. The scars that had created me screamed in my flesh, protesting the shift out of my werewolf form. I squinted through sore eyes at the milky gray sky outside my window and recalled the morning before this, the dreamy exhaustion from my night with Rafe. My fingers dug into the thin mattress beneath me, bumping against a broken spring, and I let out an animal whine at the contrast.

You could book me through the full moon.

He hadn't offered again, but I knew the opportunity was still on the table, horrifying and tempting all at once. What damage might I do to a glossy MSA apartment in my were form? What damage to Rafe?

My arms wobbled as I pushed myself up to sitting, and I

hissed as I curled up, the scratches on my calf stinging as I brushed them.

What would it be like to wake up after a full moon the way I had yesterday? I wondered. Rafe had carried me out of bed and into a hot bath, leaving me to doze and soak as he'd made me an omelet, a bowl of fresh fruit, and a strong cup of coffee.

Maybe if he'd spent the night with me in my monstrous form, that's not how it would go. Maybe there'd be bandages or wary stares, or he'd simply slip out at the first chance.

A bell blared over the speaker above the door. The moon had set, the electricity would be turned back on, and we would all scramble into our showers and hope the hot water lasted long enough to wash away the blood or sore muscles. It never did.

Maybe anything is better than this, I thought, not for the first time, and then I braced myself against the wall and struggled to stand.

CHAPTER 11
Rafe

THE FARTHER you got from downtown, the lower the roofs settled, like the peak of a mountain rolling down into hills. The average gargoyle in Chicago—there were few, so an average was meaningless, really—did what they had to for the budget to live in one of the better downtown high rises. Maybe at one point in my MSA career, I might've considered moving in that direction, but with a gradually shrinking client list that was out of the question. And actually, I liked Edgewater, far north of the crush and close to the water.

I'd managed to snag a good studio apartment near the top of one of the taller waterfront locations last year, and while it'd needed more than a reasonable amount of renovation, that helped keep the price down and saved me from wiping my savings. Which was good, considering it might dwindle if I wasn't careful at work.

I paused in front of my kitchen counter, staring down at my experimental vegetable lasagne. Thinking of work only brought one topic to mind—Hannah.

The sight of the scars rushing over her back, cast in silver by moonlight, still swollen and surrounded by red in some spots. The tangle of limbs clamped around me as I came, and the cling of her as I grew too limp and heavy for her to reasonably bear, though she didn't push me away. The way she was tense and sharp as an arrow when she walked in the door, and then as loose and relaxed as a silk ribbon by the morning, and the way that made me want to twist and wrap her around me all over again.

Except Hannah was the last part of my work I needed to be thinking about, the only client who wasn't dissatisfied with my service. I'd lost another one this week, and I…

I frowned as my knuckles scraped against my mandolin slicer, and I dropped the onion to the countertop.

I couldn't remember her name. She was a chimera, and she'd only been partnering with me for a few months. We didn't talk much during our sessions outside of quick questions and commands. She preferred me silent and obedient.

The phone rang on the counter and I startled, glancing up at the clock and bracing myself.

Right. It was Sunday, it was two, and my parents were calling.

"Hey, Pop," I answered, opening the cabinet in front of me and propping my phone up against the plates so my face was at camera level as I worked on prepping vegetables.

"He's on his way," a soft voice answered, and I blinked, looking up.

My mom was on the screen, the warm sandstone color of her cheeks so uniquely familiar to me—the only face in the world that could make my chest twinge with immediate relief and guilt at the same time. My dad was puttering in the background, a great gray shadow to her slighter, brighter shape, probably grabbing whatever scientific journal he'd gotten recently, articles tabbed and at the ready. Dad had a hard time making conversation and knowing what questions to ask, so instead he usually just came prepped with whatever information he found most interesting lately. Mom's lips twitched as he rustled papers, and we shared a private moment of humor.

My mom's dad was an imp, the only species close enough to a gargoyle to breed with one, and the species least like gargoyles in temperament. My grandpop and grandma hadn't stayed together, but he'd whisked in and out of my mom's life on a regular basis, and he was a staple of my childhood, wily and clever and delighted with my aptitude for mischief and adventure. Where gargoyles were staid, imps were mutable. They liked travel and activity and collecting acquaintances. Gargoyles preferred stability, familiarity, and routine. I wasn't exactly sure how my grandpop had landed my gran in the first place, even for the few years he'd managed to stay still, but while it was clear that where his imp genes had lent themselves to my mom's coloring, they'd trickled down to me in their own unique way.

"What are you working on?" my mom asked, recognizing the surroundings of my kitchen in the picture on her screen.

"New recipe for a client," I said.

Mom blinked, probably as confused by that answer as I was. I cooked for all my clients, although usually not with a great deal of effort. That wasn't why they hired me. It wasn't why Hannah hired me either, but it was one of the stimulation markers in her file that I actually excelled at. I was a rabid eater, cheerfully guzzling down anything edible in reach, but I was a *really* good cook. Dad's interest in science tended toward the world around us, geology and astronomy, the slow shifting changes of our universe and long-studied discoveries. I liked the faster and more immediate experimentation of the kitchen.

"Trying to see if I can make a lasagne out of just vegetables," I continued.

Mom and Dad knew about my job, and while sex wouldn't suit most gargoyles, it wasn't frowned upon by any means. My life, my choices, baffled my father. Mom, though, had grown up with an imp father who loved her beyond measure, but whose nature didn't allow him to nest for decades in the same apartment complex, in the same city, day after day.

"If anyone can…" my mother said, the second half of the sentence left unspoken, a common trait in gargoyle conversation. *It would be you*. Gargoyles saved words where they could.

"I found an article the other day," my dad announced from off camera, and I straightened my shoulders and raised my eyebrows expectantly, like I'd been waiting all week for this moment. Mom beamed at me.

They needed this. By rights, I should've been nesting with them for another decade if I hadn't gone looking for a mate. They hadn't raised a fuss when I'd announced I wanted to go see Chicago's architecture, though Mom had cried when I'd called to tell her I was staying and Dad had frowned. They hadn't objected or even seemed that surprised. So every Sunday at two, I answered their call and listened to Dad recite at least two articles from scientific journals word for word, finishing excitedly with "What do you think about that, huh?" And I told my mom about everything I'd cooked and any news from Khell or Elias, whom she'd never met, but it made her feel better to pretend she knew my friends.

"You guys should come visit," I offered at the end, now relaxing in my secondhand armchair by the window that overlooked the lake.

Mom and Dad stirred—they hadn't moved an inch since they took their respective spots in front of the camera—and talked about their schedules for the next three months, the same schedules they'd had for the past ten years.

I smiled and nodded. "When you have time."

I would have to go back to New York for a visit soon, figure out how to propose the idea in a way that wouldn't ruffle their gravel too much. But I always offered a visit here to them, just in case. I had a feeling Mom was gently working one into the future, although it'd probably be a few years away still.

"Proud of you, kiddo," Dad said, as only a gargoyle father can say to his forty-eight year old son—still young by gargoyle standards.

"Love you so much, darling," Mom said.

"Love you guys," I said, and we all nodded and smiled for a minute, and they said goodbye a few more times because gargoyles don't just hang up on a call that easily.

The timer went off as Mom finally winked at me and ended the call before Dad could reiterate for the third time that we'd talk again in a week.

I dropped my phone aside and crossed back to my barely passable studio kitchen, opening the oven to admire the golden bubbles on the surface of the lasagne. It smelled good. I'd packed in preserved lemon and a ton of herbs and my favorite brands of goat cheese and ricotta blended together. I'd even dehydrated the strips of zucchini and eggplant to make them closer to noodles before layering.

I wanted to cut directly into the dish, dissect the layers and flavors and make notes for improvement. But it needed to cool before I was allowed to poke around, and I needed to get ready for a dinner party.

"IT'S STUPENDOUS!"

I wrinkled my nose. "It needs more salt."

"Rafe, it's amazing."

"The center is completely soggy."

"It's good!"

"Quit coddling me," I said, slapping my pen down in my notebook and glaring at the faces around the crowded table.

Khell and Sunny had invited me over for dinner, along

with Sunny's best friend Natalie and her werewolf husband Theo, and Elias.

Elias was the first to break under my interrogation. "There's too much oregano."

"Thank you," I answered with a nod, picking my pen back up and starting to jot notes on the lasagne again.

"Too much lemon," Sunny said primly, and Khell huffed at her side. "I like your color palette and everything, but I think a little tomato wouldn't hurt for the acidity instead of just citrus."

I raised my free hand without looking up from my note-taking, but Sunny obliged the high five gamely.

"No meat," Theo said, shrugging. I rolled my eyes and ignored him. That was the point.

"It needs more texture, but if you can't make proper noodles from squash slices, maybe consider a layer of ground nuts," Natalie offered.

I blinked and looked up at her. I mostly knew Natalie as a friend of a friend who almost always got into drinking competitions with me at the bar. Or nacho eating competitions. Or, on one occasion, an entirely inappropriate smack-talking, vicious dance-off in Khell and Sunny's living room that had nearly taken out a vintage lamp.

"That's a really good idea," I said, and she nodded with obvious smugness.

"It's *perfect*, and I like it," Khell said stubbornly. Orcs *loved* vegetables and green energy and planting gardens and basically anything that got them as close to tree-humping as possible without the actual splinters.

"Thanks, bud," I said, and I started rewriting the recipe, absently reaching for another one of the stuffed rolls Elias had brought.

"Do you have to do that now?" Elias asked, arching an eyebrow at me as I scribbled.

I looked around the table. Everyone else was eating their dinner like a normal person, offering compliments to whoever had made each dish, sipping wine or beer or Elias's deadly ghost pepper moonshine, in my case.

"I think harshly critiquing a dish at a dinner party is kind of fun," Natalie said, and then her eyes narrowed. "But don't say a word against Theo's brownies, or I'll break your arm."

Theo draped his arm around his mate and leaned in to kiss her temple. "Thanks, babe."

I rushed through my last notes, gobbling down the roll in my hand, and then another, and then flipped my notebook shut. "There," I said through the mouthful. "Done."

Elias's nose wrinkled, and Sunny's lips twitched. "Who's all this planning for?" Sunny asked me.

I opened my mouth to answer and then shut it again, partly to chew and partly because I realized I didn't want to admit the truth. The recipe *ought* to have been for Khell's benefit. For the sake of this dinner party. But really, they were just my guinea pigs. I wanted to make this for Hannah. Which was a bit improbable, considering the amount of prep it took. I'd have to bring the whole thing with me, unbaked, to our next appointment, because I wasn't supposed to spend over an hour sautéing vegetables when I could be screwing Hannah silly on a sex ottoman.

But she liked good food, and she was a vegetarian werewolf struggling against the expectation of being a massive carnivore, and preparing something like this for her would be…thoughtful.

I tossed my notebook down into my bag on the floor. "You guys, obviously," I said. "A main and a group activity, all at once."

"Next time, bring score cards so we can eviscerate your efforts anonymously," Elias suggested, and I glared at him only to find him smirking back at me, a little too knowingly for a moth fae who couldn't read minds. I'd have to corner Astraeya at work and make sure they weren't gossiping about me behind my back.

CHAPTER 12
Hannah

"HI, I'M FLETCHER."

"Hi, Fletcher."

"I was turned a few months ago actually, but…it's just been…"

I stared at the man standing now, huge and rugged and handsome in a scraggly woodsman sort of way. He looked like a good candidate for a werewolf, a properly terrifying one. But he was standing with his shoulders hunched, a wounded flinch crinkling the scar near his right eye. He cleared his throat, and my eyes fell to my lap, too familiar with this particular wound.

"Hard," he said lamely, the single word thick with meaning. Someone in the circle hummed in sympathy, and his lips twitched. "Just hard. Don't really…know who I am anymore. Feel like the monster just has all of me."

My chest burned and my thighs ached with the urge to stand and run. There'd been other new members to our little circle since I'd joined, and some stayed while others moved on quickly. They were always the hardest stories for me to listen to, my own experience endlessly fresh.

"But I don't really wanna be that guy, so I'm…so I'm here

now. And I'm hoping you can help," he said, shrugging and looking briefly around at us through large, vivid ice blue eyes, the reddened whiskers of his beard shifting as he licked his lips. Always hungry, us werewolves.

He glanced at Diane as he started to sit, and then startled and stood straight again. "I am what I am?" he asked, guessing at the words we'd already repeated several times today.

"I am what I am," we answered him in unison.

I forced my lips to sound out the words with the others, but not for the first time wondered what they really meant. It sounded so resigned. For me, it was simply a reminder that I couldn't turn back time, *not* be running in that graveyard on the full moon, feeling quiet and calm one moment, and then panicked and frantic the next. Maybe for the others, it was a reminder to embrace our nature, all teeth and claw and hunger.

"Hannah?" Diane called, rousing me.

I found her at the front, opened my mouth to shake my head and answer my usual 'not today,' and then paused. I'd never spoken, just listened. Theo twisted in his chair to glance back at me, and his eyes were owlish behind his glasses, huge and surprised. Because I was standing up.

"I—" I was supposed to introduce myself, to let the group call back to me, but if I hesitated, heard their requisite *"Hi, Hannah"* back and faced what I was doing, I would sit back down immediately. So I just barreled ahead. "I've never transformed in front of anyone. Not even a mirror. I don't *want* to see myself as a werewolf, or know what I look like. I don't want to see the monster that made me a werewolf in a reflection," I said.

A few eyes winced away, but I was trying to keep my stare resolutely up above them all anyway, aware of the glow of Diane watching and listening, and the little reflective glimmer of Theo's glasses still turned in my direction.

"I have a...a safe opportunity to spend the full moon with someone. Not another werewolf. But someone I can't hurt... who won't hurt me. And I hate the shelter. I fucking hate being there. I hate everything about the shift. But I don't know if I can let someone else see me transform."

The room was quiet, and Diane cleared her throat to speak, but Theo beat her, which was a relief because his voice was familiar and safe—he was my friend.

"What's the benefit of *not* seeing your werewolf?"

I swallowed once, but my throat refused the motion and I had to fight through choking to do it properly. "The shelter, the full moon...it's like a- a scheduled nightmare. It's not part of my life. It doesn't feel entirely real."

Theo nodded, not encouraging, not agreeing, just telling me he'd already known my answer.

And that we both knew it was bullshit.

"I don't want this to be real yet," I admitted softly.

And because there was no hopeful way to spin this admission, no optimism burning through me to tie a bow on the speech that would make any of us feel better, I sat back down in my chair. Silence burned into my ears, as loud as screaming, and I realized I'd forgotten to say the final words.

I am what I am. And because I'd forgotten to say them, no one else had echoed the sentiment. Because I didn't *want* to be what I was, and I couldn't force myself to start the chorus for the others to follow. It was awkward, and it had turned the energy of the group down to a wounded limp. Diane's gaze held mine, cutting around the others to find me, but she didn't force me to finish, to speak. She just let the pause linger painfully—not an admonishment against me, but maybe the others. A reminder that we were here not just as cheerleaders towards progress, but as people who'd been hurt. I'd shoved that in their faces, and she'd let me. I nodded to her, and I don't know if it was acknowledgement or gratitude, but it was enough, and her eyes slid away.

IT WAS TOO much to hope I might escape the session without comment. I'd expected Theo to find me, but it was Diane who cornered me at the fruit plate.

"It was good to finally hear from you," she said, her voice all raspy velvet reassurance.

"Was it?" I challenged, glancing over her shoulder to where the rest of the group was huddling protectively around the sandwiches.

Diane smiled wryly and nodded. "I'd rather have your worst than not have you here at all."

And that...that made me want to fucking cry. No, it made me *actually* cry. No one had offered that to me, not even Kiernan. No one had said *Sure, Hannah, be the absolute shittiest, most avoidant and immature version of you today; you're welcome.* And to be fair, there weren't very many places aside from therapy that one *should* be allowed to show up as their worst self. The words reminded me of my mom, of the absolute devotion she'd raised me with, loving me determinedly even during our teen year screaming matches. *Fuck, I missed my mom.* And I was also so damn relieved she hadn't lived to this point, because I wasn't sure I could take her loving me now too. Diane let me turn my face away, doing so herself so that we were two people shoulder to shoulder, facing in opposite directions.

"You can't accept yourself if you refuse to know yourself," Diane said. I pursed my lips, but she continued, "And absolutely nothing will turn you into the werewolf who bit you, but a choice to be like them. Which you aren't going to make."

The words didn't feel true, a small band-aid for a massive burn wound, but I also couldn't really argue with them, so I just stood, staring across the room to the cluster of folding chairs until Diane drifted away from me again.

I KNEW the moment Lawrence walked in without his bass, and I think Kiernan must've understood too, but he still asked.

"L? What's up?"

"I just wanted to do this face-to-face," Lawrence said, and there was a bit of performance to the statement, to him standing there with his hands in his pockets, but his words wobbled too.

Mikey stopped fastening on the top hat, an echoing hiss and rattle carrying around our rehearsal space. We'd been awkward together, setting up to rehearse in silence instead of the usual easy conversation. Except the conversation hadn't been easy in months, and anyway my head was too full to notice until Lawrence walked in, speech ready. And still, I was busy thinking about Diane and Rafe and George and the call I needed to make to give him my decision about the tour today.

Lawrence hadn't waited. He probably thought he knew what I'd say.

"I have a spot with The Garfields," he said, rocking back on his heels, not meeting my eyes. "Label's got half a dozen songs ready, and they just needed a bassist and...and a drummer."

We all turned to stare at Mikey. Lawrence hadn't just come to tell us he was quitting the band. He'd come to *poach* Mikey. For a band a label was smashing together, probably one that would sound exactly like whatever indie darling was gathering steam lately. God, maybe even to sound like *us*.

"I'm sorry, but I can't afford to wait," Lawrence said, not sounding sorry at all. And I'd rolled Kiernan's speech around in my head for a month. I wasn't sure if any of them *needed* to be sorry. Sure, we'd been friends for a while, in the process of being a band. But where Mikey and Lawrence were concerned, it was more like co-workers you were lucky enough to get along with. "Mikey…spot's yours if you want it."

Right in fucking front of me.

"Not the move, Lawrence," Kiernan muttered, twisting away from him and running a shaking hand through his hair. Probably because he knew he should've been making the exact same move.

"I'm—" Mikey started and then paused, and I couldn't help but look back at him. He was staring at his half-assembled kit, and then at Lawrence, and then at me and Kiernan. A sort of hopeless resignation crossed his face, and I thought, *That's it, we're over*. And then he said, "Nah, man, I'm good."

Which couldn't have been true. He definitely had no reason to feel secure here with me and Kiernan, especially now that the band was down a bassist and I hadn't coughed up a decision. But he offered Lawrence a sheepish smile and a shake of his head to really set the words in stone. I wanted to walk over and grab his round face in my hands and smack a giant kiss on his forehead. I'd done that sort of thing in the past, played the part of their demanding and doting mother hen, setting the rules of our family down and praising them for good behavior. We weren't that anymore, but maybe we could end up somewhere else that wasn't so bad.

After we found a new bassist.

And actually, losing Lawrence wasn't that much of a burden. He was handsome and charismatic, and he was a good musician, but he was also a challenging dickhead who spoke over me whenever he could. There would be other bassists.

I turned back to Lawrence, who'd had lost some of the wind in his sails from Mikey's refusal, and who now looked like he wasn't *quite so sure* about this announcement he'd brought to us. I tried not to feel smug.

"I'm sorry," I said to Lawrence, shrugging.

I could've told him. It might've resulted in history's most enthusiastic about-face. Except then Lawrence would still be in the band, and now that he was walking out...I was glad.

Kiernan let out a heavy sigh and crossed to the couch, collapsing into the cushions, and I really needed Lawrence to *leave* so I could put K and Mikey out of their misery.

"Right," Lawrence said, staring at us once more each in turn. He nodded again and repeated the word. "Right."

"We'll come see a show," I said, and Lawrence's brow furrowed. Too magnanimous, then. It was making him suspicious.

"Yeah. Yeah, cool. Umm...I'll see you guys. And...good luck," he said, offering the last words over his shoulder, a little bitterly.

Neither Mikey nor Kiernan moved as Lawrence left, and I held my breath until the door that led down to the bar shut behind him.

"Fuck," Kiernan muttered.

"George will set up the auditions," I said.

Kiernan sat up, lips pressed flat and face too pale for a moment. "Will he?" Kiernan challenged.

"Look, I won't lie to you, this might go to absolute shit and you might both hate me by the end of it, but..." I took a deep breath, and Kiernan blinked, losing his frown the moment before I spoke. "We're telling George we're in for the tour. No *sooner* than we've got planned now. I *don't* know what's going to happen—"

But Kiernan was up off the couch and charging toward me, and behind me Mikey was whooping in victory. I found myself laughing as Kiernan lifted me off my feet, swinging me side to side in a crushing hug. It was more a laugh of surprise than joy, and some panic too, because now that I'd said the words, I had to follow through with them.

"Hahaha, shit, sucks to be Lawrence," Mikey cackled from

behind us, but he didn't offer to run out and tell Lawrence the good news, either. Mikey was loyal, more than I'd realized till now, and Lawrence's decision had pissed him off as much as the rest of us.

Kiernan set me down, and I couldn't bear to look at his beaming smile. "I'm serious," I whispered. "I still don't know if I can do it. But we're not telling George that, and I *will* try."

Kiernan nodded too fast, and I shot him a glare until he swallowed his grin and stopped nodding. "Han, I hear you. I know like, logistically, you're alone in this, okay? But we *are* here for you. So maybe start letting us help you figure it out?"

I wasn't sure what Kiernan and Mikey could offer, but it probably was past time to start telling them more about my new patterns and the boundaries I wanted in place.

"Let's start by figuring out how to replace our bassist," I muttered.

Kiernan snorted. "Saw your face. Don't pretend to be sad."

My lips twitched. "Fine, I won't. But I will be inconvenienced. We're gonna have to replace album art, audition, and I'm prickly now. I don't like new people."

Kiernan arched an eyebrow. "You've never liked new people, Han. Call George, give him the good news, and then drop that problem into his lap. In the meantime, I might actually have a few people I can call."

I trusted Kiernan's taste over George's, so that was a relief. It might've been dangling a golden carrot in another bassist's face that I would later yank away if I realized the tour was impossible for me, but Kiernan had been right—I owed it to our work and our music and our friendship to try. I probably even owed it to myself to seek reconciliation with the beast in me now.

I knew the first step I wanted to take, and it was coming up in a week. The anticipation was killing me, and also the anxiety, and the itch under my skin demanding *now*. Maybe I was spending a little *too* much time considering everything I could look forward to, but it was only a handful of days now. It seemed that I'd found *one* bright spot to a full moon.

CHAPTER 13
Rafe

A TWIG SNAPPED in the woods, and I paused in my work to glance out the window. But a twig wasn't an approaching car, and I shook myself and went back to readying the newly improved lasagne I'd been working on.

I'd gotten the call from Astraeya barely a week ago. Hannah had requested an alteration to our appointment. Three nights during the full moon, instead of one. There'd been one small fly in the ointment: I'd agreed to take on a new client, a gorgon, and the dates conflicted. Except it hadn't been a fly at all; it had been a relief to have Astraeya reassign the gorgon to someone else. I should've asked her to see if we could reschedule instead, considering I was running low on clients, but that wasn't what had come out of my mouth.

"Check with Benjamin," I'd said instead. "I'm staying with Hannah."

For three nights. MSA had moved our appointment out of the city and into one of their secure cottages. We'd be fenced in, but Hannah would be free to run and howl and go wild over a good ten acres of woodland during tomorrow night's full moon. I'd already checked the moon rise and set time, and we had tonight, all day tomorrow, and until eleven p.m. tomorrow night before she shifted. And then another afternoon and night afterwards. I'd always liked the day after a full moon best with werewolf clients. It was usually a lot of resting and stretching and relaxing in quiet. The idea of soothing Hannah after a full moon had me phoning up Khell and harassing him for all his best aftercare tips.

Another crunch came from outside, but this time it was gravel in the distance, and then the glow of headlights circling the kitchen walls. An odd flip bounced in my chest, and I rolled my eyes. *Client, partner*, I thought, sternly reminding myself of our roles. I hadn't been this excited for a client since my first years, before the repetition and the boredom wore me down, making me weary. It was nice to have the excitement back, but I still had to keep my head on straight.

Except when the door to the cottage opened, I dropped the giant casserole dish to the counter and ran to the hall, breathless for absolutely no reason at all.

Hannah entered the cottage quietly, but I was glad to see most of last month's tension missing from her face tonight. Her gaze skirted to me briefly—shy or wary?—and then around the hall of the cottage. It was more rustic than the apartments we'd met in previously, the modest interior clearly dressed up for Hannah's lush tastes. The ceilings were high and the rooms were wide, and I could stretch my wings out easily when I wanted.

"Hey," I greeted, the word sounding lame on my tongue. But I was busy studying her. She had an overnight bag and was wearing a pair of stylish drawstring pants. Easy to get her out of, although not as quick as the wrap dress.

"Hi. Something smells good," she murmured, hanging back by the door. I'd marveled at the way she never went on the immediate attack, but now I wanted to break her of this reserved habit too.

"Give me two minutes," I said, keeping my gaze on her as

I retreated into the kitchen. She followed, which was enough for me to turn around and focus.

I sprinkled the cheese liberally on top of the dish. Hannah's bag thumped on the floor, and I rustled my wings, offering her glimpses of my back and ass since I knew she liked to stare. I opened the oven and slid the dish inside, setting the timer, and when I turned around again, Hannah was leaning in the doorway, her jacket off. Her nipples strained through the thin material of her tank top, and we stared at one another for a moment before I recalled Elias's instructions from months ago.

I crossed to her, and the second I was within reach her hands were on my face, pulling me in for a kiss.

"Rafe," she breathed as I leaned in. She was tense, stiff at first as I grasped her hips, and she arched forcefully against me, needing more than she was willing to demand. Our tongues stroked against one another, and her fingers dug into my cheeks, trying to drag me closer.

"How long do we have?" she rasped.

Three whole damn nights, I thought gleefully, before I realized what she was asking.

"Over an hour," I said, scratching my teeth over her jaw as her hands slid back into my hair. My own were already working on the easy bow of a tie at her waist, the ribbon unwinding around my fingers.

"Good," she said, sighing on the word.

And then her hands were tugging my thick locks. I grinned at her as she forced me down, my knees bending obediently. I tugged on her pants and they fell cheerfully to the floor. She was wearing underwear this time, a flimsy lace shield, and she moaned as I burrowed my nose into the fabric.

"Don't tease me," she said, not because that was what I was doing, but because she wanted me to know she couldn't take it. Not for this first orgasm that she needed to soften the edge.

She smelled like her release, and I wondered if she'd had to take care of herself once already before she'd even left her home. I licked her through the lace, then used my thumb to pull it aside and take care of her the way she needed me to.

She came on my tongue three times, then once again on my cock, bent over the dinner table as we made the legs thump against the uneven cottage floor. There was a little line of sweat darkening the back of her tank top when the timer went off, and we ignored the beeping for another five minutes until I'd gotten her off for the fifth time. It was a good number, and I decided—bouncing on my toes to the oven as Hannah collapsed limply into a chair—that I would try to use it as a multiple for the appointment. Five orgasms, ten, twenty-five…*fifty* sounded especially nice, if she wouldn't try and kill me for it.

"Whatever you're thinking, wait until I've eaten first," she said, and I glanced over my shoulder to find her grinning too, shamelessly splayed on the chair, her brow shining and shirt askew and panties hanging shredded around her ankle.

"Of course," I said, although really, the lasagne needed to cool before we cut into it, and we'd need to do *something* while we waited, and—

Hannah growled and sat up in the chair. "Come *here*, Rafe."

I WOKE up in the night, stretched on the massive bed, and blinked up at the vague reflection over my head. The agency kept giving us mirrors over the beds, which wasn't actually standard but was fucking *awesome*, especially when Hannah really lost it while riding me. But she wasn't in the bed at the moment. I was all splayed out, relaxed, wrung dry *twice* in the night, and I lifted the watch on my wrist to find that it wasn't really night but it wasn't quite morning either.

And Hannah wasn't in the bed.

I rolled out of the tangled sheets, debated my pants, and then left them on the floor. Hannah was standing in the kitchen, illuminated by the LED glow of the fridge lamp, partially bent into the open door, eating cold vegetable lasagne with a fork. It would've been her third plate of the night, but she wasn't using a plate.

"Heathen," I said, and even the single word couldn't hide the giddy delight racing through me as I watched her.

"It's so fucking good," she mumbled through a mouthful, then paused just long enough to shoot a glare over my shoulder. "And I've got good reason to be hungry."

Which made it *so* much harder to ignore how fucking... *happy* I was right at this exact moment. I'd known after the second helping that Hannah approved of my recipe, not just because she kept saying so—and moaning and rolling her eyes up into her head and curling her toes like when I had her right on the edge—but also because she'd finished licking her plate and fingers and fork clean and then got down on the floor to lick *me* clean. And if you think it's hard to suck off a cock that's more or less made of stone and in no hurry to finish up the job, you'd be right, but she soldiered on in her gratitude.

"Fine, but it's straight back to bed with you when you're done. Tomorrow night's gonna be long, and you need your rest," I said, knowing I would take her back to bed and not let her rest till morning now.

Except she lost the flush in her cheeks as she straightened, and her eyes dropped down to the floor, and she looked almost *sick*.

"Hey—"

"I'm really nervous," she whispered.

I was already crossing over to her, and she shut the fridge

door as I approached, leaving us in the gray dark of the edge of morning, right before the sun would cut through the horizon.

I opened my mouth to point out that she'd been through a full moon before, and I reached out to pull her into my chest. She slipped away before I could, washing the fork she'd used too thoroughly, dropping it in the dish strainer, sweeping crumbs off the table. Busywork and startlingly domestic, except there was something *wrong* with this picture, which was more important than what was right with it.

"I've never been with anyone else during a full moon," she said. "No one's…no one has seen me like that."

She'd made her way around the table, almost like she was using it as a shield between us. This was the part of my work with Hannah I wasn't trained to handle.

"I…haven't made up my mind about staying completely," she murmured.

"Stay," I said immediately, lurching around the corner of the table, sighing as she didn't move. "*If* you're really not ready to be seen, then I can leave for the full moon hours, but stay here. It'll be good for your werewolf to get some time to run, and MSA will monitor—"

Hannah's brow furrowed and her head shook. "How do you know all this? How do you know it'll be good for me to run and…" She trailed off and then blushed, and the answer lingered between us.

I might be the first person to see her as a werewolf, if she let me stay, but she wasn't the first werewolf I'd spent the full moon with. There was an oddly clammy feeling along with that, the thought of other werewolf clients brought into the room again.

Hannah just sighed, and a weary smile curled her lips. "Of course. That's…a relief, actually."

Which wiped away my worry. "Is it?"

She nodded, and there was just enough light in the room

for me to see the way her muscles melted out of their tension. She looked as though she were about to drop right to the floor, but I was already marching within reach, hauling her up against my chest and carrying her back to the bedroom.

"Didn't know I hired a werewolf expert *and* an expert fuck," Hannah said softly.

I laughed, and her hands caught my wing hooks for balance as I bumped and bumbled us through the dark cottage. "Two for one deals are the specialty," I teased.

Hannah snorted. "I couldn't survive two of you."

If my pride was inappropriate to the moment, Hannah was too busy to notice, sighing as I laid her back in the bed and nestled my cock against her swollen sex. She licked her lips, and I bent my head to help myself to a taste when I noticed the flash of nerves on her face once more.

"I've only ever stayed at the shelter," she whispered. "I don't...I don't know what it will be like."

I kissed her once, wrapped my arms around her back and waist, and then threw out all my half-made plans for the next hour.

"You know what it's like to shift," I pointed out, settling Hannah down in a nest of pillows and propping myself along her side. I drew my right wing up to shield us from the sunrise, and it made our quiet words clearer between us.

"Fucking awful," Hannah muttered.

I'd known this on a basic level. Anyone watching a human turn into a werewolf could've guessed as much. Bones growing and rearranging, hair sprouting, *a tail*. One client had even told me that every time her claws came out, it was like little knife wounds in her fingers. But hearing the condemnation from Hannah made me want to *do* something about it, and there was no solution, no way to steal the transformation from her or stop it from happening.

"Usually...the werewolf already knows I'm around," I continued, twisting my own fingers into her long dark strands. "It's about fifty-fifty on whether or not you'll see me as a threat and want to establish dominance, or just be like, 'ah yes, my fuck toy.'"

Hannah grimaced, and I shook my head, reassuring her. "Hey, don't stress. I'm durable, and I know better than to present a challenge. We'll go outside. If you've never been outside during a full moon, you're in for a treat. Your werewolf will be a lot calmer."

"Shouldn't we be worried about me…getting out?" Hannah asked.

I shook my head. "Not a chance. MSA knows what they're doing, and we're all alone in this compound. You might have beef with the gate during the night because usually weres object to being penned in, but ten acres is plenty for you. Werewolves don't inherently want to go around biting other people," I said. Hannah stiffened beneath me, eyes widening and amber glow flashing, her breath cutting jaggedly through her chest. I blinked back at her and remembered, like an idiot, how she'd probably been turned in the first place. "It happens in a defensive response," I explained, gentling my words. "Startled, or territorial, or—"

"It's never…predatory?" she asked, frowning.

I opened my mouth to answer and then shut it again, thinking through my words more carefully. Words meant *more* with Hannah. "Not never, but that's not the werewolf. That's the person."

Hannah hummed, and I itched to ask questions that I had no business knowing the answers to. "What else?" she said, and she scooted closer to me, draping one leg over mine.

Gargoyles weren't especially comfortable to cuddle, but Hannah was warm and long and silky against me, and I willed myself to be as cushioned as was possible for one of my kind, just to keep her from moving away again.

"We might play a game of hide-and-seek," I said. Hannah's brow furrowed. "You have better senses as a werewolf, but since gargoyles don't have much of a scent, I'm told I pose an excellent challenge."

Offering to let a werewolf hunt me during the full moon usually went over really well with my clients, so I faltered as Hannah's frown deepened. I was in new territory with her again. *She* was in new territory with herself.

"It's going to be okay," I offered softly, and her glowing stare flicked to mine, wary and nervous. But present. In bed with me, pressing herself to my chest. I wrapped an arm around her waist and tugged her closer, and she didn't pull away. "It'll be sensory overload at first, but we'll take it slowly. We've still got most of the day too."

She relaxed at that and nodded. "And…and you're going to wear me out."

It was almost a question and almost an order, as the leg between mine moved to wrap around my hips. It was a distraction from her worries, but that was as much my job as soothing them away. And when her hand skirted around my ribs and up my back to grab the base of my wing, I was more or less helpless to obey anyways. I fell over, into the space she'd made for me between bent knees. She grabbed onto my other wing root, and her eyes were lit within by the same shade of orange that was painting the walls with the sunrise. I fell into her too, her hips arching up, eyes on mine, as she steered me into her body, our breaths chorusing on a gasp.

"Hannah," I sighed out, the heat of her biting at my cooler flesh.

She hummed, and her gaze trailed up above my head to the mirrors, a feral smile lacing her lips. She squeezed the fleshy, oversensitive knots at the base of my wings, and I cried out, surging into her. A soft growl rose from her chest, pupils dilating at the view in the mirrors.

I laughed, and it distracted her enough. "What are you looking at?" I asked.

Hannah's stare bounced between the mirror and me, but I

couldn't tell if the color on her cheeks was a blush or just the light falling in through the windows.

"Your ass. Flexing," she admitted. "I'd be on top of you constantly if I didn't like that view so much."

Hannah riding me was a personal favorite too. Hannah riding my mouth was even better. But if the lady liked to watch my ass…well, then…

"Oh, yesss," she hissed as I started to buck and thrust in earnest, bracing one hand against the top of the headboard.

And the praise was for the view in the mirrors, not the motion of our bodies crashing together, so I scooped my hand under her ass and shifted the angle, triumphant at the panicked joy written on her open mouth, the furrow between her brows, and the rising cries from her throat.

I wasn't sure any amount of fucking would make the full moon easier on Hannah's werewolf. But it was an experiment I was happy to test with her.

CHAPTER 14
Hannah

I WAS TRYING NOT to watch the clock the next night, drowsing in the bath with Rafe all wet and hard and slippery around me in the least sexual way. It was just genuinely tricky to take a bath with him and not go sliding down his chest and into the water. His arms were heavy over my shoulders, and his wings were hanging over the back edge of the massive clawfoot tub.

"We're running out of time," I whispered. Moonrise was less than half an hour away.

Rafe rubbed his cheek against my wet hair, and there was an odd squeaking sound, damp strands against his stern and polished skin. "Deep breath," he whispered.

I sucked in air like I was surfacing from the ocean. He'd been reminding me to breathe most of the night, and I'd either been too tired or too relaxed from a recent orgasm to be annoyed by the repetition. Also, it did help.

"We're not running out of time. We're just trying to spend it in whatever way I think might keep you most relaxed," Rafe said. I twisted enough to shoot him a glare, but it was obvious that I wasn't the only one who'd been thoroughly fucked in the past twenty-four hours because Rafe just beamed back at me, all casual and handsome and tempting.

It was impossible for my body not to respond to those heavy-lidded eyes, warm and dark, perfect lips full and inviting. But the nerves outweighed the irresistible attraction, and Rafe seemed to know as much, combing fingers through my hair carefully and nodding.

"Let's get dried off. Need anything to eat?"

I shook my head. If I ate anything now, I'd throw it up during the transformation. I slid forward in the tub so Rafe could haul himself out behind me. Rafe had kept me well and beautifully fed, every meal thoughtfully balanced and full of iron and protein. But my insides were tossing around like a little buoy on a stormy ocean, and I knew I couldn't keep anything down.

He groaned as he moved, hands braced on the side of the tub, and I turned to watch him, water sluicing down his body.

"Sore?" I asked, frowning.

I was sore, in a delicious but persistent way, and I couldn't imagine how I would feel tomorrow.

He shook his head. "Water and gargoyles have a bit of a beef with each other. Logically, you'd think we'd be impervious to water, but actually our skin is even more absorbent than humans'. The added weight is a trip."

"That's why you don't get your wings wet?" I guessed.

And the dork shot me finger guns in affirmation. Rafe was never what I expected. Not because he was a gargoyle or not human. If anything, it was the opposite. He was smooth and seductive with me one moment, and then almost puppyish and giddy the next. He cooked like a trained chef, but I'd caught him hoovering down a bag of sour cream and cheddar potato chips with a side of pickle spears in a post-sex refuel earlier. When we were relaxed with one another, unwinding and panting with breath, he could be outrageously goofy, almost innocent.

I hadn't expected to see so much of the *person* in him. Not that I hadn't known it would be there—I'd just imagined the professionalism of sex work might require more of a persona then a person—more guarded, or at least more carefully cultivated for a client. But there was no way the incident with the chip bag had been any form of seduction.

I knew his body in a way I'd only known a couple others, and he knew mine…best of anyone. Or at least he would by morning. But I liked the little glimpses of *Rafe* as much as his expertise in my pleasure.

Rafe dried off with a towel, tossing it in a hamper, and then grabbed another one, holding it out in front of him in offering. I glanced at the clock again. Twenty minutes and counting. My bones were already aching, and my claws clicked against the porcelain of the tub as I pushed myself out of the water.

He scooped me up, lifting me over the edge of the tub and immediately buffing me with the soft towel, humming under his breath. He wasn't watching the minutes, wasn't worried about what came next. I couldn't shake the fear, and if I wanted to send him out of the fence for the next part, I needed to do so *now*.

"You won't want it for long, but here," Rafe said, sliding one of my arms into the soft sleeve of a waffle knit robe. "I think we should go outside before you shift."

I opened my mouth to tell him to go, to leave these awful hours to me, but what came out was, "Okay."

At least one of us will know what we're getting into, I decided. Rafe finished dressing me in the robe, moving to my front to tie the straps loosely around my waist.

"I want you to stay stone the whole time," I said, and he paused with his hands on my waist.

"Hannah, I'm going to be—"

"I *can* leave scratches on you when you're not stone. And that's when I'm not even fully transformed," I said, rolling my lips between my teeth as his eyes bounced between mine. "Please."

Rafe sighed and nodded, flexing his wings once. He grew larger when he was stone, features thicker and blunter, muscles denser. I didn't usually notice the differences, but in my defense he usually turned to stone after hours of fucking, when I was more or less out of my mind. He looked more predatory like this, his horns slightly longer and sharper, jaw cut with rough angles.

"Sometimes, it's better when I'm not stone," Rafe murmured, wincing, and I caught my breath. He was familiar again, still brutal but just as beautiful.

I shook my head. "No, stay like this. I need to know I won't hurt you."

His gaze flicked up, lips parting on an automatic thought, but he shut them again just as quickly, swallowing hard. "You won't. Not because of this. But you won't. Come on."

Rafe led me out of the bathroom by the hand, and I followed with an automatic trust that made me stumble when I realized what I'd done. We were moving through the bedroom, out to the living room, through the hall to the front door. There was never a chance I would've asked Rafe to leave, because I didn't want to do this without him. It was one thing to be trapped in a small reinforced cell of a room alone during the full moon. But here in an unfamiliar place, surrounded by woods as far as I could see?

If I didn't know better, I would've said Rafe and I were walking out to meet a werewolf waiting in the dark for us, not waiting for me to transform into the beast myself. I was terrified, bracing for an attack.

My toes ached with every step over the mossy stones that led away from the cottage door, claws ready to tear free. There was a pinch at the base of my back, a tail waiting to sprout. My jaw ground against the promise of fangs and curved, threatening canines, my sinuses pounding with the slow gathering of magic that would turn me into a monster.

Transformation was the ugliest combination of science and

magic. I couldn't simply change in a swirling cloud of glitter and smoke at the first glimpse of the full moon. No, my body had to break and rebuild me. Organized chaos.

"Breathe, Hannah," Rafe coaxed, his cool and firm hand brushing over my cheek.

I sucked in the breath, and my eyes widened. Rafe's hand holding mine tightened, as if he could feel the knife's edge of the moon cutting sharply through the dark of the night, into my bones.

I screamed at the burning stab of my heart in my chest, the tearing as it grew thicker and stronger, beating with a new, ragged animal pace. My spine cracked, and Rafe released my hand as I fell forward, twigs and debris biting into my stretching, changing, toughening skin. My fingers clawed at the tie of the robe, and Rafe must've been close, because the fabric was swept off my back and shoulders at the first fiery growth of fur.

I swallowed the rest of my screams, because my lungs were changing and my jaw was breaking, and it was worse to scream than it was to let myself choke on the blood of biting my tongue with freshly sharpened teeth.

A hand passed along my side, Rafe's breath catching roughly in my ear as my ribs snapped and popped, but his touch was ice in comparison with the fire blazing through me, and I didn't know if the touch was a relief or if it compounded the agony.

Through every minute, every shattering bone, my right side gnawed at me. The scars that remade me howled through my transformation, refusing to be forgotten or ignored. It wasn't enough to be turned into this creature. I had to remember why, *how* it had happened.

It doesn't take the moon very long to rise. Not from the first little sliver to the full body heaving itself over the horizon. Only a few minutes. But even two minutes is one hundred and twenty seconds, and if every one of those seconds was the worst moment of your life, expounded upon and multiplied and made even more harrowing, it was hard to imagine surviving so many of them.

Except I did it every month, and I knew with every second there would be another that followed, just as devastating and impossible, and that even when I'd survived all two hundred of them, there would be another two hundred waiting for me in less than a month.

I looked up in the haze of the pain, in the middle of the transformation, and Rafe was there, facing me on his hands and knees. My eyes had already scratched and shredded and reshaped with the vivid, sharp vision of the beast I was now, and he was perfectly clear, right down to the pulse hammering in his throat. My nose and lungs and tongue were reshaped too, my lips parted as I hauled in air, growled through the growth of new and strange legs.

Rafe's breath was uneven, stare wide and fixed to my face, watchful…frightened.

I let out a howl, a hollow warning cry of my new voice, and Rafe sat up straighter, a flinch away from me. I could make out a glimpse of myself in his vast, dark eyes—the eerie lamp glow of my stare, the creature crouch of my twisted body, and the gaping feral grin of my mouth.

"Breathe," he whispered.

I'd followed his lead too many times—it was automatic—but with the breath came the slightly metallic tang of stress.

Rafe was frightened of me.

The seconds ticked down until the only ache remaining was that of my scars and the clawing, tugging sensation in my mind of the beast held at bay. That pain would fade too in another hour or so, bitterly dragging on longer than all the others, but the battle inside of me would last until morning.

"Hannah?" Rafe murmured, inching forward.

But the sulfur of fright was still hanging on the air, and his shoulders were high around his ears. I didn't trust the creature in me—or myself, for that matter. The world was wild and intense and unfamiliar, and the streak of fur that ran down my spine was standing on end, aware of too much, too many smells, too many sounds. Every animal that scurried to safety underground was distinct in my elongated ears, every leaf bitter on my tongue.

Rafe reached a hand out, and I gave in to the better of two urges, darting out of reach, stretching properly for the first time on my legs, leaping over the ground, low and fast. And then I was moving because I *could*. For the first time, I could *run*. My body sang with the racing movement, the metallic sheen of the gate ahead of me sending me curving to the right, darting through trees, tearing through briars, a chill licking over my stinging skin.

A bark escaped my maw, a high-pitched yip of…of excitement.

It was impossible to hold my beast at arm's length as we beat a speedy path through the woods, but she was *joyous* where I was miserable, whole where I was broken. And when she pushed forward in my mind, it was a relief, a welcome difference from my own turmoil. Diane's words echoed in my head. I didn't know her, didn't know myself. Not like this.

I reached another corner of the gate and paused, the glimmer of silver rising inch by inch into the sky, flickering through the woods outside the gate.

A bright howl rose in my chest, warm and delighted and victorious.

I gave in, and the sound exploded into the night.

CHAPTER 15
Rafe

I CURSED, dodging a tree and keeping my eyes down on the pale figure galloping wildly over the ground below. Whatever I'd expected tonight, it hadn't been for Hannah to *run* from me. Except Hannah never did what I expected, so I should've known.

I couldn't tell from up here if she was panicking, searching for an exit from the gated acres we were in, or just...had the zoomies.

She slowed as she neared the cottage, straightening her back as she crouched. The moon had risen enough now that even from above, I could make out the pucker and glimmer of the shine on her right side. I swept in a circle above her and suddenly she stood, face tipped up and eyes reflectively glowing fire up at me.

She howled, and the sound made me shiver, a slight cry in the long note. I allowed myself to fall halfway to the ground, then beat my wings once, lifting me up to the sturdiest branch I could find. Hannah's legs bent and her head tilted, watching me warily from the ground.

"You ran from me," I called down, frowning as the words came out tinged with disappointment.

Hannah straightened to a more human posture, taking a

few steps forward. Outside the gate, an owl screeched, and her head swung in that direction with the obvious impulse to *chase* the sound.

Turned away from me like that, she answered in a ragged and dark new voice. "You smelled like fear."

My wings rustled in irritation. Fear? I wasn't *afraid*. The prick at my pride was stupid and instinctive, and I was already falling from the branch to float down in her direction when I realized she was right.

Hannah stood, long and elegant, with slightly thicker thighs and an expanded rib cage. Her breasts were high and flat and inviting my mouth with round, reddened nipples. There were streaks of fur on her forearms and at the back of the bent heels of her long predator feet, and a silver-streaked tail curled around her scarred hip. She was a beautiful werewolf, a flash of movement, tense and ready to leap to action. Her gaze flickered as it traced over me, pointed ears twitching in thicker waves of fur and hair. Her snout was short and broad, a glimpse of sharp teeth gleaming from the corners. I wanted to touch her, study the flex of her legs in my hands—or better yet, around my hips—but she was shrinking in on herself as I approached, and I wasn't sure if she was bracing against an attack from me or trying to hold herself back.

"I wasn't frightened of you. I'm *not*," I clarified, and Hannah froze, on the precipice of running again. "I was frightened *for* you."

A soft whine called from her throat, and I stepped forward again. But Hannah shrank into a crouch and I stilled, the pair of us watching each other. Why was she holding still like that, staring at me out of the corners of her eyes, occasionally darting her gaze away like she was considering running again? Unless…

I crossed my arms over my chest and smirked at Hannah. "Are you still clinging to that control of yours?"

Hannah's head cocked, moonlight blinking over her huge eyes. "Of course."

"Don't you get it?" I asked. I waved a hand between us. "You're in control, Hannah. You've been in control the whole time."

She rose up from her crouch, and I spared a greedy glance for the flex of her thighs, imagining their vise grip around my hips. There was new fur there too, around her sex and on her inner thighs. I knew for a fact it would feel good against me as I fucked her.

"Even if you wanted to, you couldn't hurt me," I reminded her.

"I don't," she said, growl and whine mixing together. She blinked at me. "I don't want to hurt you."

I nodded and shrugged. "I know. So why don't you loosen the reins a bit and see what happens?"

Hannah sank deeper on her werewolf hocks, the ankle joint that led to her elongated foot, and my muscles tensed at the familiar intent in her settling expression.

"Rafe," she growled.

I feigned a grin at her and tipped my head to the side. "You want to hunt me," I said. Hannah flinched at the statement, not ready to face the truth of it, so I pushed on. "You couldn't catch me."

She huffed out a breath, rolling her eyes at the obvious bait. But it was only obvious because I knew how she'd take it. Her body grew still as she looked away from me, and my knees bent. When she darted forward, a sudden streak of pale skin and glinting eyes, I beat my wings and jumped.

I laughed as Hannah's claws swiped through the air, missing my toes by inches.

"Werewolves always think they're the biggest and baddest around," I called down to her, flying low and landing yards away. "You're puppies."

Hannah's eyes blazed, and her mouth stretched wide,

baring her pretty, sharp grin for me. She snarled and leapt forward, falling to all fours, but I was in the air again before her claws dug into the earth. I flew backwards, just high enough to remain out of her reach, and I laughed as she growled, instinctively trying to intimidate me.

"Braggarts too," I continued.

Hannah rose up at that bait. "Gargoyles are assholes."

My left wing struck the trunk of a tree at that moment, and I dropped to the ground clumsily, Hannah barking out a laugh. But she didn't waste her opportunity, racing for me once more. I ran on foot, but if there was one thing werewolves had over gargoyles, it was ground speed. I had my back to Hannah when she vaulted, arms clamping around my throat, knees hooking around my hips. I couldn't fly with her attached to me, and I stumbled at the warmth of her against my wings.

"Got you," she rumbled in my ear. And then she bit lightly at my jaw, just a nip, more of a click of her sharp teeth against my stone. I shivered at the touch. It was gentle, playful really, and not even the first time a werewolf had tried to bite me. Except the other times had all been in earnest, clients lost in the hunt. Not a teasing mark to prove a point.

Hannah hopped down from my back before I could respond, the knuckles of one hand brushing the broad skin of one of my wings. My knees tried to buckle, and my head spun. I turned to reach for her, to pull her into me, and she danced out of my reach, grinning in earnest.

"Run, Rafe."

Run, pretty toy.

I shook Sarah's voice out of my head and turned to run. Hannah howled behind me, the hunter's cry, and my wings beat, picking me up into safety. My heart was drumming heavy and fast in my chest, and I wasn't sure if it was arousal from Hannah's touch or…

I ignored the thought and spun in the air, swooping down

over Hannah's head, landing and tugging on her tail before she could swing around. She yelped, and I jumped back into flight as she dove in my direction. Back and forth we went, weaving erratically through the trees. I touched down often, aware the game wasn't fair if I spent it all in the air, but Hannah learned my patterns quickly, and more often than not my toes barely touched grass before I had to jump again to avoid being caught.

I'd had a client once, early on, who'd demanded I not fly. Another who'd climbed and leapt from tree to tree, tackling me from the air. Sarah, my last werewolf before Hannah, had simply been too good a predator, hiding from me until I let my guard down.

Hannah was simply…having fun. Growling and snapping and grunting with effort, but puffing out breaths of laughter any time she went skidding through the underbrush after just missing me.

And yet I could feel myself getting stressed. A little spike of nerves and urgency made that drumbeat in my chest falter as she nearly caught me once more. Her claws skimmed the sole of my foot, and I shuddered at the screech of those sharp tips against my stone skin, the scratch echoing up into my head. I flew higher without thinking, and Hannah paused on the ground, blinking up at me with those moon glass eyes.

"Cheater," she called.

I laughed, but the sound was ragged, and I fumbled my way onto a sturdy tree branch to catch my breath.

Hannah circled the tree trunk, prowling and pausing. Her cheeks were flushed from the activity, nipples tight and pointed either from excitement or the chilly night. She was beautiful, and I was…

What was wrong with me?

Hannah stood straight again, cocked her head, and let out a soft whine. Her wagging tail slowed. I was ruining the game for her by hiding up here. I needed to go back down. Let her catch me.

Anxiety sharpened once more, and I sucked in a sharp breath of air.

I didn't want Hannah to catch me. I didn't want her to throw me to the ground and scratch those sharp claws over my skin because…

It hurt. It hurt when Sarah would yank me back by one of my wings, when Nicolette would do her best to carve marks into my chest. It'd been part of the job, and never permanent damage, but it had *hurt*.

Hannah sank, knees bent up to her chest and arms wrapped around her shins, a little bundle of muscle and fur and those bright eyes watching me. Patient. She whined again, but the sound was soft, resigned.

I was thinking about other clients, I realized. Not Hannah. Other werewolves, not Hannah.

I don't want to hurt you.

I know.

I let out a long, slow breath of air and stepped off the branch, wings spread to catch air and slow my descent. Hannah stood and stepped back, not just making room for me but making room between us. She'd only ever been playing with me, a game we were both meant to be enjoying. I'd just gotten lost in a tangle of thought I hadn't even taken the time to notice before now.

"Come here," I said, ignoring the tremor in my voice.

I might've flinched, still stuck in my head, but I didn't have time. Hannah was pressed to my chest, her nose against my throat before I could so much as blink. She was hot to the touch, her palms crawling up the planes of my back, claws tickling against my skin. And luckily, my own instincts when it came to touching Hannah far outweighed old memories. I grabbed onto her as an anchor against my own thoughts. She purred in my ear, nuzzling my jaw.

I relaxed against her at last, cocooning us with my wings, and it was all the surrender she needed. I was on my back, breath whooshing out of me, her hands protectively bracing my wings so they had time to spread out before being crushed, and then there were three moons above my head—the one in the sky, and the pair of bright glowing eyes staring down at me. Hannah was grinning again, and she bent down slowly.

"Got you," she whispered, then nipped my nose. Her laugh was rough and guttural, and my own cracked out unevenly.

She squirmed, lying flat on top of me, still rubbing her cheeks against my throat and jaw and even down over my chest. Marking me, I realized, grinning as I sat up enough to watch her at work. Her hair curtained her face, but I could feel her breath puffing against my skin, hear the little grumbles from her throat. I had her hips in my hands, and she yelped as I hauled her off me and then threw her back into the grass and leaves, rolling to pin her there. I trapped her between my knees and hands, wings curling down to shelter us, and her eyes widened.

"Got you," I said, ducking my head to mimic the bite she'd left on my nose. Hers pinched between my teeth, and she snorted.

She reached up as I pulled away, claws outstretched for a moment, before her hand turned again, knuckles against the flesh of my wing. Gentle.

"There are…colors," she murmured, blinking and staring at my wing.

I hummed and twisted. Her vision was stronger as a werewolf. "Little fragments and particles of what makes us."

"Pretty," she said. She had the faintest lisp, her mouth not entirely used to speaking like this.

I cupped her jaw and she stilled, staring at me.

"Pretty," I said, and I bent to kiss her.

She was stiff at first—shocked, I think. But she didn't shove me away as my mouth met hers, even though we didn't fit together the same way. When she didn't respond, I sat up and rose, offering her my hand to help her up.

She took it, but she was barely standing before a feral grin stole over her face and she threw me backwards, leaping on top of me. I shouted as she laughed, and we rolled over the ground together. I wrestled with her limbs but she never snarled back, just tangled herself around me until we bumped into a tree trunk and sat up, her body wrapped around mine.

"Thank you," she whispered, and she didn't kiss me but nudged her nose to mine in something sweeter.

I nudged back and she purred, pressing into my lap briefly before turning her face away and moving to stand again.

I'd been stupid to compare Hannah to other werewolves I'd been with, or at least stupid to expect her to be similar to them. She'd never been anything like them. Except I was willing to bet all my MSA earnings for the next year on her having at least one thing in common with them, one thing she was very determinedly trying to ignore.

I grabbed her hips and pulled her down again, grinding her against my lap. Hannah growled and her eyes fell shut, head tipping back, her body rolling naturally into the motion. The sound choked in her throat and she jerked, staring at me, down at my hips where I was starting to grow thick and stiff for her.

I lifted one hand to her chin, grabbing it gently until her eyes met mine.

"Beautiful," I said, darting forward to peck a kiss to the lip pressed to those sharp lower canines. I bucked my hips up, and her breath gusted against my chin as I held those huge, pale eyes. "Sexy."

"Rafe," she grunted, but she was starting to move with me, rocking into the roll and thrust I knew she loved.

"I'll stop if you want me to," I said, shifting to rise up onto my knees. I wrapped my arm around her back, holding her to me as I thrust against her bare sex. She moaned, brow furrowing, and didn't answer. "But I'd rather do this."

I tried to lower her to the ground, surround her in my wings. That woke her up, and when she threw me off to the side, I swallowed my own disappointment. I knew she was interested physically, because that was all part of the werewolf full moon pack, but I also knew Hannah was still wrapping her brain around her transformation and that might've been a step too far, no matter what it cost her to resist.

Except it wasn't a refusal at all.

I fought off a giant smile as Hannah launched herself on top of me, claws slicing eagerly through the waistband of my pants, all the way down to one thigh. I shoved the fabric aside just in time for Hannah to come sliding down my cock.

I arched, shouting at the sudden squeezing heat of her cunt, and Hannah let out an almost human cry of pleasure. My shout turned to relieved laughter and then stolen, panting breaths as she wasted no time, riding me at a rough and determined pace, bouncing and driving her body down into mine.

"Fuck, Hannah," I gasped, gaping up at her.

Her head was thrown back, claws scratching against my chest but not deeply. The sound of that touch had no right being erotic, except that it was her, scrabbling on top of me, all abandon and appetite. She'd let go of everything, all her fear and shame and self-disgust—let go of everything but me. I reached for her breasts, pinching those ruby nipples between my fingers, and she whined and sped up. Her head tipped forward again, mouth open on noisy pants, eyes holding mine.

"That's it, gorgeous. Fucking use me," I whined.

Hannah's eyes squeezed shut, and she tightened around me so much I thought it might not take me long at all to reach the finish line, a sudden panic racing through me that I might get there before her. I kicked my hips up, pulled her down, made sure to rub her clit against my stone curls. She keened and cried, and her eyes opened again, earnest and pleading on mine.

"This is your cock," I breathed out. "I'm for you, Hannah. For whatever you need."

She grunted and groaned, falling wholly in the werewolf's mind at last, and I knew the moment I was gazing into the monster's eyes instead of the woman's.

"There you are," I whispered, meeting her body with rough upward thrusts. "You beautiful beast. Do you like this cock? It's yours."

Hannah's beast snarled her agreement, one hand sliding up to the base of my throat to keep me pinned in place for her pleasure.

"Mine," she snarled, racing faster, landing harder against me. She didn't give me orders because she wasn't about to wait for me to obey; she just took what she wanted. And she was fucking glorious.

I groaned as she tightened around me again, cunt fluttering and sucking and kissing every inch of me. And when she arched back, hands reaching for her own breasts to manage her pleasure, I held her hips and kept her pace. She howled as she came, the sound bright and brilliant and triumphant, and I ground my teeth against the grip of her. Hannah shook on top of me, and I refused to falter, holding the angle, the rhythm, the force exactly. Her mouth hung open as the wave rolled through her, and even as she twitched and sagged forward, I didn't stop.

"More," I rasped.

Her hands planted flat on my chest, head dropping down to rest there. I knew she couldn't hear my heart pounding in my chest, trapped in its stone cage. She licked my collarbone and the touch burned.

"More, Hannah," I urged, not slowing, not stopping, slapping wetly into her.

She pushed up and stared down at me, a kind of harmony on her face, curving those broad lips. "Yes," she said, and she joined me in the motion, slowing it slightly, a beautiful curve to her rocking. "Yes, more."

And then she bent and our mouths met in a clumsy, fanged, obscene kiss, her tongue twining around mine, breaths panting. I wrapped my arms around her back and held her against my chest, the racing pace of our fucking easing to a close and intimate grind.

"You know what I want," Hannah whispered. My breaths heaved as I stared up at her, and she pet my cheek once, bent to nuzzle it, and then whispered in my ear, "What's the rule, Rafe?"

She sat up, and I blinked at her. She was slowing down even more now, gliding up and down my length, stopping at the base to work herself against me.

"Rule?" I asked, lost in the view of her, all predator's grace and woman's lust.

"You know it," she said. "Say it."

I swallowed hard and stared at her. There were words on my tongue, but they were…not rules. More like a gift.

"Say it," she growled, stopping altogether.

And so I did, even though half of me didn't believe it was what she meant at all.

"We fuck till I come."

"Yesss," she hissed, moving again, cupping her long fingers around my throat. "Good boy."

I moaned, and then I was moving with her, almost frantic with need, knowing I would have to wait, that it would be worth it, that she would give me this. She kissed me again and I gave up on air, on thought, on anything but her. I would share the ecstasy; I'd make her come again and again before I reached my own finish.

The rule.

I gasped and reached between us. "Wanna feel you squeezing me again."

And Hannah arched above me, letting me rub her clit as she rode me, until she was shouting my name this time, milking my stubborn cock, drawing me in closer to the edge. We'd get there, and I'd give her everything I could before we reached that point.

"More," I snarled, sitting up and sealing her mouth to mine.

CHAPTER 16
Hannah

I WOKE to the sound of gravel falling. My body ached, but it didn't feel freshly sewn back together like it usually would after a full moon. I was bundled in cool, firm flesh, and surprisingly comfortable considering I knew it was Rafe. But the only truly hard part of him at the moment was—

The gravel crackled in my ear, and I snorted out a laugh as I realized what the sound was. Rafe was snoring and it sounded like pebbles.

His left wing was covering us, top hook pinned down into a pillow, and I reached out, recalling the little flecks of color I'd seen gleaming through the thin but impenetrable material. I stroked the flesh with my now clawless fingertips, marveling at the smooth and almost leathery soft texture, and behind me Rafe snuggled closer. I smiled to myself. He was so *sensitive*.

And such a good fuck, a rougher voice crooned in my head. I stiffened briefly, recognizing that tone and hunger. And with the voice, I recalled the night before in vivid detail—the joy of running, of hunting Rafe, of pinning him to the ground and growling filth into his ear until he was a whimpering, panting, pleading mess. And oh, how pretty he had looked as he'd come, gasping with relief, eyes wide and voice babbling gratitudes.

I was absently petting at his wing, biting my lip against the ghost memory of Rafe's wild bucking inside of me, when he released a groan in my ear and tightened his arms around me.

"*Hannah.*"

My eyes shut at my name, at the way it fell begging from his lips. I'd never heard so much need in one word. I'd never had *anyone* look at me the way Rafe did while we fucked, so stunned and rapt. It was the same power as being on stage in front of an audience, holding them in the palm of my hand right before a chorus we all knew the words to. Except instead of hundreds of pairs of eyes, it was just the one, just Rafe staring at me like he was afraid I would evaporate if he blinked.

His thigh slid between mine, one hand moving just enough to cup and squeeze at my breast. He lifted my leg and then he was sliding inside me, my hips pitching back to meet his, our moans mingling together. Simple, easy, *perfect*.

"Morning," he rasped in my ear, setting a languid pace at my back, hips circling in and out.

"Morning," I whimpered out, reaching a hand back to grab at his shoulder but stretching to find his wing root instead. Rafe grunted and I had a brief, giddy vision of being at Rafe's back, holding those tender spots in a firm grip and—

Rafe's other hand slid down between my thighs, and the thought was stolen away. I would study it later, *after*. Right now, I didn't want to waste this hazy moment.

IF I WAS DROOLING, I blamed it on the scents of garlic and onions sizzling in the skillet, and not on the outrageously pert and round ass jiggling to music on the radio. Rafe was bent over the counter, wearing an apron and nothing else—*good boy*—working on our afternoon breakfast. His wings were also vaguely dancing to the music, huge and ungainly as they were. I could've been resting in bed or lounging in the bath or stretching on one of the yoga mats tucked into a corner of the living room.

Instead, I was watching the beautiful man making me breakfast, bouncing slightly off beat to the music, chopping vegetables with a careless ease. I wondered if it was less intimidating to chop like that if you knew the knife couldn't cut you, or if Rafe had been trained.

I opened my mouth to ask when the song on the radio changed, a too-familiar bar of music blaring over the speakers.

"Oh, change the channel," I called.

Rafe stood up straight and blinked at me. "Huh?"

I scrambled off the seat as the first notes of my voice came carrying into the air. "Turn it off."

I was nearing the stereo just as he turned it off, the sudden silence as loud as Mikey's determined drumming. My face was hot, and Rafe was staring at me with amused confusion.

"You really hate that song, huh?"

My blush grew hotter and I squirmed in place, debating what to tell him and not realizing my mouth was already opening. "It's my song."

Rafe had already turned back to the counter, cracking an egg into a bowl, but he paused, staring at the egg with the shell still in his hand. "Wait, what?"

"That was...that was my band."

I pressed my lips between my teeth, and Rafe turned a comically surprised face in my direction, eyes wide and mouth hanging open.

"Your *band*?" he asked, dropping the eggshell on the counter.

I rolled my eyes and nodded, then stiffened as Rafe started to prowl closer. "No," I warned.

"Come on, I have to."

"Rafe, no!" But I was laughing, totally incapable of sounding stern.

I tried to block the stereo with my body, but as long and tall as I was, Rafe was taller, and he had no issues with crowding against me, burying his face in my throat and tickling at my sides with one hand, reaching around with the other.

I froze as the music shouted around us again, loud and sudden, my singing voice spinning through a strand of lyrics Kiernan and I had argued over. My eyes squeezed shut, and my nose wrinkled. It wasn't that I didn't like our music. I *loved* performing it. Listening back was…harder. I didn't sound like that woman any more. I didn't *feel* like her.

I cried over the stereo, long and aching, and Rafe hummed in my ear. "Oh yeah, I definitely recognize that note."

I sagged, barking out laughter, and he leaned back and grinned at me, squeezing the arm around my waist. His head tipped to the side for a moment, just listening, and I tried to escape his grip. Except I wasn't trying very hard. If anything, I might've been rubbing closer.

"I like it," Rafe mused, and then his eyes grew huge again. "Oh my god, am I fucking a *rock star*?!"

I huffed and glared at him. "If you were fucking a rock star, you'd probably have known my name to start with. Right now, all you're doing is burning a musician's breakfast."

Rafe glanced at the skillet, but it wasn't even smoking. "I dunno, I don't really keep up with music *that* much. Wow, you're on the radio! This is exciting! Grab the prosecco and juice from the fridge, we'll toast."

I'd heard myself on the radio before, but I wasn't about to turn down a mimosa or a bellini—definitely not part of my usual post full moon routine—and Rafe's excitement *was* a little infectious.

"The label's probably pushing us on air to create hype for the tour," I explained as Rafe and I set to work.

"A *tour*?!" Rafe exclaimed, with an even more exaggeratedly open mouth.

"Stop!" I laughed. "That is part of the package, right?"

He blinked and straightened, shrugging. "I suppose so. I've never really thought about the logistics of the life of a world-renowned rock star."

I didn't dignify his teasing with more than a dry look this time, and he beamed back unrepentantly.

"How do you handle full moons on tour?" Rafe asked, flippant and casual.

The shocking pop of the cork on the prosecco made me jump with tension, and I stiffened.

"They've reserved shelters for me. It's… It'll be the first time," I said, focusing too hard on the bottle in my hands.

Rafe was quiet, and when I peeked a glance, he was watching me, sober and calm now, too knowing.

"It's why I booked this weekend with you," I murmured, the words almost lost under the music—someone else's band now, thankfully—and the food cooking on the stove.

"Is it helping?" Rafe asked.

I might've said I wasn't sure. My appointments with Rafe helped because I had a plan, even in the week leading up to the full moon, a promise of relief. And they certainly made the actual full moon less tense. Except…last night had been more than less tense. It'd been kind of amazing, actually—and not just the sex. Just being able to run, to know I was safe, Rafe was safe, and to know in that moment all I really wanted was to goof off with him, have fun. My werewolf wasn't a diabolical starved monster; she was- no, *I* was just anxious, not wanting to be trapped in a box and locked away.

"Yes," I said finally, nodding.

His smile was quiet, and he nodded back. "Good. Come here. I'll teach you to flip an omelet."

I knew how to flip an omelet, but I didn't mind the excuse to be close to Rafe, so I put together two drinks for us and then slid between him and the stove, his cool body pressed to my back.

This was not what I'd expected when I'd booked Rafe. I didn't expect to be playing chase in the woods under a full moon. I didn't expect to have a beautiful man at the mercy of my werewolf and for it to be about *pleasure*, not terror. I definitely didn't expect a morning like this, laughing over breakfast, being teased like I was with my lover, my *friend*, after a rowdy weekend of rolling around in bed.

We had tonight together still, and then I would be back in the city tomorrow, living in the real world again, going weeks on end just waiting for the next appointment. Waiting for the full moon. Excited for it.

"Hmm, that was a little *too* good," Rafe said as my omelet landed perfectly back in the pan. "You were just humoring me, weren't you?"

"Yup," I said, twisting back to press a kiss to his jaw, not thinking about the gesture too hard.

I knew what we were—client and sex worker. But I also knew we liked each other, enjoyed each other's company. *Loved* the sex in an extremely mutual way.

"Go sit. Gonna make the plates look pretty," Rafe muttered.

I hid my smile and went to the table.

"Want breakfast in bed?" Rafe asked, waggling his eyebrows.

"We'd make a horrible mess, and we have to sleep in that bed. How about breakfast on the couch?"

"Pretty sure we can make a mess on the couch too."

Which was true, but at least there was a coffee table for our plates.

I settled on the floor, sipping from my glass and adding prosecco in small doses. The sun was streaming through the windows, and I had a feeling the weather outside was perfect, fall's chilly bite balanced with the sun's warm glare. Maybe I would talk Rafe into a little outside picnic blanket fucking later. Maybe he would talk *me* into it. My eyes fell shut, the corners of my lips tugging up as I daydreamed in my sunny spot on the floor.

He huffed a laugh as he entered, and I sat up. He was still only wearing the apron, but he didn't hesitate to set his bare ass on the floor, across from me at the coffee table. He slid my plate in my direction, and I sighed at the sight. Crispy roasted potatoes, creme fraiche, veggie omelet, and perfectly golden rye toast.

"You spoil me."

"That's the idea," Rafe said lightly.

And even though I knew he was paid to be here, that the response was as much a confirmation of it as anything, I still savored the warmth blooming through my chest. Affection and playful conversation had become rare in my life since the attack, but it came easily with Rafe, and at the most unlikely time of the month in my new life schedule. I needed to get Natalie a really nice gift for suggesting MSA. Maybe talk Theo into helping me plan a surprise spa day for us. He wouldn't take much convincing, I suspected.

"You know...you're one of the most gentle, careful... *controlled* werewolves I've ever met," Rafe said, eyeing me over our plates. "Aside from the full moons, what makes you nervous about the tour?"

The topic should've thrown me off my appetite, but after the past couple days with Rafe it was impossible not to be hungry, and maybe I didn't mind talking with him about it so much. That was why I was here, after all.

"I don't *feel* in control. Or I guess...I'm aware of how easily that control could slip," I said, pausing for another bite, thinking over the words to tread carefully into the truth. "My dad is a musician too. I went on a couple tours with him when I was a teenager, and I saw what it was like."

Rafe stared at me, waiting.

I cleared my throat and sat up straighter. "Dad always said being on stage is kind of like… People think you'd be exhausted at the end of a show. That all the lights and the noise and rushing all over the stage would wear you out, but actually, it's the opposite. It's like you're a battery charging until suddenly you're just a live wire, overfull and ready to throw sparks. The energy has to go somewhere."

Rafe hummed. "Partying?"

I nodded. "Partying, drugs, drinking, fighting, fucking. And I probably shouldn't have, but I saw it all firsthand. There was no control, no attempt at it. Hedonism at its finest. And for my dad and his friends, and even me, it was fun. It wasn't the part I loved most about his tours—that was…the music, the sound ringing all the way into my bones." I closed my eyes, and for a moment I could almost feel a little kernel of that joy that used to burn through me. I shook my head to clear it. "But the party culture was definitely a perk for a barely adult girl, watching fame from a sideline."

I swallowed, stalled with a bubbly, bright sip of my drink. "The week before a full moon is kind of the same as the high after a set. I am so…so *restless*. And horny," I moaned, rubbing a hand over my face. "I'm so horny before a full moon, and it's like if I even *think* about giving in, I'm cornering the nearest convenient dick. So I can't—I can't drink, I can't flirt, I can't argue, or I turn into an irrational, snarling asshole."

Rafe was frowning now, holding my gaze. And it wasn't like having this conversation with Kiernan or George, where I knew they were trying to think of the argument to counter my concerns. Rafe was just listening.

"I don't know if I can do it," I admitted softly. "It's not even about my willpower, it's… Is it possible to be on the road, with my bandmates and another whole band of people I don't know, who all want to enjoy themselves, enjoy this incredible moment we've found ourselves in, while I'm fighting with every inch of me not to give into all the impulses that I know will completely unravel my control?"

Rafe didn't answer, not that I needed one from him. And for a moment, I did feel sick to my stomach, but then I took another bite of the omelet, and *goddamn* Rafe was a good cook. I sighed as I chewed and the queasy feeling evaporated into a kind of hollow calm.

"You have to set boundaries," Rafe said.

I blinked at him, and he licked his lips.

"You just... It's not about what they can do themselves, it's more about making sure they know what you can't do and them respecting it, right?"

"I suppose."

"And I guess we need to figure out what you do with all the energy after a show," he mused. One of his knees bent up and he rested his elbow on it, holding his chin in his hand as he thought.

We.

I wish you could come with me, I thought, staring at him as he mused over my problem, all muscle and beauty, dark eyelashes fluttering and wings stretching and flexing absently.

"I like to run," I said.

Rafe smiled, eyes falling back to me. "I thought so. You have the body."

My eyebrows raised. "Oh, do I?" He nodded, smirking, and I rose to my feet, twisting side to side. "This body?"

"Those legs," Rafe said, staring at the legs in question with more hunger than he'd given his plate.

My plate was cleared. Maybe he would share...

I circled the table, and Rafe shifted, leaning back on his hands and watching me. I was in an oversized T-shirt, and I knew the hem was short enough to offer him quite a view from this angle. He reached for my calf and squeezed the muscle. I sighed and let my eyes fall shut for a moment, and he turned the squeeze into a massage.

"You know what else runner's legs are good for?" Rafe murmured, lifting my foot and drawing it to the other side of his hips.

"I do, as a matter of fact," I said lightly, blinking my eyes open and smiling down at him. His eyes were fixed to my pussy, shadowed by the T-shirt. "You didn't finish your breakfast."

"I'm hungry for something else on the menu," Rafe said, and I laughed as he grabbed my hips and pulled me down to his mouth.

My runner's legs wrapped around his shoulders, and together we put them through their paces.

THE SONG CAME in little pieces. A line that followed the whimpers of Rafe's pleas as I'd licked him clean under the table. A bridge that exploded with the stars in the sky the night I'd transformed. A final trill, the sound of the bubbles popping in the bath on our last night. I would need Kiernan to help me put it together properly, but there was a start of a melody humming in my throat.

Rafe rubbed his cheek to mine, stone body warmed by the water, solid and sturdy, arms and legs draped around either side of me.

"Whatever that is, it's sexy as hell," he rasped in my ear.

My breath caught and I stiffened in the bath, blinking at the flickering candles. Rafe's arm caught around my shoulders, stroking fingers across my chest.

I'd been…not singing, not exactly. Working out notes, an absent little call of music.

"Sorry, was I not meant to notice?" Rafe asked, chuckling a little. "Awfully skittish for a rock star."

My mouth was parted, and the room shimmered as tears rose, and my breath grew uneven before Rafe and I realized I was crying.

"Shit. Hannah?"

"I—I—" I swallowed hard and shook my head, and Rafe sat up, but only so he could wrap himself around me, drawing my knees into my chest and locking his ankles over mine, arms holding me together.

"I lost my voice."

Rafe was silent, chin hooked over my shoulder, body locked around me.

"After the attack," I continued, warm tears spilling over on my cheeks, "I didn't sound the same, and I couldn't... You can't sing when you're trying to keep your body and your mind from splitting apart. Everything is too *tight*—I can't let go. The one...the one thing I've *always* loved about myself, the thing about myself that made me love the rest of me, my *voice*...is broken."

Rafe was silent. Rafe was silent because that was exactly what I needed him to be, and *somehow* he always knew.

"And there's no music. Just *sound*. Everything has been louder and it hurts, and I wear earplugs at rehearsal, but then it's like I'm in this other place and I can't connect with my band. I'm not in my own body, I don't have my own voice, I... We recorded the album right before the attack, and now I'm not that woman anymore."

So how am I supposed to go on tour?

I shook and I cried, quiet and endless, but neither Rafe nor I spoke for a long time. Not until the water was opaque and the bubbles had popped and my tension had been exorcized in almost silent tears and only anxious sniffs remained.

"You've changed," Rafe murmured, and I let out a choked laugh and nodded my head. "But you *can* sing, Hannah.

You're in control. You have to trust yourself and let your band trust you. Like I do. The music will come back. Maybe different. But it will come back."

It had started to, here in this cottage, with this gargoyle, in little pieces of a song that I would have to take to Kiernan and make something real out of—the first bit of music that had started to play in my head in over a year.

Rafe and I softened in the water, and I closed my eyes and wet my lips and practiced the melody in a weak hum.

CHAPTER 17
Rafe

I KNOCKED on Astraeya's office door, pausing a moment to listen to the rapid click of her nails against her tablet.

"Come in," she called.

She did a double take as I slid into the seat across from her, pausing in her work to smirk at me. "Here for more of Hannah's praise?"

My wings rustled and my mouth hung open briefly. I *did* like hearing Hannah's reports, although not as much as I liked the blissed-out expression she wore after I ate her for breakfast.

"I…wouldn't mind, but actually no, not why I came in," I said slowly.

Astraeya tipped her head at me, squinting her eyes. She'd told me once that gargoyles were harder to get a read on for emotions and interests—"too hard-headed," as she put it—but I figured she had some taste of my nerves.

"Good news or bad news?" she asked.

"I…I don't know. That's up to management, I guess," I said.

Astraeya set her tablet down, her chair sliding forward, a rare seriousness taking over her. "Let me guess. You've mated Hannah?"

My wings burst open, and I let out a brief squawk of surprise at the suggestion. "What? No! She's my client!"

Astraeya arched an eyebrow. "It's happened."

"To *Khell*!" I huffed and then let out a laugh. "He was ripe for the picking."

Astraeya sighed and smiled. "Okay, what's up then?"

Astraeya's question was still sticking in my head. Why would she think I'd mated Hannah, or at least, Hannah had mated me? *Was* Hannah having werewolf mating feelings for me? Why was I more—

"Rafe," Astraeya prompted.

"Right. Uh, I want to set up some new boundaries," I burst out, startled out of my thoughts. Astraeya blinked at me. "With my clients. About…my comfort."

Astraeya frowned. "Was Hannah too rough—"

"No! No, the total opposite," I rushed out. "It's more like… I was totally fine with how things were for a long time, but it's gotten to me. Especially recently."

"Your comfort is as important to the agency as our clients', Rafe," Astraeya said gently.

And reasonably, I'd know that all along. MSA reminded those of us that worked that we had the same safety measures and ability to tailor our work as our clients did their appointments. But I'd come in to be tossed around and wrestled and scratched and tackled, and it'd all been fun. That was my role, and those were my clients. It wasn't until I realized I was anxious about how Hannah as a werewolf might treat me, that I was just as anxious about any of the other clients I worked with.

"I know, and this conversation is more the result of a lightbulb moment than something I've been sitting on, but…I mean, will MSA still need me if I'm not the indestructible guy?" I asked.

Astraeya relaxed back into her chair, offering me a smile. "You're not the first person to change your boundaries or to alter your role with the agency. We'll figure things out. Now, let's start working out what needs fixed."

I sucked in a deep breath, scuffing my palms over my knees, and sat up straight. "Most important first—I don't want my wings pulled."

"YOU WATCHING PORN IN MY BAR?"

I rolled my eyes and spared Elias a brief glare before scrolling past the video. "Don't be weird, of course not."

A tray full of baskets of food slid onto the countertop, filling the space between Khell and me, but I ignored the orc and the appetizers.

"What *are* you looking at?" Khell asked, craning across the empty stool.

I turned my phone away from his view and glared at him too, especially when I realized he had his giant hands on my basket of fried pickles. I moved to put my phone down when a pair of quick, soft-clawed hands snatched it out of my grip just as I stole back my tray of food.

"Hey!" I barked, reaching for Elias as he dodged out of the way, protected by the bar between us as he helped himself to my phone.

"Pretty," he mused, pausing on an image in the Picsapp account I'd been…perusing. His own wings rustled, and I gripped at the bar top.

"Don't dent that wood," Khell warned me.

"This is your client," Elias said, staring at me.

"No," I said, because…what else could I say? Elias could probably report me to MSA for internet *investigating* my client because yes, that absolutely was Hannah's profile. "She's…the lead singer of a band I heard on the radio."

"What band?"

"Sorry Darling. They're local," I answered quickly.

"Name one of their songs."

"I missed the song title. *You* name a song title from a band you've heard once."

Khell's gaze bounced between us, and I realized he'd gotten hold of my onion rings now. I stole those back too.

"This isn't the band's account though," Elias pointed out.

I gaped briefly and then shrugged. "So what? You've never looked at an attractive stranger's social media?"

"Hmm." Elias returned, and I snatched my phone from him as soon as it was within reach. "You're lying," he said, and I opened my mouth to argue, but he cut me off. "But that's less interesting to me than *why* you're lying."

"Who's lying? Khell, buy your own food, baby."

We all straightened, and I gusted out a relieved breath. Sunny, Khell's human mate, slid onto the stool available between us and pushed my tray of food in my direction. She was petite and rosy, with gold hair, and she tended to bring out the best behavior from Elias, although none of us, including Sunny, knew why.

"Raphael is lying about why he is internet stalking a woman," Elias said, crossing his arms over his chest.

"I'm not *stalking*," I hissed. "I just looked up the band's social media and then hers."

"Oo, what band?" Sunny asked. She was much better at stealthily mooching my food, but she would order refills of the baskets, so I pretended not to notice.

"Sorry Darling," I mumbled.

"Oh, I love them," Sunny said brightly. "They're local," she said to Elias.

"So I hear," he answered, glaring at me with those abyss black eyes of his.

"I thought they might be breaking up, actually. They sort of dropped off the radar. Their lead singer was attacked by a werewolf," Sunny added in a whisper.

My hands clenched at my sides, the sketch of Hannah's

scars vivid in my mind. "They're going on a tour soon," I said, staring down at my food, ignoring the way three sets of eyes turned in my direction.

"They are?" Sunny asked.

I nodded. "I...heard it somewhere."

"Amazing! Khell—"

"We'll find tickets, petal," Khell offered before she could finish.

Sunny hissed a "Yesss!" under her breath and stole another onion ring.

"You can come too, Rafe," Khell said, smug and obvious.

I lifted my head and held his gaze. "Perfect."

I couldn't even be that annoyed. Seeing Hannah singing live was too tempting.

"I'll have to...check them out," Elias said, arching an eyebrow at me, daring me to pick the fight.

I stuffed my mouth with fried pickles dipped in hot sauce and kept my thoughts to myself.

CHAPTER 18
Hannah

"SHE'S GOOD," Kiernan said, glugging from his water bottle and watching our new bassist, Kelsey, as she chatted with Mikey. "She's picking up the work quickly."

I nodded and accidentally caught the woman's eye as I glanced at her.

Kelsey was good. She was learning our music with a speed that was either a natural gift, or because George had offered her some homework. She was also part harpy, with glittering blue feathers around her hairline and sprouting at her elbows. Her eyes were slightly wide set and they flickered around the room like a predator's, but she didn't set me on edge like Astraeya from MSA. I suspected that was because I was the more dangerous one between the two of us.

I'd liked her best of all the candidates just from the audio files she sent in, and there was something…comforting in not being the only not-entirely-human person in the room. Not to mention having another woman in the band now.

"Mikey's going to get a crush," I murmured.

Kiernan snorted. "I'll keep an eye on it. Come on, let's get back to it. Warm up with a cover?"

I stretched, scrunching my nose as my neck cracked. "You pick."

I covered the pocket where I kept my earplugs with my right hand, but left them there. I'd asked everyone to turn their amps down for now, and it had helped with the rattle of sound I sometimes found overwhelming.

Kelsey was already moving to her bass as Kiernan and I walked over to where the gear was set up, instruments and amps arranged in a circle. We liked to face each other during our rehearsals. It was harder for me to communicate with them when we were on stage, when I was meant to be facing a crowd and not them, but this time together helped us learn each other's cues, the spots in a song where Kiernan wanted to experiment or when Mikey tended to fall off rhythm.

"Don't worry if you don't know this one, but I can mouth the chords to you," Kiernan said to Kelsey. "Pretty standard four count otherwise."

"I'll catch on." From what I could tell, our bassist was crisp on delivery and energetic while playing. I had a feeling I'd like her even more when we had time to relax around one another, but for now I appreciated how serious she was.

Kiernan started the first trickling run of notes, and I smiled, perching on my stool and cooing into the microphone, a familiar, sexy classic song we'd covered at plenty of local shows. Kiernan had learned it for his current girlfriend, and I'd always been mildly intimidated by some of the belting notes in the bridge, but this was only a rehearsal. And I had to learn my voice now, like Rafe had said.

I closed my eyes, ignoring the exchange between Kelsey and Kiernan, her soft fumble into the notes at first and then the moment she found her footing, thumping darkly along with Mikey's beat on the bass drum.

The music shook in my chest, a slow and powerful heartbeat, or better yet, the pace of a good thrust in sex. I ignored the sudden gratitude, the sting of tears in my eyes, and pressed my palm over my thrumming heart. *The music will come back.*

Rafe's face appeared in my thoughts, brow furrowed and lips parted on a pant. My body shivered with the memory of him, cunt pulsing with the phantom sensation of how he felt inside me, the detailed tease of his carved cock.

It might've been Kiernan's song for his girlfriend, but it was mine for Rafe in the moment, the need and the filth and the joy of sex. And when the bridge came, I didn't think about the notes, about the sudden rise and carrying cry that was always a fifty-fifty shot of whether or not I'd hit it.

I howled.

The sound trembled in the air and my eyes popped open, the cry ringing out, bouncing off the ceiling and snarling out of my amp. Kiernan fumbled the notes briefly and Mikey missed a beat, but we gathered ourselves back together a moment later, running steadily to the end of the song. My face was warm, and I wasn't sure if it was thoughts of Rafe or excitement, but I stood from the stool I usually rested on before Kiernan plucked out the last note.

"What the hell was that?" Kiernan laughed, eyes wide on me.

I shook my head. "I don't know!" But I did know one thing —it had sounded *good*.

"Werewolf," Kelsey said, shrugging.

Mikey and Kiernan blinked at her and then at me.

"I've heard it before," Kelsey said, "Although it was in a screamo band. But I was kind of expecting it all day."

Kiernan and I gaped at one another. "Could you do it again?" he asked me.

I opened my mouth to say I wasn't sure and then shut it briefly. I felt wild when I thought of Rafe, and that wasn't hard to do. My head tried to circle back to him more times in a day than I was even entirely comfortable with.

I swallowed and thought of a lyric in one of our songs, a place where I stretched my voice as far as I could.

The sound poured out of me again, resonant and sharp

and full, banging its way around the room, echoing and ringing darkly. And it was so easy. I shivered and gasped in the wake, alive and aroused and *excited*.

"Holy shit," Mikey murmured. "Crowds will flip."

"You already had a beautiful voice, but that certainly won't hurt," Kelsey said, with her first faint smile.

I answered it back with a grin and then turned to hide my expression for a moment. I wanted to sing. I wanted to belt. I wanted to know this sound I could make and claim it and perfect it, and I *wanted to sing*. I hadn't shared the new song I'd started playing with yet, but already I was running it through my head, searching for places to howl.

"Huh, weird," Kiernan said, but he wasn't looking at me. He was looking at his phone. "We've got…a gig offer. More like a gig demand?"

My eyebrows rose. "A demand?"

"Kind of. 'Name your price,' it says," Kiernan said, a puzzled smile twisting over his lips. "It's at a local bar. Nightlight?"

Kelsey whistled, and it was a pretty, crystalline sound, her harpy genes at work. I cataloged it for later. A whistle would be another beautiful new sound in our band's arsenal if we wanted it. *Fuck*, I was excited. And I was so happy to *be* excited that I wanted to cry and also maybe run circles around the room.

"That's owned by the moth," Kelsey said.

"By the…moth?" Mikey asked.

Kelsey stared at me, expectant, and I shrugged. She sighed. "Elias, he's a moth fae. He's…notable. And he owns Nightlight. It's a bar that mostly…our kind hang out at." She was still staring at me as she said it, the meaning delicate but obvious. *Our kind*. Not humans.

"He says he has friends who are fans of ours," Kiernan said, staring at me.

"We could use a local event to run out any kinks," I

suggested, bouncing on the balls of my feet, eager energy crackling through me. Kelsey was still new, and we had a tour coming up. She was catching up quickly, but it would be better to test out the live experience with her a few times before we were on the road.

"What's a moth fae like?" Mikey asked Kelsey.

She shrugged. "Big, fuzzy, ridiculously snobby, I think. It's a big compliment for him to be interested."

"It's a good offer," Kiernan admitted.

"Name your price" was a ridiculous offer, even if we were picking up some success lately. But it wasn't the money that made me curious.

"What kinds of species hang out there?" I asked Kelsey.

"All kinds."

Gargoyles? I wondered. *And what else?* Rafe was right—I'd been clinging to my humanity ever since I was attacked. But there was a whole world out there I belonged to that I hadn't explored yet.

"We'll need more rehearsals, but we should say yes," I said to Kiernan. "Run it by George?"

"You got it," Kiernan said, grinning.

"Man, it's been forever since we gigged. It's been—" And then Mikey stopped abruptly, remembering exactly how long it'd been. Since a week before I was attacked.

I just nodded, letting the slip float by. "We need it. This will be good."

"Lawrence will die," Mikey whispered, eyebrows waggling.

I snorted and turned away. Out of the corner of my eye, I caught Kelsey's approach.

"The moth cultivates relationships with those he finds curious or rare, like himself," Kelsey said, lowering her voice. "He probably knows more about you than you realize."

I stiffened. "You think this is about me?"

"Probably. Maybe he really does have friends who are

fans, but that wouldn't be enough to interest him. A werewolf lead singer about to go on tour? More exciting to the general mixed-species crowd. It's why I auditioned," she admitted.

"You auditioned because I'm a werewolf?" I asked, frowning.

"Because I thought I had a better chance of getting in a band that had a non-human front person. A band where it won't be…a gimmick. A 'monster band,'" she said, finger quotes in the air.

I blew out a breath, her words grinding through my head uncomfortably as I twisted my hair up off my neck. "Do you think us becoming a gimmick is a possibility?"

Kelsey shook her head. "Not with the label you have. But it would be if I tried to start a band on my own."

I stared at her, noting the feathers, the dart of her eyes. Not quite human. "Do you sing?" I asked.

"I can harmonize, if that's what you're asking," she answered, bucking her chin up.

I nodded. "Good. Let's put something together. Kiernan and Mikey can't sing for shit."

She smiled, and I turned away, hiding my frown as I reached for water. I didn't want to be a token novelty in the music scene—the werewolf's band. But I wasn't going to hide my howl or push Kelsey away because she would stand out. Part of me wanted to grab onto the steering wheel with a white-knuckled grip, map out every move we made, control the new dynamic of the band and how we would be seen. But a new instinct was growing in me, and for once, it was calm instead of aggressive. My life had changed. I couldn't take that back. Now I had to find balance—as Hannah, and as a werewolf.

I turned back to my band, shoulders square and the ground beneath me steady, if not entirely solid. "Let's work on a set list for our mothman benefactor. Kelsey, give us some clues."

A THROAT CLEARED behind me as I helped myself to the fruit buffet at the support group. I turned, smiling and expecting Theo, and then froze.

"Hi. I'm Fletcher."

The new guy. "Hey, yes. Hi," I answered, clearing my throat. He had a strong scent, sharp and warm at the same time, and he was standing a little too close, but something bristled in me at the idea of backing up, so instead I stood straighter.

"I…I just wanted to say that I…" His gaze was flashing all over my face, studying me, and I stared back. The pupil of his right eye was distorted, and I wondered if it had anything to do with the scar there, if he'd lost some vision when he was attacked. He let out a sudden breath. "Sorry, I don't know what I want to say. That I…admire you, I guess? For being able to trust someone enough to spend the full moon with them."

"Oh!" I relaxed slightly and found myself falling back a step at last, catching breathing room. "It…wasn't easy. It isn't. Trust me, I know." Fletcher nodded, but his stare was still rapt. "It was a relief though."

I'd said as much in the meeting, recalling the freedom of running with Rafe, of just collapsing into the grass with him until dawn. I'd kept some of the joy of it private, too personal, too precious to be real, almost…like I'd imagined it.

"How did you find that person?" he asked, the question desperate, his hands fisting at his sides until he stuffed them into his coat pockets.

A laugh escaped me at the thought of telling this massive man the truth. That I'd hired Rafe to be with me, that I wasn't just with a friend, that I was with someone I couldn't stop touching and fucking and playing with under the full moon.

"It's just…it can't be forced, right?" I answered, shrugging, even though that was somewhat of a lie. "Like any other relationship or friendship, you wait and see."

Fletcher frowned, lip curling slightly and brow creasing. I bristled again and sidestepped him, pleased to see Theo headed in my direction. "Excuse me."

I left Fletcher to his dissatisfaction and met my friend halfway.

"A little birdie told me you've got a gig at Nightlight this weekend," Theo said, grinning. "Actually, she screeched it at me while I was showering this morning."

I laughed. "Will you guys be able to make it?"

"Oh, absolutely. Natalie's best friend is coming too. You'll like the bar."

"I hear the owner is interesting?"

Theo rolled his eyes. "Elias is a snob, or maybe I just don't like that he ignores me and Natalie. But it's a good interspecies community place, so I'll credit him for that."

"Well, it sounds like he has very poor taste in friends," I said.

Theo paused then, starting to speak and then stopping again. "Well… Actually, nevermind. It's gonna be a fun night, and I'm glad I finally get to see you perform."

It was my turn to pause. "God, that's right. You haven't. I haven't been on stage since…"

Theo's eyes widened. "Don't get nervous!"

"I'm not!" I was.

"It's not a huge space. It'll be small, intimate."

"That's worse, actually. No lights to blind me," I said, grimacing.

"Hmmm, so you don't want Nat to bring a poster board covered in glitter and pictures of you?"

I froze, staring in horror at Theo, unable to tell on his innocent face if he was joking or not. It wasn't outside of the realm of possibility with Natalie.

"Do you value your wife's life?" I asked.

Theo cracked at last, chuckling. "She'll take that as a challenge. I'll try and subdue her."

"Whatever you have to do, Theo. Please." I licked my lips and glanced around the room, catching Fletcher watching us and shaking off the cling of his stare from my mind. "I need this show to go well. I know it's small and it's local, but—"

Theo nodded. "I know. And it will. We'll get there early and have a drink beforehand."

I puffed out a breath. "One drink. But I don't want to party."

"I understand. Mellow company, amazing night. It's gonna be good, Hannah," Theo said.

He seemed confident, so I borrowed some of that feeling for myself and hoped it would last me through the show.

CHAPTER 19
Rafe

"YOU HAVEN'T TAKEN your eyes off her."

I sighed, but I didn't feel like proving Elias wrong, not when—

"And to be fair, she's spent most of the night staring back at you."

Hannah was surrounded by my friends, some of whom seemed really familiar with her. Natalie said something in her ear and Hannah's eyes pulled from mine, squeezing shut as her head fell back and she laughed. Theo, the world's most mellow werewolf, smiled at the pair of them, and pieces of a puzzle I hadn't even realized I was in the middle of started to fit together. Natalie was the catalyst for Sunny hiring Khell. If she knew Hannah too, did I have her to thank for sending my favorite client my way? She would be insufferable if I said anything.

"What do you want, a cookie?" I asked Elias, sparing him a glance.

The bar was packed, Sorry Darling's set freshly wrapped up for the night. Some of Hannah's bandmates were tucked behind a merchandise table, and every so often someone would tap Hannah on the shoulder for an autograph. She blushed every time.

"You know what I want," Elias said in my ear.

I rolled my eyes. "Fine. You were right."

"I know," he answered lightly.

I crossed my arms over my chest, unable to fight my smile as Hannah signed another T-shirt, cheeks warm in the spotty glow of Nightlight's ambience, her gaze flicking to mine once more. She shook her head at me slightly, eyes narrowing, and it took everything in me to remain standing against the wall. I'd grabbed a spot by the hall that led to the four individual bathrooms right before the music had started, and I'd made it through the concert before Hannah had spotted me.

She'd been incredible—the whole band had, to be fair. Watching her sing reminded me of one of our appointments. She was cold at first, reserved, beautiful and haughty, but the longer she'd stood under the spotlight, the more the crowd called and cheered her, the more she unwound, until she was sweaty and howling, eyes glazed, body, mind, and voice locked into the music so completely, she was all energy and sound. I was as riveted at the sight of her singing as I was when we fucked.

"Are you going to report me?" I asked Elias.

"For what? You haven't done anything," he said, shrugging.

I wanted to. I would.

"She didn't accept the cocktail I designed for her."

I turned at the bitter note in his voice, and found him frowning at Hannah. "She's not drinking."

His antenna twitched, and his wings ruffled. "A mocktail, then. She should've said."

I laughed. "Maybe she just wanted water?"

Elias wrinkled his nose. "I'll try again. Quit lurking in the shadows. Khell will think you're mad at him."

Khell was busy trying to convince Sunny to dance with him, grinding against her back in time with the music. Or maybe he was just trying to get her alone. But when I turned to join my friends, I realized Hannah was weaving through the crowd, headed directly for me.

I held my place, and she didn't stop, her eyes widening with meaning, holding mine as she brushed against my shoulder. I glanced at the crowd once more. Natalie was eyeing us, and behind her, deeper in the room but a head taller than everyone else, so was Hannah's guitarist.

I didn't care. I turned and followed Hannah into the dark hallway, grateful for the shadows that thickened around us.

Hannah spun as she reached the end of the hall. "What are you doing here?"

"I can go," I said, aware that my attendance might've crossed a boundary for her. I shouldn't have come. Hannah was the bait Elias had dangled to catch me in a lie, and I'd let it work because I wanted to see her, see her in this new element.

"No!" Hannah hissed, reaching for my arm. Her lips were parted and her cheeks were full of color, and she looked so happy it radiated from her, filling the air. "Did you hear me? I *sang*," she said, eyes glittering.

"To be honest, I couldn't hear anything but you," I said, not thinking through the confession before it was out.

Her gaze softened and then grew warm, inviting. Short strands of hair were still plastered to her temples, and she'd cooled off since leaving the stage, but I recalled the trickle of sweat that ran down the long line of her chest, and already knew how it would taste on my tongue.

Not that it mattered. I wanted to taste her *again*.

I caught her by the neck, pulling her into my chest and ducking down. She rose on the balls of her feet, barely an inch, and that was all it took for our mouths to fuse together. My free arm banded around her waist, and her arms fastened around my shoulders, holding me as tight as I held her. She moaned into the kiss, arched her hips into mine. Our bodies were urgent, but our tongues slid languidly against one another as the kiss opened, stroking and teasing, retreating.

I pulled away to check in, but she whispered my name, her eyes shut and head tipped back.

At our appointments, Hannah was my client, but here, we were just two wildly irresponsible people, and I didn't want to question that. I wanted to be inside of her.

I released her neck to grab the handle of the bathroom on our right, grunting as it turned easily and the door open. Light spilled out, and I dragged Hannah in with me before anyone else might appear in the hall.

She was grinning, still hanging onto me by my shoulders, and our mouths crashed back together before the door even shut. We slammed it closed as I pushed her in place. She was wearing dark high-waisted jeans that made her legs look twice as long, her loose, black button-down shirt buttons ignored and hem tucked in so that the collar gaped down her smooth skin to her belly button. Her bra was black lace, visible through the soft opening of the shirt, and even more so when I pushed the fabric aside.

"Are you wound up?" I asked, bending my knees as Hannah's legs spread to make room for me. I rubbed my face into her chest, testing the texture of her bra against my cheek before nudging her shirt even farther open and sucking her nipple through the lace.

"Oh, fuck yes," she cried out, which might've been an answer to my question or just approval of the steady suckling on her tit. "Yes. But—Rafe!"

I reached into her shirt to grip her other breast, lifted one leg with my other hand to wrap it around my back, and looked up at her through my lashes. Her eyelids were heavy, lips parted and damp from the kiss.

"I don't need this," she whispered.

I brushed my thumb over her tight nipple and prepared to

pull away, but her hand sank into my hair, and every gliding stroke tugged sweetly on the roots.

"But I fucking want it so bad," she added with a toothy smile

My wings spread and beat in the air, and I was soaring with both feet on the ground. Hannah moaned and her eyes fell shut, head knocking against the door lightly as I scraped my teeth over the flesh of her breast.

"So do I," I said, and she sighed, a silky smile stretching over her lips. "Watching you sing made me hard, Hannah."

The flush on her cheeks spread down to her throat, and I stood straight, pushing the proof of my statement against her, rewarded with a strangled whimper.

I kept one thumb teasing that nipple, swirling in a circle around it, tugging it side to side so gently. I'd memorized her responses already, and I knew how wet that simple touch would make her. She'd be soaked by the time I shimmied her jeans down her hips and...

I glanced over my shoulder and grinned at the reflection of us in the mirror over the bathroom sink. She liked to watch me in mirrors. It was my turn.

"Your voice when you sing reminds me of the sounds you make when I'm inside of you," I said, pressing my chest to hers, rubbing my half-hard cock between her legs, grinning as she started to grind against me.

"Are you—are you sure?" Her eyes flew open to clash against mine, and her tongue flicked out to wet her bottom lip, the gesture snaring my attention. "You should... Oh, Rafe! You should be sure."

"Good point," I said, nodding. I stepped back, and Hannah's brow furrowed so adorably that I had to return again, cupping her jaw in my hand to draw her mouth to mine. She tasted sweet and bright, like soda, and I recalled the clear bubbly drink I'd seen in her hand, an easy disguise for a cocktail to keep others from offering her drinks.

I sucked on her tongue as she thrust it into my mouth, and she whined and squirmed against me, tearing away for a gasping breath.

"Fuck, why am I so close?"

I stepped back, fighting a triumphant smile and releasing the breast I'd tortured, taking her hands in mine. She stumbled as I guided her, spinning her away from me to face the mirror. Her palms slapped against the counter and she stared back at herself, startled and dazed, as I pulled her shirt loose from the waist of her pants.

Our hands tangled as we both reached for her waistband, fumbling at the buttons before I opened one and Hannah shoved the jeans roughly down. I covered her sex with my hand, rubbing immediately at her clit, as I unfastened my own pants. Hannah arched, breasts thrust forward, sinking her weight onto my fingers.

Her legs were trapped by her jeans, but it just made her squeeze incredibly around me as I nudged my cock between her thighs, the urgent need to be inside of her leaving me clumsy until I found her soaked core. We groaned together as I pushed in, Hannah's head falling forward, curtaining her face and the picture of her breasts in the mirror.

I paused inside of her, staring down at her back, watching the rise and fall of her unsteady breath. I tugged her shirt back to slide it down her arms just enough to show me more skin. The scars on her back were red and bright in the bathroom light, framed by the thin black straps of her bra. I reached for her hair next, pulling it back from her face, aside from the shortest layered strands. Her gaze met mine in the mirror, dark and startled and hungry. I twisted the thick locks in my grip, drawing her head back and her chin high, and she gasped.

We weren't supposed to do this.

"Fuck me," she breathed.

This wasn't an appointment. This was, if anything,

outstandingly selfish of me. But Hannah was still giving orders, and they weren't ones I had the willpower to resist.

I pulled slowly out, but my hand on her sex just guided her back with me, keeping the connection, pulling her into a deeper bend. Her breasts were small, but they still bounced as I slammed back in, and Hannah's sharp cry was every bit the note of a song. Her eyelashes fluttered, but she kept them open, kept watching me as I fucked her. If there was anyone in the hall, anyone in the nearby bathrooms, they would hear her. My fingers tangled out of her hair and then gripped the back of her neck, holding her in place. I rubbed at her slick clit, fucked her hard and quick, and wished I had a dozen more hands. I wanted to be touching those open lips, playing with her tits, stroking her hips, and tracing the line of her spine.

"I take it back," I gasped, slowing down as she started to clutch and quake around me. "You sound even better like this."

And then Hannah came, laughing and gasping and sobbing with relief, her arms wobbling as they braced against the marble countertop.

It wasn't enough. Once wasn't enough. I didn't like to be cheap. I released her hair and the nape of her neck, wrapping my arm around her chest, pushing the bra up so I could cup her breast and draw her closer to my chest, tip the angle where I struck inside of her.

"More!" Hannah growled, the sound hiccuping as my cock hit true. "Oh, fuck."

"More," I agreed, muttering the word into her ear.

My wings were stretched, hiding everything in the mirror but us. Had we locked the door? I didn't care. Sweat was glittering golden on Hannah's chest, and her hands lifted to cover mine, not guiding, just gripping me. She was still squeezing, slicking my cock as I stayed buried inside of her, just stroking her core at the right angle to make her legs go weak. They could give out completely, and I would hold her against me, fuck her as she went limp with pleasure, cunt filled, wide mouth whimpering and sighing and singing sweetly in response.

"I want you to come," she whispered. "I want to watch you."

We'd only been alone here for a handful of minutes, and no matter what Elias knew and how smug it would make him, I didn't think we'd be able to steal that much time together. Someone would come to collect her. Her band. My friends. But I wasn't going to refuse her, and it was more likely that she'd beg off before I could come, so I just…didn't stop.

Hannah came again, her hand over her breast flying back to grab onto my left wing root. I grunted as she squeezed and bit her scream off behind flat pressed lips. Her jeans were sliding down her thighs the longer we fucked, and it gave her room to spread, to let me sink in deeper, her body clasping around me.

Maybe I could…maybe if I just—

"Stone," Hannah gasped.

I ignored her at first. Werewolf or not, fucking stone for an hour would hurt her, and no matter how selfish it was to break code with MSA, to reach out to a client in her real life because she was—because I—

"Stone, Rafe," Hannah growled, and then she was gripping my sensitive wing roots with both hands, tugging me down against her back, yanking me somehow closer.

I shuddered, and the change was almost involuntary, her demand too powerful and too close to what I really wanted. I wanted to finish with Hannah every time. I wanted the pleasure she offered, no, ordered from me, and I wanted to give her the satisfaction she seemed to find when I came.

"Fuck," I gasped out. "Fuck, Hannah, you burn me."

She blinked, confused by the words, but I didn't stop

moving, didn't stop driving myself inside of her, wrapping her around me completely. I missed her legs around my waist, her arms holding me to her chest, but her back was warm through my shirt.

I buried my face in her hair, braced one hand on the counter when I was afraid I would be too rough with her breasts. I tried to hold my hand still against her slick lips and let her work herself against them, but I was trembling with tension.

Her voice broke with every thrust, but I knew the sound she made when I got a little too rough, and these brief, bright cries were only praise to my ears.

"Do you know how hard it is not to book you every week?" Hannah whispered. "Every night."

And then before I could really think about how much I wanted that, Hannah came again, her grip on my wings brutal, even against the resistance of stone. I found her eyes in the mirror, wide and startled as she scorched liquid heat on my pumping cock.

"Come for me," she breathed.

And she didn't stop squeezing. I'd found the right spot inside of her, or the correct pressure on her clit, or it was the accumulation of the moment, the fix of our stares together, but Hannah was trapped in a loop of ecstasy, her throat flexing with her struggling breaths.

I had no business being so close to the edge, except that was what she'd asked of me, and my brain was starting to associate all of these little details—being in my natural form, being inside of Hannah, the grip and kiss and clutch of her cunt on my length as she came—with my own release.

"Come, Rafe," she gasped out.

I shouted as my body defied logic to do as I was told, my hand on the counter forgetting its strength, crunching marble in my fingers as I bucked wildly, the sudden snap of electric pleasure shocking me head to toe.

Hannah's hands slapped back to the counter, holding us up as my orgasm hit and I fell into her, wrapping my arms around her and burying my face in her hair as I trembled through the bolts and licks that followed the first explosion. Her breath was loud, with soft little moans on her exhales, and she rolled back into me, milking my cock with her echoes of her own release.

I would never tell her this, but she was so small in my arms, so fragile, it almost terrified me. She spent so much time being afraid of hurting me, but in reality, I could've crushed her in my grip. Instead, I searched for the perfect hold, the one that let her soften and sag and go limp against me as we caught our breath.

Every night.

I hid my grin in her hair, imagining how absurdly perfect it would be to just…be at Hannah's beck and call. Would she still want me to come every time. Would it be the rule? I didn't care if it wasn't—I wasn't sure I even cared if she never told me to finish again. Would she let me experiment with new vegetarian recipes? Make her dinner every night, let her use my body to unwind from the adrenaline high of being on stage?

I was drowsing in my fantasy when she started to move against me, to slide away, and my arms tightened briefly before my head cleared. I pulled back and hissed as Hannah dragged away from the exquisite fit of me inside of her. My arms loosened, almost dropping to my sides, but she was only turning to face me. Her hands held my jaw as she rose for the kiss, and in another moment we were tangled back together, arms around one another as we tasted and nibbled each other's lips.

Nightlight's bathrooms were pristine, but it was still a cold interior, and I wanted to roll and find a mattress to lay us down on, to keep kissing Hannah until we were either falling asleep or she was wiggling and searching for my cock at her opening again.

Behind us, the door handle jiggled, clicking as the lock held. Hannah stiffened and bit briefly at my bottom lip before pulling away, both of us turning to stare. The handle jerked again, but there was no knock, and it went silent as we held our breath.

Hannah sighed and swiped her hand through her hair, and her eyes were wide on mine. "I…wasn't expecting… Was that…?"

I grasped her face in my hand, pulled her in for a firm kiss, cutting off the question. That was selfish. That was us. That wasn't part of MSA. That was fucking fantastic.

She relaxed, and her eyes were slightly hooded as I pulled away again. We fixed our clothes, smiling at one another, and when she opened her mouth to speak again my heart rattled in my chest.

"I'll see you in less than a week," I said.

Because I was an idiot and afraid she would thank me or offer me money. Or worse, that she might invite me home with her, which I would absolutely say yes to and then probably lose my job—like Khell, but without the resumé and backup plan to cover my ass. Or even worse than that, that she wouldn't.

She blinked, but her smile didn't falter. "Six days."

She was counting the days.

"Six days," I echoed, itching to reach for her again, pull her into my chest, wrap my wings around her, and pretend we were just a few steps away from a bed.

I turned, tucking my wings close and heading for the door. The hallway was empty. Whoever had interrupted us either gave up or found a different restroom, and even the bar seemed to have thinned out.

Hannah's fingers slipped under my shirt, grazing a line across my back. Her head was high as we walked down the hall together, but no matter how casual she looked, there was only one conclusion anyone could make if they looked at us. I brushed the back of her hand and turned, heading for the door without another word.

Six days.

CHAPTER 20
Hannah

I SMOOTHED my hands over my skirt as the car bumped down the lane in the MSA woods, headlights twisting and flashing around tree trunks in the dark. The driver seemed to inch closer to our destination, and I wondered briefly if I could throw myself out of the backseat and run there faster. Another part of me considered asking him to slow down, because I wasn't quite ready to see Rafe again yet.

The weight of him on my back. The crack in the marble countertop. His breath, cool in my hair. The thick cock filling and stroking inside of me.

Six days had taken six years or six minutes. Just a few aimless days of being horny at home, where nothing satisfied my itch but replaying memories, and a few good rehearsals with the band. They dragged by until suddenly, they were gone and I had only one day of waiting left. Just eight hours to idle through before taking the train to the suburbs, arriving too early at MSA, and sitting in a lobby until a car was ready to drive me to the cottage in the woods.

Until finally, *finally*, the guest service car parked, headlights golden through gauzy curtains.

"Enjoy," the driver said, mild and neutral.

My hands were sweaty and my legs were numb, and I

stared out of the backseat passenger-side window for either a moment or an hour. Time was all sideways and backwards since…

I'd only meant to tease Rafe for coming to the little show at Nightlight, maybe tell him how hard it was to remember my lyrics while he was undressing me with his eyes from the corner of the room. And then he'd kissed me, and it had been reflexive and perfect and exactly what I'd needed—the outlet for the bright, electric buzz running through my veins.

The driver's throat cleared, and I jumped out of the car, making it three steps away before I remembered my bag and had to fling myself back to the door before he pulled away.

Wake up, calm down.

The bag and its contents—what the hell was I thinking when I'd packed?—thumped against my side, adding to my nerves. The air was cold, a bitter reminder that I'd dressed in thin silk and a long coat, no protection at all from the wind coming off the lake. It cut through my skirt, biting between my legs, turning icy where I was slick, a somewhat cruel proof of my arousal.

I opened the door to the cottage, and the air was heady with spice and garlic and onion, something warm and yeasty in the background. I was immediately warm, immediately relaxed, immediately wanting.

I dropped my bag and hurried for the kitchen, pausing in surprise to find it empty. There was a pot steaming on the stove, a loaf of bread on the table. No gargoyle.

A shadow loomed on the wall, and I smiled as firm arms wrapped around my waist and a cool chest pressed close.

"Hungry?"

"Not yet," I said, even though my mouth was watering.

Rafe's hands slid up, sliding over my breasts, and I leaned forward as he pulled my coat off my shoulders. "Bath?"

It was probably already started, also steaming, the bathroom all glittering with candles and scented with rose petals in the water.

I shook my head. "I want you to put me on the bed and eat me out until I beg for mercy."

Rafe groaned and pressed close, nuzzling his face into my hair again, a habit he'd picked up with me, his hands sliding back down my chest to pull my hips back to his. He was half hard, and there was a very good possibility that I would change my mind and beg for him to be inside of me rather than for mercy.

And I knew, with absolute certainty, that he would do it. Rafe wanted me.

The kiss. The broken countertop. The devastated joy on his face as he came.

"I like your taste in clothing," he murmured, stroking my hips and thighs and over my sex and ass through the silk.

And then he scooped me up and carried me to the bed.

"WOULD you like to explain to me what this was doing in your bag?"

I was face down on the bed, starfished and naked, fully prepared to either sleep another four hours or wake up with Rafe's face in my pussy. His tart tone permeated my foggy head first, and the words translated through my fuck-drunk confusion.

I sat up with a start, scrambling through the tangled sheets, wincing at the slice of sunlight cutting through a curtain.

"It was just an idea!" I shouted.

But Rafe was laughing, arms stretched above his head as I ran for him, keeping his stolen treasures out of my reach. The purple dildo wobbled side to side in the air above our heads, but I managed to snag at the leather harness, ripping it from his grip and tossing it on the bed behind me.

"You didn't mention it last night."

"You need to stop digging around in my bag," I huffed out, trying and failing to climb him.

His free arm wrapped around my waist, and I grunted as he lifted me. But I put my own arms around his shoulders, sagging in his hold and glaring down at his beaming face.

"I would, but I always find something fun in it," Rafe answered, and he grabbed my ass and hoisted me higher around his waist. "I knew you liked my ass, but I didn't realize how much."

My face was on fire, so I hid it against his cool shoulder as he carried me out of the bedroom. "Rafe."

"I have to admit, I wasn't expecting this—"

"Rafe," I groaned, but the damn man was carrying me to the kitchen where I smelled cheese, and he and I both knew he was going to be forgiven for teasing me as soon as I'd had my first bite.

"But I've always been curious to try it."

I lifted my head at that. "You haven't before?"

Rafe shrugged and his wings rustled, and my hand couldn't help but reach out and brush over the boning, his eyelids sinking in pleasure at the touch. "No one's asked."

You could've asked, I thought, and then realized that wasn't really true. *You could've asked* me.

"We've got lots of time before you shift to try it out," Rafe said, waggling his eyebrows.

I glanced at the clock on the stove. It was close to noon, so we did have most of the day. I knew now how a day with Rafe went—we ate, we fucked, we got lazy in the bath, we fucked, we napped, we ate. Aside from when I was a werewolf, being together in this cottage reminded me of the dreamiest moments of a new lover, when you couldn't stop touching and kissing, and silence was profoundly intimate and conversations were trivial and meaningful at the same time. I didn't forget that I was Rafe's client, that this was his job, but I also knew our chemistry and connection was genuine.

"We could...we could save it...for tonight," I murmured, half-hoping he hadn't heard me. Except I was still right by his ear and there was no chance of that.

Rafe set me on my feet, and I remembered I was naked at the exact moment he pulled his long sleeve shirt off over his head and then dropped it onto me.

"This is a craving, isn't it?" he asked, and I struggled my arms into the sleeves and popped my head through the collar to find his eyes glittering down at me. He reached over and pushed my hair back from my face before I had to do it myself. "Your werewolf-y urges have been thinking about this."

"I think so," I said. I knew so.

Rafe nodded. "You're definitely more dominant when you're shifted. It's hot."

I was blushing, but he just turned and pulled a plate out of the oven. And bless his juicy firm ass and carved cock, it was loaded with breakfast burritos, and the counter was dressed with bowls of salsa and guacamole and there were beans simmering on the stove.

"I'm going to have MSA send us some lube and plugs in that case. You gotta work for it," he added, winking at me over his shoulder and then shaking his ass.

IT WAS EASIER SAID than done to get anything up an ass as tight as Rafe's, especially when his flesh was significantly firmer as a gargoyle. I nearly broke a finger when he clenched, and lube helped, but also made things so outrageously slippery it was like a game of evasion to get the plug in place. Finally, Rafe had to push the little stainless steel bulb in himself because I was too nervous.

But the sight of him with his legs spread and his brow crunched with effort and his mouth falling out in a garbled cry as it sank in was worth all the frustrated laughter and my bruised index finger. And the sounds he made as the plug wiggled and pushed inside of him as he walked around made my thighs press together.

And the way he gasped and squirmed on the floor, eyes wide as pressure forced the plug deeper while I rode his cock at the edge of moonrise, made the burn in my thighs sing up into my cunt and the sweat trickling down between my breasts a licking caress.

"Oh fuck, oh Hannah, fuck," he hissed, squeezing his eyes shut as I leaned back against his bent legs and tried to push him endlessly deeper inside of me.

My transformation was already prickling under my skin, but I was so close and so was Rafe, and I wanted to see how many times I could make him come tonight, because he fucking deserved to feel as wrung out tomorrow morning as I always did.

"We're running out of time." I had my eye on the window and then the clock. We were minutes away from moonrise, but I needed this—I needed this last moment of relief and ecstasy before the torture of the shift.

"Don't stop, please."

Rafe had a beautiful whine. He teased me now about how I sounded close to singing, but his voice, all broken and begging, was musical too.

I snarled and threw myself forward, claws gouging into the floorboards on either side of Rafe's head, driving myself down onto him roughly, grinding into the curls over his pubic bone. He was already stone, and his feet stomped and scrambled against the floor, scuffing loudly as he arched his back and let out a long, startled shout. His wings were pinned, but they drummed into the carpet as he came, body bucking up just enough to tip me over the edge.

I howled as I came, head thrown back. I was the wolf, crying to the moon, but my call was for Rafe alone. Strong arms banded around my back, pulling me into his chest, head turning and mouth searching for mine. He moaned into the kiss, still fucking into me, hands stroking up and down my back. He was cool to the touch as always, firm and comforting and familiar beneath me, and I collapsed into his embrace, forgetting anything but the lovely haze of the afterglow.

And then my spine snapped.

I stiffened and screamed into Rafe's shoulder, and his arms circled tighter before I could wrest myself away.

"Stay, I have you," he whispered in my ear.

I fought briefly, skin on fire, scars carving into my muscle, and Rafe kissed my temple in answer.

"Stay, Hannah. Let me hold you."

It wasn't less painful to be held while the transformation broke and rebuilt me. Rafe's gentle words in my ear didn't make time pass quicker. There was no relief for what I was and what I had to become.

But there was something better about it this time. Even if the torture never ended, as it always seemed, it would've carried on indefinitely while I was held against the cool chest of someone I liked, who didn't say it was 'okay' but just that they were there and wanted to be.

And it did end, as it always did, and I was on my side with Rafe sheltering us both with his right wing, soothing the tension out of my muscles with firm strokes of his hands, a furrow between his stone brows, dense with worry and anger. For me. It eased as I met his gaze, and I shivered as he reached up, scratching his fingers into my hair.

My tail thumped against the floorboards in answer, and he smiled.

"Want to run?"

I did. I wanted fresh air, the dark forest, and room to run, but only because I wanted something else even more.

"I want to chase you," I said, and a slight growl escaped with the words.

Rafe just grinned. "I won't make it easy for you. Unless you say I can't fly."

I snarled, and I rolled us back to where we'd been, my claws clicking against his skin but not digging in. "Why would I tell my pretty gray bird not to use his wings?"

Rafe's lips parted slightly, pupils dilating. "You know," he rasped out, and he licked his lips and swallowed hard before continuing, "I really like when you look at me like you're going to eat me."

I was aware of how toothy and sharp my smile appeared in this form, but Rafe remained unphased. "You mean it makes your lovely, thick cock hard," I purred.

He nodded, and his chest fell and rose quickly under my hands. "Yeah. That."

For a brief moment, the human part of me that'd been tucked away for the evening came crying out, tearful and full of gratitude for this man, this moment, the ability to enjoy being a werewolf. And then Rafe took advantage of my distraction, throwing me to the side and scrambling up. He ran for the door, the plug in his ass winking in the dark.

My laughter was rough and growling as I stood slowly, giving him plenty of a head start. I wanted to give chase immediately, the sound of his feet pounding against the ground, the crunch of frozen grass and brittle twigs perking up my ears. But I wanted Rafe on his hands and knees for me when I caught him too.

I let him run and anticipate and wonder as I reached for the delicate harness, stepping awkwardly into its openings with my altered feet and legs. I'd avoided looking at myself before spending the last full moon with Rafe, but I was growing more curious now. My legs were more muscular as a werewolf. The body hair—the fur—was unnerving, but it was also glossy and soft. I huffed as the harness twisted in the wrong direction, but then it was up around my hips, snug and comfortable around my strong thighs and ass. I reached for the dildo next, a modest size in the firmest silicone they made. It jutted out proudly as I fit it through the small gold ring, the base pressing securely against my pubic bone.

I buckled myself in and took a moment to study the effect. I felt a bit silly, but aroused too, and the fantasy of having Rafe pinned to my hips, plugged with a cock, was every bit as imperative as it had been when it'd bubbled up in my thoughts days ago.

"Hannah?"

I grinned at Rafe's call from outside. Was my gargoyle missing me? I bent forward, loping with my elongated arms, not thinking about my changed posture but just falling into the ease of the movement.

I was learning to be myself as a werewolf. I would still be learning for years to come, but was that really so different from being human?

The air outside was sharp, but my flesh was denser and now furred and my blood ran hot, insulating me against the cold. Somewhere above—I paused to listen and found it was coming from the west—a pair of heavy wings beat once in the air, preparing for flight. I ran, and Rafe leapt down from whatever tree branch he'd been hiding in, coasting toward the ground, a massive, dark shadow of stone. I jumped as he neared, and he laughed, throwing himself higher so only my claws teased along the bottom of his foot. I laughed with him and circled, racing his shadow as it fluttered over the ground.

It was time to hunt.

CHAPTER 21
Rafe

HANNAH WAS WEARING THE STRAP-ON. I didn't notice at first. She was bent forward, giving in to her body's new shape and running with the help of all four limbs. Her tail was high, twitching and turning and revealing what direction she would turn in next. I wouldn't tell her that though. At least not tonight.

She rose onto her feet and sniffed the air as I took a moment to hide in the trees again, and I saw it, stiff and straight between her legs, a profane interruption to her elegant lines. I tilted my head and wondered if my own cock looked like that when it was erect. She moved forward and it swayed slightly, bobbing. I shifted, and the plug inside of me teased at the edge of perfect pressure, just a fraction shy of where I needed it.

I wanted to be caught. I wanted Hannah growling in my ear, wanted her breasts pressed to my back, to my wing roots, wanted her claws in my hair as she fucked me. I bit my lip, watching Hannah prowl, and my body tensed with the urge to throw myself to the ground, to land at her feet and bow my body to her command. The base of my wings throbbed and I recalled her grip on them, imagined her at my back, holding them and using them to pull me onto that eggplant-purple cock she wore.

"You're thinking of it, aren't you?" she called from the ground. "I can... You smell different."

I grinned, proud of her and not understanding why. "I am."

I jumped and paced my fall as she spun to face me, knees crouching and ready to pounce. "Do you want to be caught or do you want to surrender?"

The suggestion made me shiver, and I tucked my wings back to fall and land at her feet, dropping to my knees seamlessly and staring up at her. The moon rose behind her, outlining her tangled hair and tall ears. I'd pet them while she slept last time, held back my laughs as they twitched and flicked, tickled by my touch. Werewolves wanted to believe they were terrifying and monstrous and powerful. I thought they were kind of cute, really, wagging tails and fluffy ears.

But at the moment Hannah was not cute, towering over me with her heavy-lidded eyes and her canines peeking out from full lips. And that pretty purple cock taunting me in front of my lips.

Hannah arched her hips forward at the same moment I leaned in, our minds in sync as I parted my lips and she pressed the tip of the dildo to my tongue, snarling softly in approval. The taste of silicone was nothing to write home about, more of a turn-off than a turn-on, but Hannah's purr and her stare on my face made up for the fact. Black claws slid into my hair, a rough palm rubbing at my small horn, and I groaned as she fucked my mouth.

"Make it sloppy," she ordered, pushing deeper, forcing me to salivate as she teased the back of my throat.

I would do anything she asked, I thought in the background of my head.

"Squeeze around the plug," Hannah murmured.

I groaned as I did so, my own hips bucking in time with her careful thrusts. My wings flexed and stretched, wanting to beat and drive me into her, pin her to the ground and fuck her until I came—and she came five times at least.

"Pretty bird," she whispered, and then she pulled away, leaving me whining, on my knees, my cock hard and throbbing and my mouth sorely empty. "Bend over for me."

My hands thumped hard on the ground, denting the soft earth, and my wings spread wide and flat, exposing my back and ass. Hannah had to circle farther around to avoid them, and I waited, tense and trembling. She stirred leaves on the ground behind me, a long, clawed foot nudging one of my legs to the side, then the other, until the stretch extended into my balls, even into my ass. I huffed into the ground. The cottage was in front of me, inviting and sweet and safe, by all rights a better location for this moment.

I liked it here in the woods, under the moon, with the wild creature behind me.

Hannah pushed at the ring of the plug, digging it into me, and my cock bounced, knocking against my stomach. I released loud and eager sounds for her, and my wings shook, stirring up debris.

"Have I mentioned how much I like your ass?"

I laughed, and the sound was ragged, a crack in the tension of waiting. "I might've noticed."

Hannah purred, and her claws grazed over my back, around the globes of my ass, up and down my thighs. She knelt and her body was hot against mine. I twisted to stare back, catching a glimpse of her study over the rise of my wing, the gleam of her eyes. And then the plug was tugging inside of me, and I crumbled forward as she pulled and pushed and pulled again, easing it out of me and re-stretching my opening.

I whimpered, waiting for the kiss of the dildo, but instead came the shocking, delicate scratch of a claw, tracing around my gaping hole, sliding inside. I stiffened, stunned, but my cock made it clear how I felt, dribbling with approval, jerking and bouncing and begging to be inside someone. Inside Hannah. I reached for my own length, wondering if I needed permission, when she gripped my balls in her other hand and stuffed another sharp-tipped finger inside of me.

"Holy fuck!" I gasped, head drooping, yanking on my own cock.

"Claws good or bad?"

"Good," I managed, moaning as they touched inside of me. "Very fucking good. Don't know why."

"This is one time you won't talk me out of being careful," she said, more to herself.

I wouldn't try. It was an outrageously vulnerable act. But outrageously stimulating too, and my body could handle this—it was just the *shock* of the blade sharp touch, applied so gently as if to tickle. I repeated my curse into the ground, resting my forehead in the dirt, and Hannah hummed as my body opened to her.

"I don't normally have gender envy, but I do like feeling you like this. It's a shame it's just silicone."

I wanted to tell her she didn't even have to use the strap-on—what the fuck did I care when she had two fingers in my ass and a hand pulling on my balls? It would have been nice if she had more hands to touch me everywhere else, but then she was drawing her hands free and pushing in with the dildo next.

The ground didn't muffle my shout. The toy wasn't super long, but it was thicker than the plug, stiffer than her fingers, and it was demanding my body *make room* as it entered.

"Good or bad?" Hannah asked, pulling her hands away to stroke them up and down my back.

"Good, good, so fucking good. Hannah, fuck, don't stop."

She laughed and rocked against me, and my whole body wanted to fall flat to the ground and spread itself to its limits and just *take* this. Very fucking good.

"Keep touching yourself," Hannah coaxed. Apparently, I

had stopped. My tugs and strokes were uneven, distracted by every little shift, the nudge of her knees against mine as she scooted closer, sank deeper. "Hmm, where did I set the—Oh, here it is."

There was an obscene squirt, an awkward sound, but then she was slick and pumping smoothly inside of me, opening me with every drive forward, my body squeezing and begging for her return as she retreated. And like she had read my mind, one hand slid up, squeezing the back of my neck and then sliding into my hair, and the other gripped my right wing root. I was crying out, babbling praises, fucking into my hand with her thrusts in my ass, and I managed one clear order, snapped out in a near growl.

"Harder."

Hannah huffed, but she bucked against me, pulling on my wing root and my hair to yank me backward into the motion. I shouted to the moon, to her, howling my approval as she snarled with the effort of fucking me. It seemed a shame she couldn't feel anything more than the motion. I would have to make it up to her.

She pulled harder on my hair, lifting me from the ground, and released my wing to wrap her arm around me. Her breasts were pressed to my back, her breath hot on my neck, and her fucking was a shallow motion but deep inside of me. I whimpered as she shifted and the cock she wore pressed lower against me, my hand on my cock shaking and slippery with precum.

"I want to know every way there is to make you come," Hannah said in my ear, words dark. "You are so pretty when you come. Such destruction on such beauty."

"You've—you've already found more ways than anyone else," I said—wheezed, really, because I could barely catch my breath and she was striking an obvious spot inside of me that made my stone body turn to weak jelly.

My cock was spurting little bursts of fluid, but I wasn't

there yet. I wished there were two Hannahs—one to fuck me and one to fuck. Hell, I wished there were a dozen Hannahs, all tormenting me at once. I was discovering that I was shockingly selfish when it came to sex. At least I was if I could get away with it.

"I'll find more," she said simply, and then the hand on my chest slid up to my throat, holding me in place. She wrapped her other arm around me and joined my messy hand in stroking my cock. She was crueler and rougher than I'd been, but it was *perfect*. I was so sensitive, every nerve possessed by Hannah's touch, so powerful and potent. I wished I could share it all back with her.

It *was* destruction. It was like someone had lit a stick of dynamite and shoved it up my ass, something I would tell Hannah later and make her howl with laughter. I didn't care. I came in an explosion, bursting in our shared grip on my cock, throwing myself back into her embrace, arching into her hand on my throat. She licked my ear and rubbed my still gushing release over my length, down on my sac, up over my stomach, and then returned to stroking me as I finished shuddering and shaking.

It was the first time we'd had sex and Hannah hadn't come first. Hadn't come at all.

Suddenly, I wasn't selfish at all. It was *imperative* that I make her come. She huffed a laugh as I scrambled away, still full of aftershocks and as wild as if I were right on the edge again.

"Rafe—What? Oh!"

I scooped her up under her legs, and the dildo slapped against my forehead as I found my way to her cunt with my mouth. She was silky-wet and slick, and she gasped as I latched onto her, thrusting my tongue inside, nuzzling her clit with my nose.

"Ohhh, is this—Fuck! Is this my thank you?"

I nodded against her, and Hannah stirred in my grip. Her

legs wrapped around my shoulders, and I was holding her up, kneeling on the ground with her riding my mouth. She unbuckled the harness, laughing and sighing as she pulled the dildo out and tossed it aside, giving me more room, more of her to kiss and lick.

"You're very welcome," she rumbled, and her hands rubbed my horns as she worked herself against my face. "Ohhhh, Rafe! You're very welcome to *keep* doing exactly that."

And I would. As long as she let me.

HANNAH WAS beautiful the day after the full moon. Well, from what I knew she was beautiful every day, but I found a unique kind of satisfaction seeing her like this. Exhausted, at ease, foggy with the double transformation and a whirlwind of sex all packed into a few days.

And right now she was cuddly, latched to my side and only stirring to try and scoot closer. There was no closer. There'd been no way for us to be closer than we'd been quite a few times during this appointment.

"You know…you're my favorite client."

The words came unbidden, uninvited. For a moment, I thought I might've only thought them.

"I'd be offended if I wasn't," Hannah murmured, smiling lazily.

It was the *last* thing I was supposed to say to a client, a reminder that there were others, a totally unprofessional choice to offer any sense of ranking. But Hannah didn't blink, just teased calmly back.

I should've cleared the air, brushed the statement aside. But the words were true, and they'd been said and I didn't want to take them back.

So instead, I kissed her. She arched and twined herself

around me. We only had an hour or two left before she had to leave, but that was an hour or two to be touching, kissing, talking. She sighed as I nipped her bottom lip, spread her legs, and ripped the sheet out from between us.

An hour or two to be inside of her.

I would take it all.

CHAPTER 22
Hannah

"I THINK...I think I might've met my mate."

My head shot up and I blinked, turning and finding Theo in the circle, his own expression recovering from the initial surprise.

Nancy laughed softly at all of us. "Yeah, I know. I wasn't expecting it either. Definitely been taking my chance to just... sample the buffet, I guess you could say. And that was totally the plan, but she..."

I kept my gaze on Nancy as a few others around the circle tried to stifle their reactions—mostly men tittering and clearing their throats.

Nancy stumbled in her speech and took a moment of pause before smiling slightly. "She just makes me happy. As a werewolf. And as a woman, of course, but no one's ever...you know, made my tail wag before."

Can't be that hard. Rafe makes my tail wag all the time.

Around the room, the mated werewolves chuckled and smiled at Nancy.

"And I thought mating would be aggressive or possessive, but it's not. It's just feeling sure of my place with someone. Excited to be with them, but relaxed too. Feral and domesticated. In control."

Everyone was beaming at Nancy now, her joy infectious, but I had my hands clamped around the metal ridge of the seat.

"And the human part of me is overthinking all of this. It happened really quickly, and I had a mindset of not forming a romantic attachment yet, just learning myself. But I know myself better when I'm around her. My werewolf feels like me, and vice versa. And that's the part of me that has no doubt that this is right and permanent."

"Werewolves have good instincts," Diane offered gently, cheeks rounded with her smile.

Nancy huffed out a laugh and nodded, and I watched them all from a distance, my heart kicking and punching in the cage of my chest.

Don't make something up just because it sounds familiar, I warned myself, but the thoughts were already racing, toppling like dominoes, little moments recalled through the rosy filter of Nancy's words.

"Yeah, yeah, I'm learning that. I guess that's what I'm offering today. Don't fight the good things this change can offer you. Don't talk yourself out of the best parts."

Don't jump to conclusions, I told myself, trying and failing to push the thought of Rafe's lazy grin and dark curls from my mind. But even the thought of him settled me and stirred up a flurry of warmth in my chest. Feral and domesticated indeed.

I am not mating my sex worker. The words were my new mantra, but they didn't stop the satisfying zipper-click sensation—tines sewing themselves perfectly together—as I thought of Rafe and compared my time with him to Nancy's description of how mating felt.

"Hannah?"

I startled, sucking in a breath, and found the circle all staring back expectantly at me.

"Anything you'd like to share today?" Diane asked.

"No!" I realized my mistake as the word burst out of me. Theo's lips were twitching, and his brows rose behind his glasses. I shook my head, clearing my throat. "No, not this week," I said, recovering my senses slightly.

I sank deep into my folding chair as the conversation turned, but a few stares remained fixed on me, gazes reading me too clearly.

"HEY—"

I jumped as a hand caught my elbow while I was trying to flee the scene of the support group. Theo was grinning, hands raised at his sides when I spun.

"Sorry. You're jumpy today."

I shook myself and glared at my friend. "Don't ask."

He pressed his lips together and nodded. "How about an invitation to dinner?"

I sighed, glancing back at the doors to see more of the group heading for the exit. Including Fletcher, who'd once again tried to catch my attention afterwards. I started walking again and Theo followed, keeping pace with me.

"Dinner sounds good," I said, because Natalie would probably talk enough to distract me. Maybe.

"Sunny and Khell will be there too, just as a heads-up. You met them at—"

"I remember," I said, offering him a smile. The couple had been at the show at Nightlight, and while I'd been pretty distracted—getting railed in the bathroom—I remembered the pair. Her name suited her, a pretty and bright sunbeam of a woman who shined cheerfully even while others dominated the conversation, and most especially while she leaned into her massive orc boyfriend.

Mate, I corrected, recalling the word Khell had used to introduce Sunny. It'd seemed such an innocent and sweet word then, not at all capable of making me break out in a cold sweat.

Khell had set me on edge at first, just because of his enormous stature and obvious strength. I was learning that my werewolf objected to proximity to what she deemed as physical threats. But a few minutes around Khell, and that tension had evaporated. The orc was one coat of soft fur away from being an enormous teddy bear.

I also knew that Sunny and Khell met through MSA. And that we had a…mutual friend.

"Anyone else?" I asked, proud of how I managed to make the question sound light.

"Nope," Theo answered, just as lightly, and probably just as false.

Had he noticed me disappear with Rafe that night? Had Natalie told him I'd gone to MSA for help? I sped up, marching nowhere in particular, and at my side Theo cleared his throat.

"So, where are we going?" Theo asked.

I slowed. "Um…to your car?"

He fought his smile again, the smug bastard, and shook his head, pointing his thumb over his shoulder. "My car is that way."

My breath puffed out of me, and I swallowed the whine that wanted to follow as I stared around the street, wondering where I'd put my brain today. A brightly painted window glimmered back at me, waves of frosting gliding along the frame, a row of college students gobbling cupcakes at a bar top. "I…can grab dessert for us?"

"We love dessert!" Theo said, patting my shoulder and guiding me across the street to the bakery.

"WHY DIDN'T Theo tell you we had dessert covered? I don't understand. Not that I mind cupcakes, but—"

"He was just letting me save face, I'm all…" I waved my hand and trailed off as Natalie stared back at me.

Natalie waited for me to finish the thought, but since I didn't know what I was trying to say, I just shrugged at her. "I see. Does your" —she waved her hands in the air, imitating me— "have anything to do with you skulking off with Rafe at Nightlight?"

I tried to turn away from her but since my entire face was going up in flames, there was no hiding my answer. Natalie gasped and grabbed my arm.

"Please don't," I squeezed out.

"I knew it. He's your partner, isn't he?"

"Oh my god," I moaned, covering my face in my hands.

"Sorry, sorry. I know this is personal and we are still getting to know each other, but—Hang on. We need Sunny."

"Natalie—" I growled.

She pulled my hands from my face, and what I found was not humor or glee, but a sympathetic and crooked smile. "I know. But Sunny's been in your shoes, so if you're uncomfortable I'm sure she'd be really reassuring right now. And we can send Theo and Khell out to the yard."

"To the yard?" I asked, laughing through my strangled voice.

"Khell can throw a ball, Theo can fetch. It'll be fine," Natalie said, back to flippant.

I snorted, but I didn't fight her as she led me out of her kitchen with a firm grip around my arm. And as we reached the hall, Theo was already leading Khell out the back door to the small courtyard in the back. He'd overheard Natalie.

Oof.

We found Sunny rearranging knickknacks on Natalie's bookshelves in the living room, and she did a double-take glance at us before pausing. "Uh oh, what's up?"

"We have cupcakes," Natalie said.

"I like cupcakes," Sunny answered. "But I meant why are you holding Hannah hostage like that?"

Natalie shrugged. Ah. So she was going to make me speak for myself. Forcibly hold me in the room, yes, but leave the rest to me.

"I...am a client at MSA," I said, reminding myself that there was no shame in that fact and that Sunny had been one herself.

Before she and Khell mated.

"Oh," she said, and her cheeks went pink. "I suppose... Natalie mentioned Khell and I..."

"I did, sorry, but—"

Sunny shrugged and slid over to the couch, falling into it with the ease of a familiar visitor. I moved more stiffly to join her, and Natalie sat on the floor, placing the cupcakes on the coffee table between us.

"I'm not embarrassed. Khell and I did have to have an awkward conversation with my parents about how we met, but at the end of the day..." Sunny's smile was silky. "I took my man home with me."

"How did that happen? If it's okay for me to ask," I said, reaching for the triple chocolate cupcake at the center of the plate, putting all my focus into peeling back the paper wrapper.

"Well, I mean, obviously I had no idea Khell was forming a mating bond, but I knew pretty fast I was in big feels," Sunny said.

Big feels, I thought, nodding along. Big feels was much easier to swallow than a permanent attachment. Maybe that was what I was dealing with now. Not mating. Just big feels.

"He says he knew he was in deep shit around the same time as me, but I'd just broken up with a long-term boyfriend and we were in the awkward stage of being in an MSA contract, so when I left on my last day I did think that was sort of…the end of it," Sunny continued, frowning to herself while accepting the cupcake topped with a raspberry that Natalie passed to her. "Except I just couldn't not see him again, even though I knew my feelings for him were super inappropriate. So I booked another appointment, and I found out then that he'd quit and had just come back to me as a freelancer. Khell says I should've realized that meant he really wanted to see me—"

"You absolutely should've realized," Natalie said, then held up her hands as Sunny glanced at her. "Sorry, just listening."

"Anyway, I tried to back out and Khell chased me down and told me about the mating thing, and even though that was way too much to hear under fairly confusing circumstances, it was enough for that night to know he really wanted to be with me, and that was the only reason he'd quit MSA," Sunny said, blushing again and then pausing to blink at me. "That was a lot. Sorry. I got carried away and—"

"No! No, that's good to hear," I said.

"Soo…what species are you paired with?" Sunny asked, waggling her eyebrows.

I knew it would give the whole thing away if I said. Gargoyles weren't common, and these were Rafe's friends, and the whole thing was completely tangled and totally against any confidentiality clause, probably…but I was already in a mess, wasn't I? I'd developed *big feels* for my contracted sex partner.

"Gargoyle," I said.

Sunny's mouth rounded to an O, and then so did her eyes. "Oh," she said unnecessarily. And it was just a single note of a sound, but it said too much. *Oh, no. Oh, dear. Oh, I'm sorry.*

"Yeah," I sighed out, sinking back into Natalie's couch and taking a massive bite of cupcake.

"NO, no. Rafe didn't do anything wrong," I repeated. "He was a perfect partner. Please, is there any way I can talk to him directly? I don't want him thinking I had complaints."

"But you're canceling your appointments," the tight voice on the end of the line replied, not for the first time.

I sighed. "Not because I want to. I'm sorry, listen—I can…I can keep my next appointment, but I should say this to him, and if you can't connect me to him—"

"We owe our agents and workers as much right to their privacy as we do our clients."

I paced my apartment, canines biting down on the inside of my lips to restrain my growl, claws twisting around strands of my hair and tugging. "I understand that, of course," I said.

But your worker and I fucked in person once for fun, and I don't think he'd mind a phone call.

"Ma'am—"

"Hannah, please," I snarled.

"I'm not going to reschedule an appointment under these circumstances when you're asking for personal contact information. This is irregular and inappropriate." This was definitely that little antlered bureaucrat I had dealt with after appointments sometimes. I wanted to growl and remind him that in the hierarchy of the food chain, I definitely was the one looking down at him like dinner. "You can give your exit interview, which will be passed along to your former partner."

"Fuck," I whispered, falling still in the center of my living room. Fuck.

I'd fucked up. I'd been letting Sunny's story about how she and Khell got together roll through my head for days. My appointment with Rafe was looming closer, and I was seventy-five percent terrified of seeing him and knowing for certain how deeply I'd let myself fall, and seventy-five percent excited because it'd been weeks and I missed his voice and I missed his cooking and I missed the sex and I missed the conversations—

"Ma'am."

"Yes, all right," I said, and there was no growl or snarl, just a weak sigh of resignation. "I am…I am canceling all further appointments because I am emotionally invested in my connection with my partner Rafe. I think…I might be forming a mating bond, and I…"

And I should be telling him this, I thought, eyes stinging. I'd considered digging into Natalie or Sunny, seeing if there was a way to just call him, but that felt like crossing one boundary too many.

"And I don't want to impose my emotions on his work if he doesn't feel the same," I said softly.

The answer was clipped, and I flinched. "I see. Anything else?"

Fuck.

"Tell Rafe he was perfect. Tell MSA too, whoever needs to hear it. He was everything I needed, above and beyond, and I…I'm so grateful. And I…really hope he feels the same way."

Fuck.

Keys clacked on the other end of the line, the coldest possible response. "Well. You've done the right thing."

I was pretty sure I hadn't.

"You'll…pass all of that along to Rafe?"

"Yes, he's entitled to the entirety of the interview."

Which was not, *"Of course, we'll call him immediately and let him know how you feel."* But it was probably all I was going to get. Still, I had to try.

"If you could even just patch a call through—"

"Good day, Miss Shay," the agent said, and then there was only silence.

Fuck.

I stared out my bay window toward the water, the gray glimmer of Lake Michigan just visible on the horizon, through the park. I'd made a mistake. I should've waited to see Rafe. I hadn't meant to cancel our appointments, I'd only said I might need to, and then everything had spiraled and—

I snarled as my phone vibrated in my white-knuckle grip. Fuck. Dad.

My thumb hovered over the screen as my head whirled. MSA would be pissed, but maybe I could reach out to Natalie, get a phone tree to Rafe going, at least to let him know I wanted to talk. Or I could keep the appropriate boundaries in place, pass the ball into Rafe's court to make his own decision without trying to hunt him down. Maybe that was better. Maybe it was appropriate to let him learn about my feelings without the pressure of an appointment to respond favorably?

There were too many variables, and I needed a distraction. I swiped.

"Hey, Dad,"

"Hey there, kiddo! Guess who's in town?"

I laughed. Dad had been in town for three days, actually. I'd seen it in the Red-Eye yesterday, but three days before a call wasn't bad for him.

"Welcome back to home number three," I teased.

"Always good to be back in Chicago and nearly swept down Wabash at the first chance. Hey, what say you to a little get-together tonight at mine? Dinner and drinks. Bring your band. You can schmooze before your tour!"

I wanted to say no, except Dad would zip out of town again before I knew it and I did like to see him when I could, even if it was only a few sincere words mixed in with all the hype and gaiety he surrounded himself with. And the band would lose their minds to get invited to one of Dad's infamous parties. I owed them moments like this, especially Kiernan and Mikey, who'd months of waiting for me to come out of hibernation.

"That sounds perfect," I said, forcing a smile even if he couldn't see it. It would be good practice for tonight.

I'd messed up, but I'd salvaged what I could. Rafe would see my message. All I could do was cross my fingers and hope to hear from him.

CHAPTER 23
Rafe

I SQUINTED at my backsplash tile, licking my lips and tilting my head. Had I added too much salt, or was it perfect? Did it matter if I wasn't using a measuring spoon anyway? Probably not, because it'd be a guessing game again on Tuesday when I saw Hannah, but I wanted the sauce to be perfect.

I wanted everything to be perfect when it came to my appointments with Hannah.

I would've liked to say that it was because Hannah was still my only client giving me good ratings and singing my praises to MSA, but I knew that wasn't the truth. I wanted my performance with Hannah, the food I cooked for her, the time we spent together, to be perfect because I liked Hannah and she deserved the best. Because she'd made a rule that I got off when we were together. Because she was fun to spend time with, and I could feel the good it did for her to be free and wild and a werewolf.

I paused, spoon held in front of my mouth, wings stretching behind me, and fought off a wild and irrational urge to go flying through Chicago to find Hannah at that exact moment and—

My phone chimed, and I dropped the spoon down to the

stovetop to pull it from my pocket. A calendar alert, which meant either bookings or…

Cancellations.

I sighed and swiped, already prepared to lose my latest gorgon client. We'd had fun. She'd been fairly nice, and when I'd set up new rules with MSA she hadn't fussed, but I knew the difference now between the chemistry that was natural and the appointments that required my performance. Hannah was—

I blinked at the screen.

Hannah was my cancellation. Cancellations, plural. I'd only had two more appointments left with her before her tour, and I knew she wouldn't be able to book during those months obviously, but she'd…she'd cut the others. She'd cut Tuesday. That was less than a week away, and I was making sauce.

My body was suddenly made of lead, and I could've sworn I was dropping down through one floor after another of the building, right down to the ground. At least my stomach was.

Fuck. I'd lost Hannah.

I had told her she was my favorite client, which was true, and she'd teased back, but I hadn't thought… This couldn't be right. I knew Hannah enjoyed our time together. I'd made sure of it, damnit!

Or had I messed up? Maybe I'd gotten too selfish. Maybe she'd wanted more than what we had, rougher or rowdier, more chasing and scratching and…

And I would've given her that if she'd wanted it. She could've pulled my wings and thrown me down a hill and scratched me till I bled, and I still would've begged to be inside of her.

I clicked the stovetop off, red sauce bubbling in the pan, and pulled up my email. There was nothing from MSA, although they'd pass along Hannah's exit interview within the next day or so. And it would offer insight, but it wouldn't let me change Hannah's mind.

I wanted a drink, but the only place with any that actually made me feel anything was Nightlight, and I absolutely did not want to run into Elias or Khell, so that ruled that out.

The other option was flight. Which sounded good. It sounded better than standing in front of my stove, staring at something I'd been cooking for my latest client who'd canceled on me. My favorite client.

Hannah.

"I quit," I said, glaring at the bubbling sauce.

I pulled my phone back out of my pocket and pulled up emails. With Hannah's cancellation, I had three weeks before another appointment. With Hannah's cancellation, I wasn't even going to make ends meet with what I had left. It was over. It was time to move on. At least I had Grandpops's imp genes to make that exciting.

Except I wasn't excited. I was miserable.

My two-week's notice to MSA was as dismal as my apparent performance to their clients, but then that wouldn't make me much of a loss. I sent all three sentences off to Astraeya and crossed to my living room, opening my largest window and tossing myself out.

A bit dramatic, but my wings were ready, catching the air and cutting through, sending me soaring toward the lake. It'd been a while since I'd gone for a good flight. I was overdue.

I SHOULD'VE CURLED my wings and turned back the way I'd come the second I saw the lights in the apartment. It was the first time there'd been any sign of life there during one of my visits, and the view of the lamps glittering through hammered glass was more beautiful than I'd expected. I wasn't Elias, but the glow drew me in closer when I should've turned away.

Raucous music thumped inside of the beautiful gothic stone of the Chicago Tribune Tower, and a mass of bodies writhed through the warped glass. There was a party going on, voices blurring together, laughter cracking through the dull harmony. It was bitterly cold out tonight so the high-rise balcony was deserted, and I found myself a shadowy perch at the top of one of the ornate archways. If anyone looked out, they would assume I was a feature of the building, rather than stony flesh and blood.

I couldn't make out features through the pebbled texture of the glass windows, but there was enough detail to surprise me. The music blaring was rock, old classics leading directly into new hits, a strange collection of songs and a playlist no one in the crowded room seemed to pay much attention to. Jewelry glittered on the throats of men and women, bodies stacked together on furniture, and a thin haze of smoke floated up above heads to swirl around lamps.

Not the crowd I'd expected to find in the ritzy reputation of the tower. Still, the room looked warm, cheerful, and celebratory. Not my mood at all.

I shifted, preparing to leap and take flight again, when a balcony door cracked open. I paused, curious at first, and then stunned as a tall, slim figure stepped through, shrouded in a massive black coat.

"Hannah." I greeted her on instinct, but Chicago's wind whipped the word away from my lips and sent it into the city rather than to her ear.

Her head was down, and I wasn't sure if I was imagining the stress hooking her shoulders tighter or if it was just her defense against the cold, but I found myself go as still and solid as if I really had been a bit of ornamentation carved into this arch.

She shut the door on the noise from the main room and

lifted her face into the quiet. There was a lamp behind her, casting her face in shadow, but my eyes were sharp enough to cut through the darkness to see the folds in her brow and the clench of her jaw. Her hand pulled free of her coat pocket and brought out her phone, the glow illuminating her frown as she searched the screen briefly and then tucked the device away again.

Hannah sighed, heavy and hollow, and my body tipped toward her, barely maintaining my balance on my post as she looked up in my direction.

No. Not my direction, I realized as her eyes widened. At me.

"Rafe?"

And there was no escape from my name. Even the wind conspired in Hannah's favor, floating her voice to my spot above her.

She stepped forward and I stiffened, torn between jumping down to meet her and throwing myself into the air.

"What are you doing here?" I asked, at the same moment she said, "How did you know where to find me?"

We stared at one another, her mouth parted, face so open and startled. I tried to fix my expression into nothing.

"This apartment is one of my dad's places," she said.

My internet not-stalking had offered up information about her dad and who he was. The crowd inside made sense now. Hannah did too, in a way. Daughter of a rock star, becoming one in her own right.

What would she want with a gargoyle who she met through sex work?

"It's my favorite building in the city. I wasn't looking for you," I said, blinking up at the peaks and carved stone, trying to understand the sense of betrayal eating at me, as if it were the tower's fault I had to see Hannah in this moment.

"Oh," she said, and then her face went blank too. "You got the cancellations."

I nodded, and my wings started to stretch and flap, wanting to carry me away. My heart's rhythm didn't match, slower and uneven, too heavy in my chest.

Hannah licked her lips, standing there in the shadows below me, hands in her pockets and beautiful body shrouded from my gaze. "Rafe…did you—?"

"It's fine, Hannah. I don't keep clients forever," I said.

She reared back as if I'd struck her, eyes wide and wounded, and I couldn't stand to stay and receive some half-hearted apology or excuse for why she was canceling her time with me. I jumped, and the wind caught my wings and launched me back, sailing me in a new direction.

I HUNCHED my shoulders and ducked my head down as a rustle of furred wings passed behind me. Not that it would do any good. Elias was unlikely to miss my presence at his bar.

"He's been here all day," the pixie bartender behind the counter murmured to her boss. "He keeps groaning."

I lifted my head to glare at her, stuffing another spicy pork bao bun into my mouth until it made my cheeks swell. Elias wouldn't want me to talk to him while my mouth was full.

"I'll handle it," he said, shooing her to the other end of the bar, where a pair of naga were twined together and staring in horror at me. "Khell is on his way," Elias said to me.

"Uh-uh," I answered, shaking my head and then lowering it again.

"If you wanted to be alone, you wouldn't have come here," Elias reasoned. "Therefore, I'll assume you're in need of… company. Camaraderie? Companionship."

I groaned, and he shrugged, staring at me while I chewed and swallowed.

"Just here for the menu. Though I'm pretty sure it's giving

me food poisoning," I added just to spite him. And then I ate three onion rings at once.

"My food is not the problem," Elias said. "What are you going to do for work?"

I gaped at him, battered onion sticking out of my mouth, and he stared back, unflappable. The bar door opened, winter snapping ruthlessly in for a moment before it was blocked out by Khell's enormous frame.

"You quit MSA?" he shouted toward us. "What are you going to do for a job?"

"Whyyew boff know dat?" I asked, and Elias shuddered and looked away from me.

Khell planted himself on the stool next to me, and my shoulders loosened. Maybe Elias was right. Had I come here…hoping these two jokers would find me?

Yes, because they're your friends, my mother's voice offered in my head.

"MSA rumor mill," Khell said. "I could use some help with some jobs."

"If you're going to eat all my food, you could always, I dunno, cook some of it," Elias offered, studying his own claws rather than meeting my eyes.

I stared at them both for a beat, and the nonstop gut punching discomfort that had plagued me since I'd left Hannah on the roof of Tribune Tower last night kicked up to a faster tempo. I pushed all the baskets of food surrounding me away, groaning and falling forward, resting my forehead on top of my folded arms.

"I'm sick," I moaned into the bar top. "Elias, your food poisoned me."

"What did you eat?" Khell asked, playing along.

"He's not sick," Elias snarled. "He has a stone stomach. These are emotions, you idiot."

I scowled into my arms.

"You developed feelings for a client. She, for all intents and purposes, severed your relationship. Now you're upset."

"Chill, Elias," Khell said softly.

Elias's wings rustled, and he sighed. "Fine. You also…possibly…have indigestion. But only because you're trying to eat my entire menu."

"She was my client," I moaned.

"Sunny was mine," Khell reasoned. "It happened. Do you know why she canceled?"

I swallowed the bile trying to rise up my throat because Elias, annoying as it was, was right. It wasn't the food I'd eaten, but the disappointment and…and heartache, of being tossed aside by Hannah. Who I liked. Who I…

"I haven't wanted to look," I admitted, lifting my head and wiping the grease from my face. The bar top was cleared in front of me, Khell and Elias effectively stealing away my coping mechanism while I wasn't looking.

They were quiet for a beat, glancing at one another.

"What?" I asked, fighting that surging sensation in my gut again.

"You should check," Elias said, too neutral to be trusted.

"Maybe the explanation isn't…bad?" Khell asked, voice a note too high.

My eyes narrowed. "What do you know?" I asked.

Elias's eyes rolled and his mouth opened, but at that moment the door to the bar banged open once more, startling everyone in the room. A tiny bullet of pink and violet and sapphire blue charged toward the three of us, and I grabbed onto the bar top, bracing myself to be struck.

"We had it under control," Elias drawled.

Astraeya stopped inches away from me and glared over my shoulder at the moth fae. "If that were true, he wouldn't still be sitting here smelling like a deep fryer. What is Khell even doing here?"

"I'm useful in a crisis," Khell said, chest puffing up.

Astraeya rolled her eyes. "Arguable." And then she turned her full blazing purple stare onto me, glaring and threatening to reduce my lifespan by decades. "Read. The. Exit. Interview."

She produced a tablet from the inside of her draped blue coat and shoved it under my nose without ceremony.

The words jangled and rearranged at first glance, but there was enough there to catch my interest.

Emotionally invested. Maybe my mate? Possibly boundaries. Feelings. Relationship.

"Fuck," I hissed, snatching the tablet from Astraeya's hands and gluing my gaze to the screen until the pieces settled in the right order. "Fuck!"

I don't keep my clients forever.

"Oh, fuck," I moaned, hands shaking. I hadn't finished reading, but I didn't need to. I knew enough to know why Hannah had looked so bruised last night. I looked up at last and found my friends staring back at me, expressions smug. I would be angry with them for that later. I had bigger issues to deal with now. "Astraeya, please. Where do I find her?"

She sucked in a breath, lips pursing briefly, and I knew what she risked by telling me information that was meant to be protected by the agency.

"No, no," Khell said. "She can stay out of this. This is why I'm here. I have a phone tree," he said proudly. "Sunny texted Natalie, who asked Theo. Here's her address."

"I forgive you for stealing all the food I ordered," I gasped, snatching his phone and memorizing the address. Gold Coast, by the water, sixth floor.

"Ignore him, he put it on your tab," Elias said to Khell.

"I have to go," I said, jumping off the stool and finding that I did not, in fact, have food poisoning, but possibly an entire summer's worth of butterflies swirling in my chest.

"Obviously," Astraeya said, snagging her tablet from my fingers before I could race to the door with it.

"Good luck!" Khell called.

"He doesn't need luck. They're in love," Astraeya said softly.

"Doesn't matter. He's an idiot. He needs luck," Elias muttered.

And then the door to the bar swung shut, and I was startling a young woman walking her dog as I leapt into the air and took flight.

CHAPTER 24
Hannah

"DO you know why Natalie would need to mail something to your apartment?" Theo asked me, frowning at his phone. "She's being suspiciously pushy."

"Hm?"

He paused and stared back at me. "Hey. You okay?"

I nodded, even if the opposite was true. I wasn't okay. Seeing Rafe—barely, just the outline of him against the orange glow of the city sky at night—had made any doubt that he was my mate disappear. The way all the worry and the nerves and the confusion had gone quiet in my head. I'd just been happy that he was there. If I'd had my tail, it would have been wagging.

And then... *I don't keep my clients forever.*

What did it mean for a werewolf to have a mating bond rejected? Had it been my fault for finding Rafe through MSA? Maybe I'd never really gotten to know Rafe as himself. All the humor and the smiles and the *you're my favorite client* had just been work.

"Han?" Theo prompted, reaching for my arm.

I was a raw nerve, and the full moon was right around the corner. I inched away and nodded. "I'm good. Nat...Nat can mail me whatever she wants."

Theo glanced between me and his phone for a moment before nodding and answering the text. I slipped away before he could question me again, sliding through the mingling crowd of the therapy group, heading for the door.

"Hannah!"

Fletcher stepped in front of me and I skidded to a halt, stifling the growl that bubbled up from my throat.

"Fletcher."

He'd talked today about finding his balance as a werewolf, about embracing his instincts. He was making good progress, better than I had, until I'd met Rafe. Now I wondered if I was backsliding. My hackles were high, and I wanted to shove this man out of my way.

"Sorry, I'm heading out, actually," I said, trying to sidestep him.

"Sure," he said, turning with me. "I want to ask if you'd like to grab dinner together."

My steps slowed. I didn't want to walk out with Fletcher, have him following me like a puppy.

"I ca—"

"I know I'm being kind of…forward," he said, offering me a crooked smile, his body hunching to appear smaller. "It's just…I feel really drawn to you. Comfortable."

No.

The word was so clear in my thoughts, I had to stop myself from shaking my head in answer. I wasn't drawn to Fletcher. I wasn't comfortable.

I wanted Rafe. And that had gone up in smoke, so…

"I'm not available," I said. Another day, and I might've tried to soften the words, but I let them sit, flat and honest. I wasn't available today. I wasn't available to him.

His eyes winced and I turned, marching for the door without anyone at my side.

Chicago winters were brutal. Every year, I considered the idea of moving to somewhere like Los Angeles, where I'd actually find some vitamin D in December. But every year, the view of the frozen lake, barely visible through the coating of frost on my drafty pre-war windows, made me fall in love with this city and its harsh winter again.

And at least today the sharp wind gave my eyes an excuse to water and shed tears that froze and chipped like shards of glass off my cheeks, trying to seal my eyelashes together. It gave my skin a reason for the raw yet numb sensation that had seized me since the night before. It was a punishment, throwing itself into me as I headed south to my apartment. Chicago was a moody city in winter, temperamental and petty, and that suited me fine.

I passed the cemetery where I'd been attacked on my way home, and the hairs at the back of my neck sharpened and rose in warning, the memory haunting me with the sensation of being watched, hunted.

It followed me home, the starving wolf of winter and the worst night of my life. By the time I turned the corner onto my street, my door in sight, I was convinced I was being watched all over again, dissected from afar.

And in a way I was, but the figure waiting on my stoop made my heart leap into my throat for an entirely different reason than fear. Or maybe it was fear—fear tied to hope, afraid to have it cut away again.

Rafe's wings curled around him, bracing against the wind, and his head hung. His elbows were on his knees, body hunched over, and he almost looked like a statue someone had left on my building's doorstep. But then ice crunched under my boot and his head lifted, eyes darting around and landing on me. He jumped up, and I knew.

I knew this was my mate. And I knew that whatever he said next, it wasn't going to hurt. My cheeks warmed and my tears thawed, and I smiled at him as I walked closer. Rafe grinned back, laughing, eyes bright and light. I wanted the explanation, to know what he'd been thinking last night when we'd seen one another outside of my dad's party, but not right now. Right now, I only wanted one thing.

I ran forward, and he jumped down two steps, still beaming at me. I leapt, my heart taking flight with the motion, and he caught me around my waist, hauling me into his chest, our heads tipping in perfect harmony. We were both smiling too much, teeth bumping briefly, breaths panting in laughter as we nuzzled into one another. My arms tightened around his shoulders, toes just barely finding room on the step where we balanced together.

"I was upset, I didn't know," Rafe breathed.

I nodded, and then I slid my hand over his shoulder, cupping his cold face, and our smiles settled for us to kiss. The taste of him, the cling of the winter cold to his stone, reminded me of scooping snow by the handful as a child, biting into the ice and letting it thaw on its way down my throat. I shivered, and he tried to pull away but I wasn't ready to let go, feasting on firm lips, nibbling at the tongue that stroked against my mouth.

Rafe gasped and I surged in, claiming him and clutching him closer.

Mine, my head and heart growled in unison, the sound following from my chest. Rafe's wings were shielding us from the wind, creating a quiet bubble where our breaths and moans echoed around us. I shifted one arm down to circle his waist, pressing our hips together and rubbing myself against his firm length, whimpering into my starving kiss.

"Hannah," he groaned, hands tightening onto the heavy wool of my coat. "Take me—"

"Yes," I hissed, trying to push him down so I could climb onto his lap and—

Rafe laughed and pulled away, grinning down at me. "Take me inside."

I blinked and glanced over my shoulder, shivering once more. The sky was turning the murky mauve of evening in the city, and my toes were frozen solid in my boots, and we were just a handful of staircases away from my warm apartment—an infinitely preferable place to be naked and sweaty with Rafe. After we defrosted.

"Right," I said.

Rafe turned us, keeping his wings around me to shield me from the wind as we shuffled to the front door. I pulled my keys from my coat pocket, and Rafe crowded against my back, tangling his horns in my hair as he rooted around for my throat to kiss.

The key missed the lock twice, and I had to shimmy free of his hands before they found their way under my coat. Rafe paused, glancing around the small interior landing of my building.

"Tour later," I rasped, unlocking the door on the left that led up to the upper story apartments.

His hand was freezing in mine, and I mentally revised my plan to throw him down on my floor the moment we got inside. Temperature play was fun in theory, but I was already too cold to enjoy icy fingers.

We passed the two second-story apartment doors, but Rafe grew impatient on the half landing before mine. Or maybe it was me who pulled him to the corner wall. Either way, we were out of sight of anyone, alone under the small art deco light fixture that illuminated my stairs, arms wrestling out of coats and around one another.

Rafe sucked on my tongue, and my hands gripped at his horns when I realized I didn't have the first clue about getting a jacket off Rafe's back. Damn wings.

He groaned, untangling me from around him, reaching back and unsnapping the shoulders of the coat.

"Come on," I said breathlessly, snatching my coat from the floor and running safely out of reach up to my door.

Rafe slowed as he followed me inside of my apartment. I owned the top two stories of the building, a wonderfully renovated layout in a classic lakeside graystone, and Rafe paused at the threshold of the great room. I hesitated too, suddenly nervous to be here with him. It was all well and good to feel that hungry certainty that Rafe was my person, but the reality of us was that we'd only really known each other in neutral territory. This was my home, my den. Part of me was deeply, instinctively satisfied to bring Rafe to this space, the rightness of having him in my home a tangible warmth and weight in my chest. The other part was vibrating with nervous anticipation. What if he didn't like it?

But he smiled as he took in the rich fabrics, the deep jewel colors and the layers of textures, the delicate antiques and sturdy, decadent furniture. "Feels like you," he said. He met my eyes, and I was twitching with the urge to leap again, to hold him in my grip and never let go, but his smile faltered as he stared at me, and a nervous dropping sensation hit me. "Hannah, why didn't you wait until our appointment to tell me?"

I heaved out a sigh and tossed my coat onto the hook. When I crossed to Rafe, he didn't hesitate to reach for me.

"I meant to talk to you before the appointment, but I got anxious and fucked up. I was on the phone with some squirrelly MSA agent, and suddenly I was having to explain why I wanted to talk to you."

Rafe hummed and nodded, hands on my hips tugging me closer. But those beautiful hands were bricks of ice without the protection of my coat, and I shivered again for less pleasant reasons.

"I only saw your cancellation last night, not the interview," he said, eyes flicking back and forth against mine. "I was afraid you were going to apologize."

"I was," I admitted. "But not for not wanting you. Just for wanting you too much."

His expression relaxed, and his eyelids drooped as he

gazed down at me, all the warmth of his stare pooled low in my belly.

"Well, in that case, I owe you an apology too," he murmured.

"Rafe. You really, really don't." I rose to my toes, and he yanked me into his chest, our mouths sliding together. But where I was starting to feel the tingle of my hot blood warming my skin again, Rafe was still ice cold. I hissed into the kiss and then leaned back, reaching up to comb icicles from his hair. "What's the fastest way to warm you up?"

His grin was lazy. "I think you know."

I laughed and tugged him along with me, guiding us towards the stairs up to my bedroom. "Second fastest?"

"Hot shower."

I nodded. "Good. We'll be efficient and do both in that case." I turned away to walk up, and Rafe groaned behind me, his hand tightening around mine.

"Fuck, Hannah. Have I mentioned how sexy you are when you're all wet and slippery?"

I bounced on my toes as I dragged Rafe along with me, entering my massive bedroom. It took up most of the second floor, aside from my bathroom and a small balcony that overlooked the local buildings' garden.

"Well then you'll be excited to know that I am extremely wet and probably very slippery at the moment," I teased.

Rafe growled, and then chilly arms snatched me up, charging for the bathroom door I'd been leading him toward. "Jesus, this really is a rock star's apartment," Rafe murmured as we entered. "We should've been having appointments here."

MSA had suggested it, but at the time I'd been too terrified of myself to let my werewolf roam free here. Now that I knew that the only damage I managed was in the heat of the moment with Rafe, and generally just to whatever linens we were in contact with, the idea of spending the full moon tucked away in my home with my…gargoyle sounded lovely.

"I don't suppose they'll let me rebook now," I laughed.

Rafe paused, setting me down on the large woven mat in front of my walk-in shower. "Well, I hope not 'cause…I kinda quit…yesterday."

I'd been in the middle of pulling off my shirt, and I was tangled inside of the cotton when he spoke. I wrestled my way out and found Rafe blinking at me, eyes wide.

"You what?"

"I lost my favorite client," Rafe said, shrugging sheepishly, his eyes already sliding down to my chest with an eager glint. Which only made the part of me not currently startled by the declaration more determined to shove the conversation aside and warm up with Rafe in any possible way. "I'd…already lost my enjoyment working there, but I didn't know what else to do. And then you showed up, and suddenly I really liked keeping my job because it meant time with you and—"

My control snapped, and Rafe grunted but he met my kiss with equal force. And I didn't care that his fingers were frozen —it just made my skin sing and quake and tremble. I leaned into his chest, my nipples pebbling and aching in my lace bra, and Rafe's hands tightened on my ass, holding me to him as I kicked my boots off. This time I knew the secret to his clothes and I grappled at his back, finding the snaps that loosened his shirt.

"It's not the same," he breathed against my lips. "Nothing with you was ever the same. It wasn't even work lately. Did you mean what you said in the interview?"

His shirt was drooping down his chest, and I stepped back, watching greedily as he finished stripping it away and then moved to his pants.

"Hannah," he prompted, eyebrows bouncing even as he pushed his pants down his hips. And how was I supposed to focus on questions when it'd been weeks since I'd seen his cock and my mouth was watering and my cunt was throbbing? "Do you really think I'm your mate?"

Except that was an important question. My breath caught, and I blinked up at him. Part of me wanted to hedge around the truth. *I think so.* But all Rafe had ever asked me to do was to let go and embrace what I wanted. Which was almost exclusively him. The thought startled me and made the answer clearer than ever.

I can lose the band. I can lose the record.

I cannot lose Rafe.

"Yes," I said.

And Rafe beamed at me, smile so startlingly bright and full I nearly fell back another step with the force of it. "Then we'll figure it out."

Just like that.

I threw myself against him, and he was ready. He always caught me. We grappled at my clothes in the kiss, but I was still wearing my bra and my socks when we tripped into my shower. Rafe yanked the water on high, and one cold stream struck my back, drawing me out of the starving haze of the kiss and making me stifle a screech before he spun us, wincing as his wings created a shield.

We stared at one another for a moment, Rafe's expression twisted as the initial cold blast of water beat against him, and I broke out laughing. I hopped in place, pulling my socks off one at a time and tossing them with a wet slap to the tiled floor outside of the shower. I reached for my bra next and Rafe caught my hand, stopping me, reaching out and pinching one of my nipples through the lace, his eyes staring.

"Leave it for a bit. You like it when I lick you through lace," he said.

Steam was starting to billow up from his back, and his wings were stretching and folding, flexing under the warming water before settling and tucking close.

"Hmm, you think you know what I like?" I asked, shuffling closer, the steamy air warming around us.

Rafe scoffed, lips twitching. "I know I do, Hannah."

I grinned briefly and then hid my smile away, gazing up at him. "Prove it."

Rafe's gaze darkened, everything still for a moment. And then suddenly I was off my feet, cold, firm arms banded around my back, a rough kiss pulling on my breast through my thin bra. I might've considered stifling my moan, but Rafe forced it out of me before I could play any games with him.

I didn't want to play games. I wanted this. I wanted what he'd given me from the start—genuine interest, curiosity, abandon. I pulled my arms free of his grip, arching my chest into his mouth, his tongue swirling around my right nipple. His hair was still frozen on top, but the hot water had thawed the strands against the back of his neck, and I held him there, stroking my fingers against the tense muscle, down to where his wing roots thickened his skin.

Rafe turned again, and I gasped, eyes falling shut as the water sprayed down on me, soaking my hair and burning my still cool skin beautifully. My knees bent, and my legs wrapped around Rafe. With a gentle twist of my body his mouth slid to my left breast, treating it with the same sucking kisses and teasing twirl of his tongue before latching onto my nipple and drawing roughly.

I was rocking shamelessly against him, taking the smooth and subtle friction of his stomach against my core, and Rafe kissed his way up my chest, nesting his head under my jaw. I turned my head, resting my cheek between his horns, and we paused like that, wrapped around one another.

"Hannah," he whispered against my collarbone.

"Mm?"

"I fucking need you."

I blinked at the simple words, not understanding their significance. That was our aim, wasn't it? A messy, wonderful union to celebrate being together again? His head tipped back, and my heart tripped in my chest at the sight of him, eyes wide and frightened. He pulled me down an inch, and I gasped at the brief press of his cock to my sex.

"I should be on my knees," he said, staring up at me. "I should have you screaming on my tongue, make you drench my fingers. I know what you like, but I—"

But he needed me. And we weren't client and partner now. I bent my head and kissed his forehead. I wasn't sure if it'd ever been entirely selfish between us. I'd craved his pleasure from almost the start, and he'd been devoted to mine.

"Take what you need," I murmured. *You are what I need too.*

Rafe groaned, and it only took one easy correction between us before I was sliding down onto his cock.

I whimpered as he bucked, holding me to the hilt, and his chest rumbled, eyes falling shut. I stared my fill of him, as stunned by his beauty as I had been that moment I first saw him, walking into the MSA apartment. His eyes opened slowly, lips curving.

"We are never going an entire month without this again," he said, the words thick and low.

My lips parted on a gasp and Rafe turned, pressing me to the tile wall and thrusting in, hard and fast. I cried out at the bone deep shudder of pleasure, and Rafe swallowed the sound with his kiss. He was relentless, hands everywhere, massive body pinning me to the wall as he fucked me.

I didn't need to be in control. Rafe's mastery of my body was more than enough. I tangled myself tighter around him, kissed his throat when he pulled away to moan, let him ride me up the wall with his force, my own voice ragged and broken with praise.

Everything was going to change. I had a mate, and I barely knew what that meant, but in this moment only one thing was clear and important.

"Fuck, Rafe, yes!"

His mouth found mine as I leaned forward, begging for his kiss. His tongue stroked in, fucking against mine with the same pace of his cock pounding inside of me. He was staying deep, rocking into me with short thrusts, those beautiful dense curls at his base grinding sweetly against my clit. My nails scratched at his back, and I surged suddenly to the edge of an orgasm, blade sharp and fire bright.

Rafe snarled, driving in as deep as I could take him, sealing my shout with a kiss, moving with a steady, curving rhythm that made the pound of ecstasy drum harder and higher until it broke with a sudden boom. His mouth smeared over my cheek as I whined and shook against him, sliding to my ear and licking inside, drawing out the trembling aftershocks with his relentless rocking. When I was limp he eased out, just a fraction, enough to pull me closer and let my head fall weakly back, our gazes meeting.

"More?" he asked, but his smile was smug and hungry.

"What's the rule?" I rasped out, voice cracking in the wreckage of pleasure.

Rafe's eyes shut, and his lips pressed closed, chest rumbling with a groan. He nodded. "More." I grinned as he pulled me away from the wall, hoisting me against his chest and turning off the water. "I hope your bed is reinforced."

CHAPTER 25
Rafe

HANNAH WAS FIDGETING next to my boneless body, her fingertip tracing over my chest and her feet rubbing against her own legs, little cricket movements in the aftermath of our reunion sex marathon. I'd just come for the third time of the night, and the sun was starting to warm the color of the sky outside of Hannah's bay window. I was more than ready to fall asleep, outrageously sated, but her tiny movements were a warning.

If she was always this insatiable before the full moon, I was going to end up chafed, if such a thing were possible.

I grinned at the notion.

"Are you going to get another job?"

"S'pose," I said, shrugging.

Hannah nodded, but her little legs just started shifting faster.

I sighed and started to roll toward her. "Okaaaay, but you're gonna have to do most of the work," I said, my face split wide with my smile so she would know I was teasing.

Hannah barked out a laugh and pushed her hand against my chest. "Rafe, I will go up in smoke if we have any more sex."

Well, I didn't want that. I propped my head up on my hand, and Hannah's eyes slid away from mine. Interesting. This was nerves.

"You change your mind?" I asked, feigning casual indifference.

And she just rolled her eyes at me. And to be fair, I had been joking. She'd been growling and calling me *mate* through most of the last three hours, her wolf pinning me to her bed and giving her gaze a brilliant glow as she'd rode me into my final shocked orgasm of the night.

"Don't tease," she murmured.

"Don't just lie there freaking out and not tell me what's going on," I answered, arching an eyebrow.

She froze for a moment, gaping at me, and I remembered that I hadn't challenged her very often in our appointments. Only when she'd needed it for her own sake, like now. And just like those times, Hannah's initial response was to freeze with surprise, eyes narrowing in offense. Then she blinked, desire darkening her gaze and softening her lips into a smile. I'd told her tonight that I knew what she liked, but I wasn't sure if she was ready to be told that she liked it when I pushed back. We'd figure that out eventually. We had plenty of time now.

Her hands reached for me, stroking over my chest in aimless appreciation. "Fine. I'm not totally sure how to propose this, but…"

She chewed at her lip for a moment, and suddenly I was the one fidgeting. "Hannah," I pleaded.

Her eyes flashed to mine. "I wanted to ask if I could…hire you to be my personal chef for the tour?" she breathed out in a sudden rush. "But I feel like we're just stepping outside of this, like, work relationship boundary. And obviously, you know, I wanna fuck you, and like, I'm falling in love with you, so—"

I dove down, slamming my lips to hers in a clumsy and graceless but necessary motion. She made something better of the kiss, opening her mouth just enough to seam us together, her hands on my chest gliding up to stroke my throat and jaw. I wrapped my arms around her waist, pulling her to press against me, head to toe, and we stayed like that until her breath was catching. She sucked in air as I released her.

"Can I just come as your boyfriend?" I asked, my own breath uneven, heart racing as fast as a gargoyle's could. Faster, I suspected, thanks to my grandpa. And the invitation to go on tour, to travel with Hannah, might've been out of the question without Grandpop. It would certainly send my parents' heads spinning when I told them.

Hannah's cheeks pinked, and we stared at one another with dopey smiles as she nodded.

"Your 'I'm falling in love with you too,' boyfriend," I corrected gently, bending down and kissing her with gentle brushes of our lips.

"As long as you're with me," she murmured, chin tucking shyly, but she held my gaze. "Like you said, I don't ever wanna go an entire month again."

"I also really love cooking you food, for the record. That's absolutely on the table." I pecked her lips firmly, making her smile twitch back into place. "No more steaks, I promise."

She laughed, head tipping back, and I ducked down, decorating her throat with more kisses, whispering menu suggestions as she squirmed closer, tangling long limbs around me. She found my face, lifted it to hers, and pressed a long, simple kiss to my mouth.

"Will this make me your groupie?" I asked.

She grinned again, nodding and giggling. Happy. Hannah was happy.

And so was I. My own grin stretched and my face hurt from how much I had smiled tonight.

We cuddled into one another, the rising sun glowing across our skin, falling asleep at last as morning clawed its way over the horizon.

"LOOK AT ALL THESE BEANS!"

"Rafe."

"Hannah, this is incredible! Look at your pantry, it's bigger than your shower! I can stretch my wings all the way—this is insane."

"Rafe!"

"Why do you have two juicers? I don't care, I'm using them both. What produce do you have? Open your fridge," I demanded, emerging from the pantry, arms loaded with spice jars and high-end cooking gadgets.

Hannah was perched on the counter. Her hair was a rat's nest and her inner thighs were faintly marked from my hips, and she was wearing a deep wine red robe and a pair of the softest black underwear I'd ever fondled a woman's clit through. She had one foot braced against the counter, her arms wrapped around her bent leg, and she was trying to hide her beaming smile against her knee.

"Rafe," she attempted again through giggles.

"Don't distract me, babe. I've never been this excited to cook in my life."

"Baayabe," she cooed, teasing the word out into a song.

My haul clattered onto the counter, and I glanced warily at her out of the corner of my eye. "Don't."

"Baaaaabe," she purred, unfolding and sliding off the counter, toes pointed as they touched the ground. Those legs. They were my weakness.

"Hannah," I warned, inching away. "Breakfast."

But her gaze was hooded, and her pace was slow and

predatory. "You're not making me beans and juice for breakfast, Rafe," she said, a giddy smile peeking through the intent.

"Huevos rancheros," I said weakly.

She paused and licked her lips, and for a moment I thought I might've won and was just a little disappointed by the fact, until she tensed.

"After," she said.

"After?"

And then I found myself pinned to the counter, Hannah's teeth nipping at my skin, tongue tracing patterns, hands mapping me. She was wild, everywhere, kissing and biting and grasping at me, and I was every bit the trembling prey to her hunger. She snagged my bare nipple in her teeth, and I swooned for her, moaning at the electric snap of sensation racing down to my cock.

And she was running kisses down my chest, hunching at first and then lowering to her knees, cupping me through my jeans and stroking.

"Hannah," I rasped, glancing once more hopefully at the juicers, as if they could save me now from a fate I didn't really want to escape.

"Just a little appetizer," she murmured, fingers graceful with my waistband, button popping cheerfully from its hole. She gazed up at me, amber eyes glowing and the hint of sharp canines in her smile.

She didn't tug my jeans down but let them fall open, sagging around my hips as she nuzzled inside, kissing the curls over my pubic bone, sucking on my sensitive skin. I bucked toward her, and her hands grasped my ass, squeezing hard.

"It'll...it'll take too long," I whispered. *Don't talk her out of this, idiot!*

"I'm very tenacious," Hannah said cooly, kissing the base of my cock, smiling at it as it jumped for more, my jeans slipping a little. She glanced up at me, feral and exquisite, and I shivered in her stare. "And you're worth it, babe."

I groaned and rolled my hips, shimmying off my jeans. Hannah greeted my cock with a long wet stripe of a lick, and I fell back on my elbows, grateful to be at the mercy of my insatiable werewolf girlfriend.

IT WAS ONLY two days before the full moon, and rightfully Hannah should've been a bit of a wreck. Instead, it was me who was pacing circles around her as she got ready for the day. She smiled at me in the reflection of the mirror, painting her lips in the most unnecessarily erotic shade of plum, a color I now wanted smeared around my cock.

"Just grab a bag and meet me back here. Or come to the bar," Hannah said.

I nodded, pausing and leaning against the doorframe of her bathroom. She was wearing long, loose black pants and a black lace bra, her nipples full and flat against the lace, teasing me with the peek. She had her right foot hooked behind her left ankle, hip cocked as she played with the strands of her hair, teasing them in different haphazard directions.

It'd been a long time since I'd been in a relationship, and I couldn't remember ever being as fascinated by a woman getting dressed and ready to go out. Hannah's pleasure in beauty extended to herself, and while she'd always dressed with a kind of elegant ease, it was fun to see the process of choices and the care of details that created the result.

"What's wrong?" she asked.

"Nothing," I said.

Hannah turned, and I withheld my groan as she braced her hands against the counter, offering too tempting a view of all her long angles. She arched a dark eyebrow, and I sighed.

"It's…been a really good three days," I said.

Hannah smiled back at me. "It has, but why does that make you look anxious?"

I bit my lip and debated honesty before rushing across the space. Hannah seemed to fall forward into me, the natural magnetism we found near one another, our chests pressing close even as her head tipped back to hold my gaze.

"It's the same amount of time as our appointments. It feels like the…the bubble's about to pop, or I'll wake up from the dream, or—"

Hannah's smile softened and those richly stained lips lifted to mine, her arms circling my shoulders as she pressed a soft kiss to my mouth. "It's not," she said simply.

My own smile hitched, and she kissed me once more. "Oh. Okay," I said, only a little sarcastic.

"Grab some stuff, come to the bar, meet the band since you'll be spending at least five months in close quarters with them. The bubble will continue to float," she said gently. "But it's not a dream."

I nodded and she mirrored me, smile widening before she added, "If anything, meeting the band should really set reality in. If you see us in rehearsal, you'll realize what a control freak I am."

I grinned. "Hannah, babe." I leaned forward, watching as her pupils dilated. How had one silly little word become such a siren call between us? "I knew that already."

She huffed a laugh into my kiss, mouth parted and tongue flicking out to swipe at mine. I pulled back before we could get carried away. She looked perfect, and I didn't want to muss her. Or I did, but I'd rather she was on her way to rehearsal and I was getting my things and we were standing in the same room again as soon as possible. I wanted the knowledge of us having time together to sink in. That there wasn't a clock ticking down the minutes to zero.

"Okay, I'm leaving," I murmured, more to myself, considering I was still helping myself to little sipping kisses.

"M'kay. See you soon," Hannah answered, her hands combing through my hair, tugging at my roots. I groaned and she laughed again, nudging me away with her hip, turning again to the mirror and picking gold chains off hooks that hung along the top, still fussing with her final accessories.

I'd managed to drag myself out of the bathroom and into the bedroom, hunting down my shirt, when I found myself charging back to the bathroom door.

"Hey," I blurted out.

Hannah fought her smile, eyebrows raising. "Hey."

"You're fucking beautiful."

Her cheeks flushed, which was the perfect accessory. I pulled my shirt up my chest, snapping the shoulders in place, and left her to get ready.

"So are you!" she called as I reached the stairs.

I grinned, jogging down. I hadn't given her enough compliments while I worked with her. At least not ones that didn't feel slightly staged in retrospect. And it had been the agency that provided our venues with flowers, not me. I made myself a mental list as I gathered my things and left the apartment. I would get flowers on the way to the bar to meet her, hopefully make her blush again in front of her band. I would call Khell and plan a double date.

No.

We needed dates just for the two of us first. Maybe a vegetarian cooking class. Or just a night at the local BYOB double feature movie theater.

I needed to call Khell and see if I could get some work with him before we left for the tour, save up some more money to cover my bills and take Hannah out on dates. She thought she was forming a mating attachment, and I was going to prove to her why that was absolutely the best news.

I double-checked the lock on Hannah's apartment as I

stepped outside and then paused on her stoop, considering flying home to my apartment. But Chicago hadn't changed its mind about winter, and the wind was brutal, beating hard against my coat and the tight fold of my wings the second I stepped outside. My only route home would be to fly up along the lake, and I'd be fighting against wind the whole time. Finding the bus wouldn't take much longer, and it would be less likely to leave me sore, exhausted, and frozen.

I ducked my head, hunched, and drew my wings in tight, turning to march north up Lake Shore.

I made it as far as the tiny, dark alcove between Hannah's apartment building and the next, my eyes widening as something cold and tight snagged my wing hooks, yanking me backwards. I opened my mouth, yelping as my heels skidded over ice, and another binding tug wrapped itself under my wings, tying them shut.

I tried to twist when a hand slapped over my face.

Werewolf. Wet dog and pine. My brow furrowed, and I was about to teach this fucker where he and I were respectively on the monster food chain when he stepped close behind me and growled into my ear.

"She's mine, you know." The breath was sour, and the words made me stiffen to stone, readying to tear my wings free. And then he added, with sick, dark pride, "I made her."

White-hot rage stilled me in place, my gaze sliding left to make out the fuzzy shadow behind me. He was big, I would give him that, but he was still soft meat flesh compared to me. Something I would've been happy to demonstrate if he hadn't just admitted to being the man, the monster, who'd torn Hannah open under a full moon and shattered her life to pieces.

I was considering my options—shoving him back into the brick, knocking him unconscious, dragging him back to Hannah like a cat with a kill, or maybe straight to the police—when a sudden, shattering pain blanked my vision brilliant white. I screamed into the hand that stifled my breath as a cracking pressure in my wing sapped my knees of strength.

A fucking chisel. Stabbed into me like a dagger, forcing a crack through the flesh of my wing—a small injury, but painful enough to shock my system. Whoever was behind me knew what he was doing, how to hurt me.

"Move," he hissed, and he dragged my numb and stumbling feet deeper into the shadows.

CHAPTER 26
Hannah

AT SOME POINT in the past two hours, I'd become obsessed with the hands on the clock at the corner of the rehearsal space. Maybe it was because I was fairly certain the battery was dying for how *slowly* the seconds seemed to tick by.

Or maybe it was—it definitely was—because I'd expected Rafe...almost two full hours ago.

It was three hours since he'd left my apartment and that wasn't an unexpected amount of time, but he'd acted like he hadn't wanted to be more than a few feet apart. It was sort of silly. We'd been stuck to each other for three days. I was ready for a breather...right?

I tore my gaze away from the clock once more to glance at my bandmates. Kelsey was stretching, Kiernan was winding cables, Mikey was texting, and now I was staring at the damn door, torn between the petty and wholly unreasonable worry that I'd been stood up and just...*worry* for my mate.

"Wanna tell me what's going on?" Kiernan asked, pretending to focus on the cord he was wrapping around his arm.

"Hm?" I dug my phone from my pocket for the third time

in the past five minutes and frowned once more at the blank screen.

"Han, you came in with a shit-eating grin and an *actual* swagger in your step, and now you look like a pin drop away from…I dunno what," Kiernan said, tying off the cord and dropping it to the pile. "What's going on?"

"I…my boyfriend was supposed to be coming here to meet you guys. I just kinda thought he'd get here a bit ago," I admitted. "But we didn't set a time and—"

"Your boyfriend?" Kiernan asked, smiling at me. He wagged a finger at me. "I knew it. I knew you were…" And then he laughed and shook his head. "I'm surprised you invited him to rehearsal though, Miss Our Music is Our Business."

I rolled my eyes. "I'm bringing him on tour. I wanted you to meet him."

Kiernan sobered at that. "Wait, you're what?"

His arms crossed over his chest, and my gaze bounced between him, the door, and the clock once more. Behind the happy haze of the past three days, I'd known this was going to throw the band for a loop. Bringing Rafe along for the tour would solve a lot of *my* problems, but it was also the matter of introducing him to the others, telling them rather than asking them that I needed Rafe with me. And I'd really wanted to do it *after* they'd met him. Preferably after a dinner at my apartment, so Rafe's cooking could win the crew over.

"I…" My hand itched in my pocket, and I wanted to draw my phone free again, but I was already hovering on the brink of an argument with Kiernan and that would be the last straw for him. "I wanted you guys to meet before I said something, but Rafe makes everything easier for me. As a werewolf. And I know that doesn't necessarily mean it will be easier as a band having another person on the bus, but—"

"Is he your mate?"

I turned and found Kelsey shamelessly listening into the conversation, her head tipped, and Mikey crossing to join us.

"I think so," I said softly.

"Congratulations!" She offered me a bright smile.

And for a moment, my heart soared, because yes, this was something to be happy about, something to celebrate. Kelsey belonged in the same world as me, or I belonged in hers, and she didn't question how I could've been mated, or if I was sure—the way the human part of me wanted to. She just was happy for me. Happy for the certainty and the joy that having a mate brought.

"Thank you," I said. I turned to Kiernan, and to his credit, he was staring at Kelsey, interpreting the meaning of our exchange without having to ask the questions. "It's recent. Things have changed since the last time we all met up."

"They do that with matings," Kelsey said, simple and straightforward, and I was outrageously grateful for her presence.

"He helps with the full moon?" Kiernan asked.

I nodded urgently, something like a laugh bursting out of me. "So much. And the mood swings. And he's a *really* good cook. You'll like him." And I glanced at Mikey to include him. Realistically, I thought Mikey and Rafe would probably hit it off the best of the group. They had a similar brand of boisterous enthusiasm.

"I'm glad. But you get that you're springing this on us?" Kiernan asked.

"I do, honestly. And I'm not trying to pull a power move. If you want Jess to come with us too, we'll figure it out."

Kiernan rolled his eyes. "Jess has to *work*," he said, and there was a dig in the statement that I chose not to examine for the sake of keeping the peace. And then his head tilted. "But I bet she could take a week off. She's always wanted to travel abroad."

"If I *was* going to pull a power move," I said slowly,

catching Kiernan's eye again, "I'd do it with the label, not you guys. I could probably swing us a better travel arrangement. I don't ask Virgil for much, and he'd be thrilled to lobby."

Kiernan's eyes widened, and his lips twitched. "*Wow*. You *really* want me to play nice with your boyfriend."

"I do," I admitted, wincing, finally glancing at the clock once more. "I know we're done for the day, but if he's on his way, would you guys stay to meet him?"

Kiernan shrugged and turned to pack up his guitar. "Was planning on grabbing a drink anyway."

"What species is he?" Kelsey asked bluntly, and I caught Kiernan tripping slightly at the question.

"Gargoyle," I said.

"Surprising. They're usually very staid."

"Was he the guy you fu—snuck off with at Nightlight?" Mikey asked. My eyes widened as I turned to my drummer. He grinned. "Oh, did you think no one noticed?"

I would've bet money on *Mikey* not noticing, at the very least.

"Congrats, Han," he added. "Happy to meet him."

My hand was already in my pocket, pulling my phone free. Rafe's number was freshly added, and I drew it up with a mix of nerves and excitement. I twisted on my toes, turning my back to the others, as the phone rang. Once. Twice. Three times.

And then a sudden, heavy silence. I frowned, pulling the phone away from my ear just enough to see that the timer was running and the call had gone through.

"Rafe? Are you flying?" I asked, although there was no sound of wind rushing like there ought to have been.

Instead, a low, dark chuckle cracked through the small speaker. "No…not flying. He won't be flying for a while."

There was something familiar in the tone, and I tried to recall the voices of Rafe's and Natalie's friends I'd met. Was this the orc? Or the mothman who'd hovered around me at his club and tried to bully me into elaborate drinks?

The call was quiet again.

"Who is this?" I asked, the worry that'd been itching at me for hours now finding sharp focus, cutting into my heart.

"Your mate," the voice answered. And it was not Rafe. "Your maker."

My what? *My...*

Terror and rage were hot, burning through me, the rising growl vibrating through my bones before escaping my clenched teeth.

"Where is Rafe?" I snarled.

Kiernan was approaching my side and I held my hand up, claws extended, to halt him, unsure of what my own coiling anger might result in if he reached out.

"You'll find us. You and I have a connection. Follow it."

I gaped out at the dark sky outside of the window, and the silence on the phone changed, dulled, the call cut off from the other end of the line.

"Hannah?" Kiernan prompted.

My head snapped in his direction and his eyes widened, steps falling backwards, instinct tugging him away from the threat I'd become in just seconds. Kelsey stepped between us, feathers bristling.

"What's happened?" she asked.

"Someone has Rafe," I said, and the full moon was too close for me to clear away the growl now lodged in my throat. "My..." I refused the word he'd used, shuddering at the thought. "The werewolf who attacked me. He says...we have a connection?"

Kelsey's head tipped, shaking slightly. "That's not true. It's not like vampires. Your only connection would be to your mate."

He called me his *mate.* I was going to be sick at the suggestion, my body rebelling any claim such a beast might have on me.

"Can you feel Rafe?" Kelsey asked.

I already had my phone up again, my finger sliding through old calls, searching for the number I needed most in the moment, but I paused at her question, trying to breathe through my panic and finding it snapping my heartbeat faster with every passing second. I closed my eyes and swallowed hard, a clawing ache running down my throat. *Rafe*. I needed to get to Rafe. Was it too soon? Or was the voice on the other end of the line right, and I'd only wanted him to be my mate? Had the claws that had marked my skin and changed my life taken possession of some other part of me too?

No.

The answer was clear, and it gave me the first reprieve. No, there was a tug in my chest and an ache in my shoulders, worry and nerves spiraling like a top waiting to catch its breath and crash. And it'd been there for hours. I'd assumed it was my own excitement to see Rafe, the honeymoon jitters of a new relationship, but what if…

I leaned into the feelings rather than trying to push them aside, and I found myself swaying to the left, my steps stumbling, a frightened but *safe* echo calling for me. Rafe.

I opened my eyes again, turning and running for the door, hitting the call button on my phone.

"Hannah! What do we do?" Kiernan asked.

"Hannah?"

"Ray! Please, I need your help. He has my mate."

There was a slam of a door, the buzz of voices in the background, Ray's breath uneven. "Hannah…we… I have a lead. I was waiting to tell you. Do you know where they are?"

"No," I snarled. And then I closed my eyes again, searching for that hollow tunnel towards stress and pain that was pleading for me. "West."

Ray grunted. "Where are you? I'm coming."

I STARED at the photograph in my shaking hands, blinking at the torn face in the center, the starving gaze staring back at the camera. Familiar features, and yet an almost unrecognizable person.

"You know him," Ray said.

"He said his name was Fletcher. He showed up at my group therapy," I murmured.

The scars on his face were ragged, barely held together in the photograph. I'd thought they were still healing, but only because I hadn't realized how deep they'd been to start.

Fletcher hadn't been turned into a werewolf this year. His transformation was almost a decade old.

I looked up, gasping, my mind fueled by my werewolf's instinct, steering Ray along the springy band of connection I had with Rafe. "No, no, turn right," I cried out.

Ray tensed in the driver's seat and yanked hard on the wheel, but his lights and sirens were on and no other cars moved into our path as he corrected.

"We're close," I whined, sitting up.

"We have to wait for the others. You gotta let us go in first, Hannah," Ray said.

I growled, but I was too focused on the road, on the barely visible path we needed to wind to take us to the edge of Humboldt Park, almost out of the city entirely.

"Trust me when I say that you, more than anyone, deserves to have a crack at this fucker," Ray answered, his own voice growing rough. "But we gotta do this right. Can't make any mistakes if we're gonna make sure he stays locked up this time."

"I don't care about *him*! Ray, I *need* to get to Rafe," I moaned, the seatbelt strapped across my chest biting into my throat.

Fletcher, whose real name was actually Kirk Fincher, had

attacked another woman. It was how he'd received the scars. Not from a werewolf, but after his first transformation. He'd hunted down a young woman, and she'd gouged her handful of keys into his face. But the CCTV footage had been blurry, and Fincher's defense team had made a strong argument that it'd been the woman who'd attacked first, prompting Fincher to defend himself. He'd been charged only with not seeking an appropriate safe haven for the full moon and was out on probation within a year.

I didn't blame the woman. If I'd been ready to defend myself, been facing Fincher's werewolf instead of left vulnerable with my back to him, if I'd *known* what was coming, I would've struck first too.

But not now. I meant what I'd said to Ray. The police could do whatever they wanted or had to, and I would stay out of their way...up to a point. The point being I needed to get to my mate.

"Please. I don't...I don't think you can *stop* me, Ray," I admitted, wincing and knowing that might just prompt Ray to cuff me in the backseat of the cruiser to keep me out of the way.

But he sighed. "No, I doubt it too. Can't believe you didn't introduce me to him," he muttered.

Something that ought to have been a laugh huffed out of me. A brief fantasy of dragging Rafe to meet Ray with me at Chicago Diner bubbled up in my head. *Ray, meet Rafe, my sex partner who's been helping me with full moon cravings. Rafe, meet Ray, the detective assigned to my case who's become a surrogate dad to me.*

Except then I wanted to cry a little, because I really *wanted* to have that moment between them. Just maybe not in those exact words.

"Stop!" I cried out, suddenly aware of how *close* we were, like I'd wound the tether between Rafe and I around my finger and suddenly found there was no more room to twist.

I turned in my seat, and when Ray put the car in park, I tore the seatbelt loose, reaching for the door.

"Hannah," Ray snarled in warning, and I froze, fighting back all the terror and anger and the instinctual demand that I slash him with my claws for daring to stop me from getting to my mate. "Please. At least let us go in together."

I licked my lips, but even my tongue felt dry in this moment, scraping over where I'd bitten too roughly. I nodded. Together. Together, we would help distract Fincher, make it easier for me to get to Rafe.

He was here.

Ray was quick, jumping out of the car before I'd even slid out of my seat, probably wanting to make sure he didn't lose me. He pulled a radio from his left hip and a gun from the right, calling orders into the mouthpiece, demanding backup. But he followed me as I paced a circle around his car, searching for the tether to Rafe. We were at a rundown corner of the neighborhood, vacant brownstones with broken windows facing a carryout with faded window peel advertisements, a faint glow emitting through the chipped illustrations. I paced toward the brownstones and then froze, my gut yanking me backwards.

"Hold your breath and focus for one minute, Hannah, and I swear this will go smoother and easier for us," Ray said in my ear, shoulder to shoulder with me. "Can you feel him? Is he alive?"

I nodded, whining, because Rafe was beautifully alive, determinedly hopeful, and in so much *pain*.

"You let me and the team rush in first, and you'll have a clear path right to your mate," Ray said as my feet dragged me closer.

For a second the scene, this strange, impossible moment, sank in. There was a street lamp in the corner flickering, and this far from downtown, the sky was a deeper shade of ink blue. If there were witnesses watching from windows, they hid from Ray's police car lights.

But Fincher would know.

"Hannah," Ray coaxed.

I sucked in a breath, trying to see the reason Ray offered, to convince myself that it was the right move legally and logically in this moment. But then a sharp, cracking sound came from inside, and I cried out at the faded echo of pain in my leg, launching myself forward.

Ray cursed, but he didn't grab me or try to settle me again, just charged to the door at my side. His radio was bleating at his hip, but he had both hands on his gun.

"Open the door and stand back," he said to me, pressing himself to the right of the opening, his back to the window. We were both wearing heavy, plated vests for protection, and the wolf in me wanted to disregard every word, charge inside, and follow the magnet drawing me to my suffering mate.

But Rafe had always praised me for how much control I had, teased me for it, and I held onto that, even as my claws flexed in my aching, trembling hands. I opened the door, shielded behind it.

"Kirk Fincher, come out unarmed, hands up," Ray called, but he didn't wait for an answer. His eyes widened on me once more, a new call of sirens rushing closer. "You should *not* be here," he hissed, one final protestation, and then he twisted and charged inside, gun raised.

He was right, and I hoped it didn't hurt his case, but I didn't hesitate to swing around the open door and follow him in.

"Downstairs," I whispered, focusing on the gut dropping sensation that called me down underground to Rafe. My eyes glanced wildly around the bare shelves and hollow black freezers. A single lightbulb in a cage rested on the floor down one aisle, extension cord trailing into a freezer.

But my instinct only pointed to Rafe's location. A shot thundered through the air, bouncing wildly off metal shelves and glass doors. Ray was faster than me, his arm around my shoulders yanking me to the floor, shoving me toward the dark backroom, just as one of the freezer doors on our right banged open.

"Go!" Ray snapped at me, holding me down by a hand on my back as he stood and turned.

"You found me," Fletch- *Fincher* shouted, almost jovial, and I spared him one glance. His scar was white and wild, and he was splashed with a strange, shimmering silver that made my heart pound in fear. His eyes were on me. "I told you," he said to me. "We have a con—"

I flinched, and I tore my gaze away as another shot sounded, trying hard not to assume which man was yelping. I scrambled up to my feet, rushing forward and finding the stairwell closer than I expected, nearly toppling face-first into the darkness before catching the rhythm of the stairs, running and stumbling down.

"Hannah?"

I answered Rafe's ragged voice with an animal cry, racing around a corner in the stairs, pausing at the sight of him below. Now I knew where the silver had come from.

It was Rafe's blood.

He was chained to cement blocks, wings bound with what looked like a metallic netting, and he was bleeding in sheening silver rivulets that almost blended in with his gray stone. His cheek was gouged. His wings were cracked. His clothing was torn and sullied.

"Rafe!"

There were glittering chisels on the floor, three of the four already broken and stained with silver.

Rafe looked haggard, his stone darkened under his eyes, but he flashed a smile at me as I tripped over my feet and fell to the floor in front of him, hands grappling for his chains. He grunted as I pulled at them uselessly.

"Fuck. How do I—?" I glanced over my shoulder, wondering if I had to go back upstairs. Was Ray okay? Was he *alive?*

"Cutters," Rafe said, nodding his head to the corner of the room.

My claws gouged at the dirty floor as I skidded over to the corner and came back, massive bolt cutters in my grip. Rafe groaned as he flexed his injured wings, pulling the chain taut and giving me room to maneuver. Over our heads, voices shouted and feet stamped.

"Oh god, Rafe, are you—"

"Gonna be fine," he hissed, his breath hitching as I snarled and crushed one chain link between the teeth of the cutter, freeing his left arm. "Gargoyles bleed slowly too."

A soft cry escaped my lips, but it blended into the huff of effort as I cut his other arm free.

"Gimme those and sort out the net?"

I shoved the bolt cutters into his hands and swallowed back my next cry as I rounded his back to face the wreckage of his wings. The edges were ragged. Fincher had chipped away at their beautiful curves, and there were so many cracks I was almost afraid to touch him, wondering if the net was all that was holding the flesh of his wings together at the moment.

"It's gonna be okay," Rafe whispered.

And since I was meant to be the one rescuing him in the moment, I pressed my lips flat, silenced my whine, and searched the surface of the net until I found the hook that tightened the links together.

Rafe sagged, the metal jaw of the bolt cutters clattering against the floor as the top of the net drooped open. I was gentle, pulling the metal threads free from his wing hooks, and I held my breath as it dropped to my feet, but Rafe's wings immediately stretched open and closed, like a pair of lungs taking their first breath in hours, and my own lungs burned as if they'd done the same.

My knees crumbled and my hands pressed to his back, his wings dripping blood faintly to the floor but not shattering to pieces as I'd feared.

"Rafe," I moaned, pressing my face into his neck, breath catching on a sob as his wings reached back and gently brushed against me.

"He thinks you're his mate," Rafe said.

"I *know* you're mine," I answered, growling a little, my hands sliding down to grip his sides.

"Me too," he whispered, hands covering mine, a drip of hot silver blood hitting my sleeve.

Relief left me weak, and if Rafe had asked me to stand in that moment, I would've failed to do so.

Not until Fletcher, *Fincher*, came charging down the stairs. His own blood was red, and it wept eagerly from his leg as he thunked, limping, but he had a gun held in his shaking hand and it was pointed directly at Rafe's spread wings.

I knew, in the most imperative way, that if he fired and it struck, Rafe's left wing would shatter.

I could not stand.

But I learned to fly.

A feral snarl ripped from my lips as I leapt over my mate toward the stairs.

"Hannah!" Rafe screamed.

Fincher's grin was wild and forced, all the ferocious energy he'd buried that my instinct had shied away from now revealed. But he didn't fire. Not at *me*.

I wasn't his mate. It'd taken him months to find me, and it was his search—joining and leaving werewolf group therapies around the city, signing up for and quitting shelters—that had finally left enough clues for Ray to follow. If I'd been his mate, he would've been able to do what I'd done tonight for Rafe.

He was just a man who'd tried to take what he wanted from a woman, and then created a fantasy to support his greed.

I scratched hard at the wound on his leg with one clawed hand, snatched the hand holding the gun with my other, and tackled him onto the stairs. The gun went off, but it was pointed high above Fincher's head, and he was howling and snarling, trying to kick my grip off his injury. I only dug deeper.

"You *found* me," he snarled up at me, still grinning. His eyes weren't focusing, fully black and dilated, but he was still clinging to his claim, the one some part of him knew was a lie.

"No," Rafe announced from behind me, and then he was looming over my back, one heavy stone foot planting itself on Fincher's chest, pinning him down. "She found *me*."

CHAPTER 27
Hannah

RAFE'S ARMS tightened around my shoulders, his breath hitching, but he laughed in my ear at my low snarl, and he wouldn't let me turn and glare at the medics who were tending to his wings. Swarms of police and medical officials and journalists flashing camera lights circled around us, but I kept my back to them all, holding on to the only thing that mattered.

My mate.

"I'm okay, babe," Rafe said, pressing a kiss to my temple.

The endearment was placating in a way that felt almost weaponized, but I settled in Rafe's embrace. We had nearly gotten ourselves separated by arguing with the medics about letting him hold me, and Ray had to step in on our behalf.

Speaking of…

I leaned forward, searching the swirling crowd until I saw my friend, head down and shoulders up, heading in our direction.

"Did we mess things up too much for you?" I asked Ray when he reached us.

His lips pursed, and he shrugged in a way that said 'a little.' "No one was here to see you shove me out of the way and run inside," Ray said, glancing at me and raising his eyebrows.

I fought my own grateful smile. "Right. Sorry about that."

He grunted. "But nah. Should be okay. He's talking too much now to make a good case for himself."

"Was he right?" Rafe asked, drawing mine and Ray's attention. "Could he have had a one-sided mate bond?"

"No," Ray and I said at the same time.

Rafe rubbed his cheek against my head, soothing me, and Ray continued, "No, and there's a trail of reports about him stalking women. This is a pattern of behavior, not a romantic impulse or whatever the fuck—" Ray shook his head, turning briefly away, gaze blazing.

"Thank you, Ray," I murmured.

He turned back to me, tension melting. "I'm gonna get you two outta here as soon they're done patching you up."

Behind Rafe, a medic spoke up. "Pretty much there. Gargoyle clotting makes good mortar."

I twisted to shoot a glare at the man, a large and cheerful orc, but Rafe was just grinning.

"Just need to be careful for a couple weeks. No flying, and definitely no pressure on any of the fractures for the next few days," the orc added.

"How many interviews have they put you through already?" Ray asked me.

"Three or four," I said.

He nodded. "I'll clear you. We'll talk after the full moon. You'll introduce me properly," he added, arching an eyebrow and glancing at Rafe significantly.

The full moon. It was tomorrow and Rafe was injured, and I was one wrong word away from losing my shit.

"I'll make us dinner," Rafe answered easily. He stroked the side of my thigh, and the silver sheen of the fresh scar on the back of his hand glimmered blue and red with the police lights. "Come on. Let's get home."

THIS IS A MISTAKE, I thought, growling. *I shouldn't be here.*

I was hunched on my living room floor, moonlight rushing through the bay window to coat my fur, muscles still spasming from my transformation. Downstairs, my neighbors were blaring their TV to cover the sounds of my howls, the noise too sharp for my enhanced hearing. One of my claws was caught on a strand of black yarn, torn loose from my carpet.

And above my head, pacing footsteps.

"Can I come down now?"

I snarled, but I was immediately rising on quivering limbs, darting toward the stairs before forcing myself to stop.

My front door was just to my left. I could leave. I should've left hours ago to stay at the full moon shelter, except—

"Hannah," Rafe called down from my bedroom. "Come on. It's gonna be okay."

"What if—" I flinched at the coarse tenor of my own voice, shaking my head. "What if I'm too—"

"Okay, that's it, I'm coming down."

I skidded toward the door for a moment, and then froze almost immediately. The cool, soft scent of Rafe floating down the stairs drew out a whine. My claws were noisy on the tile of my hall, my feet slipping clumsily, and I raced back to the stairs as fast as I'd tried to run from them.

"You're not going to hurt me. I'm your mate," Rafe said.

I stood, watching his approach with a starving stare. He was whole, aside from the little ragged edges on his wings, which he promised would heal within a few months. He was marked with silver, his blood sealing the wounds Fincher had inflicted, giving his stone time to harden and set. He was *mine*.

Just the thought drew out a growling purr, and Rafe smirked in answer, pausing three steps above me. I was vibrating with the need to touch him, while trembling with the fear I might hurt him. Also my tail was wagging at a wild, galloping pace, in time with the beat of my heart.

"Even Theo uses chains," I murmured.

"That's because Natalie is kinky," Rafe said, grinning. "I don't want you in chains. You *could* put me in chains."

"Rafe," I growled, trying very hard *not* to picture Rafe chained to my bed, helpless and hard and—

He laughed, and I was too distracted by the image in my head to dash out of reach when he descended the last few steps. His arms were around me before I could protest, and then refusing him was impossible, not with him pressed to me, safe and mostly whole, my muzzle tucked against his throat, hands splayed flat on his back to keep from scratching him.

"See? Isn't this better than being stuck in some dismal hotel room?" Rafe asked.

"Don't be smug," I muttered, leaning more heavily into him for a moment before remembering that we needed to be careful.

I thought I'd made up my mind to go to the shelter tonight —it seemed like the obvious choice—and then Rafe had asked the simple, seemingly innocent question of "What if something happens to me while you're gone?"

I'd nearly lost my mind.

So here I was. A werewolf. In my lovely lakeside apartment. Trying very hard not to cause further injury to my gargoyle boyfriend-slash-mate who I desperately wanted to pin to the floor and… That part was less clear at the moment. It wasn't quite sex I wanted, or not simply that. I wanted to press myself into his stone flesh and fuse our entire beings together, to know for certain that there would never be anything else that would ever come between us, that would harm him or me.

I'd always been a cat person, and this was why. Codependency was galling.

"We need to either tell them to turn it down or go upstairs," Rafe said, because the soap opera-like argument playing downstairs was audible word-for-word in our quiet embrace.

"Both," I said, instinct warning me that we were currently too close to other people while my mate was still vulnerable.

Rafe leaned back, and his injured hand dug into my hair and fur, my eyes rolling back gently at the wonderful, warm tingling his touch rushed through me. "Want popcorn?"

I wanted to cry. Mostly because he was perfect and he was right and I *did* want popcorn and I'd almost lost him the night before.

"You text, I pop," I said. It was Rafe who'd introduced himself to my neighbors anyway, planning ahead for this night even as we arrived home from the crime scene exhausted and, in my case, on edge.

And when Rafe's hand linked with mine, following me step for step into the kitchen, I sighed with relief, needing him within reach. He texted and grabbed a spice blend as I pulled a popcorn packet from the box, scowling at the way it slipped clumsily in my claws. He stretched our arms between us as he pulled butter from the fridge. When I flinched at the popping sounds, he dragged me closer, wrapping one arm around me, covering my ears, and warmed the butter in a pan on the stove with the spices. I was meant to be taking care of him, or at least that was my intention, but something was cracking inside of me, mimicking the lines of silver now decorating his skin. His hand soothed down my back and paused over my scars.

"Hmm. We match now."

It was too close to my own thoughts. Fincher had grabbed

Rafe as punishment and as bait. I was the reason my mate had been put in danger, if not the one to blame. And Rafe was just…being calm and cute and never complaining, even though I'd seen him wincing in the shower earlier when the water had rinsed over his wings.

A werewolf weeping is a peculiar sound—a woofing, barking, whining noise, my human cries mingling in my animal throat.

"Shit, sorry," Rafe whispered, shoving the pan from the heat and gathering me fully against his chest, squeezing too hard to be safe for the crack of silver along his ribs. "I'm all right, Hannah. I'm okay. I'm here."

"He could've killed you!" I snarled, my hands hovering at his sides, wanting to clasp onto him but afraid to.

"Nahhh," Rafe said.

I leaned back, eyes wide and baffled, and gaped at him.

Rafe blinked down at me. "Woulda taken a really long time. Gargoyle thing," he said, shrugging. "And he had shitty tools."

My jaw hung open, and Rafe's eyes were big and honest, his expression even. I had other points to argue—mainly that Rafe being slowly chiseled to death wasn't *better* than Fincher being quick about it—but Rafe's hands rose to cup my face and he leaned down, pressing a kiss to the tip of my nose.

"I knew my mate was on her way," he murmured, head tipping to kiss my jaw, then leaning in and burrowing his face into my fur.

I shuddered, and my arms wrapped tight around Rafe's back, my eyes fixed to the rivulets of silver that marked Rafe's wings, matching us as a set, and wished I'd taken the opportunity to tear Fincher's throat out when I'd had the chance.

RAFE WAS heavy on top of me, an anchor as the transformation tore through me the next day, leaving me panting on my bed, sore and exhausted. But the night had been quiet and easy, the pair of us staying tangled up together. Whatever anxious urges I ought to have had were pushed aside with the need to touch and soothe and cuddle with my mate. It was almost restful, if only my mind hadn't been caught in a spiral of intrusive thoughts.

"Shower?" Rafe asked, stretching on top of me as my body settled back to human.

A shower would be good—a bath would be even better—but I shook my head. He lifted himself up on his elbows and stared down at me.

"What's wrong?" he asked, frowning.

I blinked up at him, trying to find the right words in the right order to explain myself.

"I...still wish it hadn't happened," I answered in a whisper.

Rafe's brow furrowed. "I mean, listen, I'm not saying I had a good time either."

I pressed my lips together and shook my head. "Not that. I mean, obviously I wish Fincher hadn't been able to hurt you, but I...mean I wish he hadn't turned me into a werewolf."

"*Should* you wish he had?" Rafe asked.

"Shouldn't I?"

We stared at one another for a moment, mutually puzzled, and then Rafe's expression cleared and softened. His lips curved and his head ducked, resting against my forehead. He was warmer like this, after we'd spent hours cuddling and lying in the sun, his stone soaking up the heat.

"Because you being a werewolf is why we met?" Rafe asked.

I nodded, and he rose up just enough to share his grin with me.

"Like, I want us to be *us*, and....and I want you to be my

mate, and none of that happens if I'm not a werewolf. I'd almost actually gotten to a place where I was…" I trailed off in my ramble. Before Fincher had grabbed Rafe, I'd not been thrilled to be a werewolf, but I'd been moving toward acceptance.

"Nothing changes our relationship now, Hannah," Rafe said, still smiling. "You don't have to run hypotheticals, and I'm not going to be hurt or offended that you wish you hadn't suffered through Fincher's attack or what he put us through. We *are* mates, even if the chain of events wasn't ideal."

I huffed at the understatement of Rafe being kidnapped and *chiseled* as 'not ideal,' and Rafe shrugged.

"I love you," he murmured, reaching up and stroking the backs of his fingers over my cheek and down my throat. "And because I love you, I'm never going to look at your scars and say to myself, 'gosh, I'm sure glad Hannah was hurt so we could have a reason to fuck each other straight into matehood.'"

I snorted, and Rafe's expression brightened at my growing smile. "I just thought I was supposed to say something like… like about how I'm grateful it happened 'cause it brought me to you."

Rafe's lips pressed flat and his cheeks turned warm even as stone. And then he let out a sharp bark of laughter, and I rolled my eyes.

"Sorry! Sorry, that just…doesn't sound like you," he said.

I sighed and softened into the bed, reaching a hand up to pet at his smooth chest. He'd told me once he was more sensitive as stone. It meant he'd felt those chisel marks even more intensely, which made me queasy to think about. It also meant…

I stretched up, kissing his shoulder as Rafe hummed and sighed.

"I love you," I said, brushing my lips over the same spot again and again until I thought Rafe's stone was starting to prickle with goosebumps. I shimmied down into the sheets, giving myself access to more of his chest to touch and kiss. "You are the tastiest, sweetest, funniest, sexiest part of my life now, Rafe."

And maybe I wished Fincher hadn't attacked me, but I wouldn't have turned back time to change it either.

I licked over Rafe's nipple, humming as his cock stiffened against my side. "How do we make this work so I don't hurt you?" I asked, tilting my head back to find his soft and hungry gaze on mine.

Rafe blinked slowly, smile crooked. He shook his head. "I don't know. But you've always managed it before." There was something secret in those words that I would ask the meaning of later. For now…

I slithered back up, pushing pillows out of my way and raising my arms up over my head to grab onto the iron bars of my headboard. "I think you'd better hold me down."

Rafe's eyes widened. "Really? You don't want…you don't want to be in charge?"

I blushed. "We haven't really had time to get to know each other's tastes, I guess. I…I'm only a control freak when a full moon's coming up. The rest of the time, I kind of like when…" I glanced over at my posed arms and back at Rafe, strangely shy of what I was asking for.

But Rafe looked like a kid who'd just been told to pick out everything he wanted at the toy store. He sat up on his knees, now fully erect, and stared down at the bare stretch of me. His eyes were on mine as he scooped up my right ankle, swinging it around his hips to hold me open. I hummed and rocked my hips up in invitation as Rafe laughed.

"Huh. Now I'm the one nervous about hurting you. I'm… heavy like this," he said.

"I love it," I said, smiling. "I have since that first night."

He licked his lips and then leaned forward, his hands

cupping around my wrists, pushing them down into the mattress. I sighed at his grip, firm and immovable.

"I'm stronger too," he said, staring at his hands on me.

I curled one leg, rubbing it against his hips. "That just means I can struggle and still not get my way," I said, arching my back to show him how tight my nipples were at the thought.

He swallowed hard, voice dropping. "And if I get too rough?"

I bit my lip at that. "We should be careful till you're healed. But…I dare you to try."

Rafe groaned, and then he gifted me with that weight and strength, with a rough and hungry kiss, tongue plunging in to stroke against mine. His hips landed between my legs, cock stroking against my sex, slow and careful. I moaned when I tried to pull my hands free and found them thoroughly cuffed in his grasp, and Rafe pulled away, beaming in response.

"Oh, Hannah…I have a *lot* I want to do," Rafe murmured, nuzzling our noses together.

"I'm yours to play with then," I said, nipping at his lips. He bucked against me, breaths huffing. "Your toy. Your mate."

Rafe let out an uncharacteristic growl, and I yelped as he plunged inside of me with one deep thrust. I was wet, and he was gloriously polished, but the demand of the stretch and depth was enough to wipe all teasing from my mind.

"Mine," Rafe snarled, baring his teeth, gaze glowing down on me. He moaned as he pulled out, grunted and winced as he slammed back in.

I wanted to tell him to be careful, to consider his injuries, but I'd offered him the reins and he'd looked too thrilled for me to take them back now. Also his rhythm was robbing me of speech and thought—rough and heavy and briefly brutal, sure to leave bruises on the inside of my thighs.

I gasped, my hand twisting to grip the headboard, eyes

wide at his force, and Rafe paused, staring down at me, his hunger fracturing.

"My love," he whispered. I relaxed and arched my neck for his kiss.

Rafe's hands swept mine together, and then his newly freed arm banded under my chest, holding me closer as he took my mouth in a feasting kiss, biting my lips and laving the bruises with his tongue. His cock surged and stroked, buried deep, and my legs twined around his hips.

"I love you," we gasped out together—a panting, pleading, praising refrain as fire lit in my veins. "I love you."

His hands grew too greedy, unsatisfied with binding mine any longer, and then he touched and gripped and stroked me everywhere. I took his face in my palms, afraid to touch his wings, and sealed our lips together in rich and messy kisses that muffled my cries as I came in bursts of heat and clinging trembles.

And in spite of what I'd said to Rafe just minutes ago, I was suddenly desperately grateful to anything and everything in my life that had brought me to this man.

CHAPTER 28
Rafe

"TAKE THAT! HA!"

"Go to *hell*, Hannah."

I grinned, watching Hannah trounce Natalie at another round of darts. At my side, Theo sucked in a breath and swallowed the last of his drink.

"I need to go intervene," he said.

I raised my eyebrows. "Do you?"

Theo's smile was sheepish. "Natalie's a sore loser."

I was going to say that Nat had never seemed sore during our games, and then I realized that was because she'd always won. I cupped my hands to my mouth and called across Nightlight.

"Good job, babe, you kicked her ass."

"Oh, thanks, that helps," Theo muttered, stifling his laugh as Natalie glared daggers at me and Hannah just rolled her eyes.

Elias passed Theo, and it took me a moment to register seeing the mothman out from behind his bar. He had a basket of fried pickles in one hand and a shot of what looked like his ghost pepper moonshine in the other.

"Here," he said, passing me the food and drink. He pulled

a stool out from his bar and sat down next to me, staring at our friends. "How are you?"

Hannah was twisting her hair up off her neck, revealing a hickey I'd left that I was pretty sure she didn't know about yet. Natalie was still fuming, but Theo and Hannah were smoothing the way with some distracting conversation, from what I could tell.

"I'm really good," I said, grinning in a way I knew would baffle Elias.

But when I glanced at him, I found his stare fixed to my scars. "And your wings?"

I blinked. "Were you worried about me, Elias?"

"A bit," he said, meeting my eyes.

Which was startling.

"Khell told me you were healing," he said.

Khell had texted after the full moon to check in on my "mating progress" with Hannah, and I'd updated him on the events that had passed. Hannah had spoken with Theo too. One direction or another, the news would've reached Elias, but I hadn't reached out to the moth fae directly.

Smirking, I opened my phone and started a group chat between Khell, Theo, Elias, and myself, sending a pickle emoji and nothing else. Elias pulled out his phone and stared at the text, at the screen, at the names listed, and then put it back in his pocket.

"How did it happen?" he asked instead.

"Uhhh. Fincher followed Hannah home. Must've been watching us, 'cause he—"

"Not that," Elias said. "I read the police report—"

"Elias, *how* did you get the police—"

"How did you end up in love with a client?"

I gaped at him briefly and then shook my head, popping the questions that bubbled up. He wouldn't answer them anyway.

I had asked Khell a similar question when he'd quit MSA,

unable to fathom forming an emotional attachment to any of my own clients.

"I fell in love with Hannah," I said, shrugging. "Not a client. I got to *know* her because… I dunno. She wasn't what I expected, and that made me curious about who she *was*. And it seemed impossible, until it didn't. We have to know what pleases our clients, what arouses them and relaxes them, what their boundaries are. And generally that's part of work, a list to follow. But then this *one* time, everything was just really natural. She fit with who I am and what arouses and relaxes me, and what my boundaries are too."

"Do you think Astraeya knew that when she paired you?" Elias asked me, black gaze somehow sharper than usual.

"I don't think she could have," I admitted. "I wasn't really being honest with MSA at the time about some of my boundaries. I had changed. *But* Astraeya is really good at her job, and ya know, a succubus too, so who knows? Maybe."

Elias hummed and nodded, turning back to stare at our friends.

A faint, itching suspicion rose in my mind, and my eyes narrowed. "Elias…*why*?"

"I'd like to try it."

"Try…?"

"Falling in love," he said.

I gaped at him for a moment, and it was impossible to tell with his eyes, but I was fairly sure he was glancing at me out of the corners. One hundred arguments to pose against Elias's clinical curiosity to "try falling in love" rose to my tongue. Love wasn't an experiment. MSA had been more of an obstacle for me and Khell than a boon. *Hunting* for love was sure to end in disaster.

Except, damn, it would be fun to watch.

"*RAFE!*"

I groaned, pressing my face into Hannah's throat, my fingers digging into her back, tucked under her loosened shirt. I *really* loved it when she said my name like that. She grew limp in my embrace, giving over to the wave of sensation rushing through her, and I tightened my arms around her waist, beating my wings against the sudden whip of wind.

I forced my eyes open, refusing to give in to the plea of her cunt clasping on my length, aware that my body was already a little too focused on Hannah in my arms instead of keeping us safely in the air as I'd promised.

Hannah's legs twined around my waist as she settled, her own cheek coming to rest on my bare shoulder. Her skin was chilling, and I needed to get her back inside soon, even with her warm werewolf blood pulsing through her veins.

"Is this the mile-high club?" she murmured, giggling almost drunkenly.

"Not remotely!" I grinned and kissed her cheek, bundling Hannah closer, trying to shield her against the wind even as we had to turn and brace into it to reach the spires of Tribune Tower.

She'd brought me up to her dad's apartment after I'd explained why I was hovering outside of it the night of the party. He was safely back out of town now. Making out by the windows had become fooling around on the balcony, which had somehow turned into, *"Can gargoyles have sex while flying?"*

We could, as it turned out. I hadn't tried it before.

"Oh my god," Hannah squeaked out, fingers clutching against my skin.

"I told you not to look down."

Her thighs clamped tighter around my hips and I laughed, tucking her face back into my shoulder as I flew us the few feet back to the tower.

"I had to peek," she breathed. "Not inside yet! Just maybe…somewhere with something we can hold onto."

I found an ornate perch along the balustrade in front of her dad's apartment. It'd been my usual spot anyway—I could enjoy the architecture of the building, but out of the way of rough winds.

"You hold onto me, and I'll keep us steady," I said, bringing my wings up just enough to shelter Hannah. She was already starting to shiver, so we wouldn't be outside for much longer, but her eyes were drinking in the city eagerly, and she stretched on my lap to peek around my wings.

"I never get sick of this view," I said, staring at her, smiling to myself as she hummed in agreement. Another gust barreled into us, whipping Hannah's hair around her face, and she squeaked slightly, clinging to me. "Are you scared?" I asked.

The time to be scared had been when I was thrusting into her four hundred feet off the ground. Not that she'd been capable of much thinking at the time.

"I…" She blinked and glanced at me. "A bit. I talked about how scared I was at the meeting today."

I leaned away just enough to catch her eye. "Of Fincher?"

She frowned, shaking her head. "No, I mean…no. Of…of the tour. Of the future. Of what life will be like if the band becomes famous, or if it doesn't." She waved a hand and then sank into my chest. "I know I don't have to worry, but I do sometimes."

I fit her head under my chin, spread my wings, and curled them around us to block out the wind and the noise and the cold. Worries came and went, even I knew that. I worried about being a useless mate, about how Hannah might feel burdened on the tour, essentially supporting me. About how presumptuous it would be to ask to move in when we'd only really started dating. She had the mating bond, I knew, but she'd still been human up until the past year, and I didn't want her to feel cornered or rushed.

But in this moment, with this woman, I was calm and content in a way I hadn't been for most of my life.

"Although now that you mentioned it, I am starting to feel the height," she mumbled, huffing a nervous laugh.

I stroked her back, kissed her hair. "I won't let you fall," I said.

Hannah twisted, kissing my jaw and then finding my gaze, and my promise took on more weight, wanting to fill the gaps to all her fears, not just the height.

"I know," she said, smiling. I ducked my head to meet her lips with mine, catching her murmur. "I won't let you fall either."

EPIL☾GUE

RAFE - SEVERAL MONTHS LATER

"THANK YOU SO MUCH, London, you've been incredible! We've got one last song for you tonight, and to be honest, it's a bit of a dumb dad joke my boyfriend suggested." There was an inexplicable cheer from the audience, and I grinned as Hannah glanced over her shoulder toward me in the wings of the stage, her eyes rolling lightly. "Yeah, I have a soft spot for those too. So here's a classic—"

Vic stepped up to my side. He was the orc stagehand for our touring partners, The Disasters, and he'd become a fan of Sorry, Darling and cheerfully lended his help whenever he could.

"*I saw a werewolf with a Chinese menu in his hand,
Walking through the streets of SoHo in the rain.*"

Vic barked the words of the verse out with Hannah, but he and the whole audience held their breath as she howled.

"*Awoooo, werewolves of London!*"

The crowd erupted and Hannah faltered, just for a

moment, a husky laugh following seductively after her sharp howl.

It was the last night of the tour. Virgil Darwood had a chartered plane, and it was waiting to take us home in the morning. My mate was flushed and sweaty and giddy, bouncing across the stage with the microphone fisted in her grip. We'd just come off a full moon, and she'd still had the slightly stiff gait of bruised bones this morning, but all of that tension had unwound by the time she reached the stage. Ilsa, the lead singer of The Disasters, had watched the set and had said, in a perfect offhand, that Hannah had the kind of natural performance energy of her father. I hadn't mentioned that one to Hannah yet, not sure how she'd really take it, and I'd never seen Virgil perform, but I suspected Ilsa was probably right. Hannah held the audience in the palm of her hand from the moment the stage lights rose and she stared out at them from those vivid, hooded eyes.

And as soon as the stage lights went down and she'd taken her final deep breath of the cheering and turned toward the wings, she was all mine again.

I stretched my wings slightly, arms parted in invitation, and Hannah sighed as she took her place in my embrace, my cooler temperature a relief against her stage light flushed skin.

"You did it."

"I did it," she whispered back, tucking her chin over my shoulder.

I backed us carefully through the churning traffic of backstage activity as Vic and the others set up for The Disasters' set. I tucked us into a clear corner, and Hannah sagged against my chest, snuggling closer.

"So when's the next tour?" I asked, fighting my laugh as she growled into my throat. I had a tender spot there where she'd nearly chipped her tooth trying to mark me when we'd gotten a little rowdy and playful on the previous full moon.

"Don't let the others hear you," Hannah muttered, and over her shoulder I saw Mikey play wrestling with the other band's drummer, and Kiernan and Kelsey cheersing one another with frothing red cups.

The tour had gone smoothly. No, that was an understatement. It had been a huge success for Sorry Darling. Their first released single was already starting to chart, gaining them their own loyalty from the audiences at the start of the concerts. But Hannah had been right in guessing the insane hours and close quarters would challenge her as a werewolf. There hadn't been any blowups, just a few sharp words and some tense silences when the togetherness grew to be too much, but I knew she was exhausted, and I had elaborate plans for us to take some time in isolation together when we got back to Chicago.

"I know we should stay and watch and celebrate with the others," Hannah started, her voice barely audible beneath the bustle around us, "but do you think..."

"I was going to suggest we see if we can fly up and fuck on Big Ben—"

Hannah laughed and leaned back in my arms to share her huge smile with me. "London would send the sky patrol after us."

Paris certainly had. As it turned out, Notre Dame had its own gargoyle guards for just such a purpose, and while they'd been sympathetic with me, Hannah and I had probably narrowly avoided getting arrested.

"Then I guess we could just walk back to the hotel and fire up the jacuzzi jets," I said, shrugging.

Hannah sighed, her smile softening and her eyes sliding shut as she nodded. "Please."

We said our goodbyes for the night—we'd see everyone in the morning for a big tour breakfast at a restaurant we'd reserved—and then slid out of the backdoor of the venue, into the muggy summer air of London. Hannah paused on the top step, taking a deep breath, but her nose immediately wrinkled and I pulled her down and away from the dumpsters, out toward the busy streets. Our hotel was only a few blocks away, and we walked hand in hand in silence, letting the city flow around us.

"What's today's menu for the supper club?" Hannah asked, leaning her head on my shoulder.

"I've been thinking about the egg rice we had in Japan," I said, a little flutter in my chest. Hannah nodded against me and I continued, telling her about all the new dish combinations I'd been imagining composing together for my first ever supper club event. It'd been Elias's idea, actually. I might want to be a chef, but I would always want to be with Hannah when she was on tour, and that made owning a restaurant pretty unrealistic. But with Hannah and Elias's help, I'd managed to organize a rental space to run as a test kitchen for my recipes and an event space to hold an exclusive, eight-course dinner party. Elias had sold out the tickets for me before I'd even fully reconciled myself to the plan, and every time it seemed a little impossible to imagine, Hannah would talk me back from the ledge and listen to me ramble for two hours about all the different sauce preparations I knew and flavor combinations I wanted to try.

"Two months probably isn't enough time to—"

"Two months is how much time you have. Elias definitely isn't letting you change your mind now," Hannah said, cutting me off before I could spiral again. "And anyway, you really only have a month before Gilda Buckingham comes to your test kitchen to give you feedback."

My steps stumbled, and some poor Londoner ran into one of my wings at my sudden stop in the middle of the sidewalk.

"Gilda Buckingham?! Hannah! Did you—?"

She shook her head, smirking. "Virgil. I warned you. He loves to meddle. And Gilda is a fan and a friend of his. Dad told me today he made the plans for you."

I gaped at Hannah and ran a hand over my face. Gilda fucking Buckingham. In my kitchen. Trying my food. *Telling me what she thought.*

"Don't panic. You'll have another month to use the feedback. And you've already given this so much thought. You're just stalling at this point."

I glared at Hannah but she shrugged, unrepentant, and tugged on my hand, pulling me back into motion and through the doors of our hotel.

Virgil did seem to like to meddle, as Hannah put it, although after meeting the man I was pretty sure that flexing his influence was the only way he knew how to show his love for his daughter. And once Hannah explained the mating situation to Virgil, he'd seemed to cheerfully take me on as a son-in-law, occasionally texting me to let me know what kind of reservations he'd made for us on our travels. Our fairy-rock-star-father.

"Only having one month to prepare for Buckingham really cuts in on my plan to spend two weeks locked in the apartment with you without seeing or speaking to anyone," I said.

Hannah frowned at that for a moment, realizing the sacrifice she'd just made, but then she shook her head. "Nice try. But we have to eat. You'll have plenty of time to experiment in my kitchen."

She pressed the button for the elevator and it dinged immediately, doors opening to let us inside. I hit the button to close them behind us before anyone else might appear, then crowded Hannah to the glossy brass wall. She laughed, that same low and smoky note of humor she'd shared with the crowd back at the concert, and I nuzzled down against her throat for a moment before lifting my head once more to meet her gaze.

"I love you," I said.

Hannah's eyes watered, and she wet her lips before answering me. "I love you too."

"I love our future." There'd be more tours, more traveling. I'd make this damn supper club a success, and Virgil would probably talk me into holding one in London next time we were around.

We had scars to match, and we had one of the less conventional starts to a relationship—then again, we weren't even the first in my circle of acquaintances to meet through the agency—and we'd probably never be the picket-fence couple. But I'd never be bored, and Hannah would never be scared of herself, and we'd walk hand in hand toward whatever came next.

"I love our future," Hannah murmured, rising on her toes to slide her lips against mine, a perfect fit.

Afterword

Welcome to the Monster Smash Agency!

This series is a fun model for me where I post in progress chapters on my Patreon and then later rewrite, edit, polish and publish the series wide!

I am currently drafting and posting a new series on my Patreon (omegaverse Gaslamp fantasy dragons anyone??) but as soon as that book is wrapped up I'll be working on Lessons with the Mothman! I'm really excited about Elias's book. I haven't named the FMC yet, so I'm open to suggestions, but I can say their story will include consensually non-monogamy and two people who absolutely do NOT understand the concept of love trying make sense of romance.

If serial chapter reading isn't for you, I promise to bring Lessons with the Mothman to book seller platforms later in 2024!

Also by Kathryn Moon

COMPLETE READS

The Librarian's Coven Series

Written

Warriors

Scrivens

Ancients

Standalones

Good Deeds

Command The Moon

Say Your Prayers - co-write with Crystal Ash

Secrets of Summerland

The Sweetverse

Baby + the Late Night Howlers

Lola & the Millionaires - Part One

Lola & the Millionaires - Part Two

Bad Alpha

Faith and the Dead End Devils

Sol & Lune

Book 1

Book 2

Inheritance of Hunger Trilogy

The Queen's Line

The Princess's Chosen
The Kingdom's Crown

Tempting Monsters
A Lady of Rooksgrave Manor
The Basilisk of Star Manor (novella)
The Company of Fiends
Sanctuary with Kings

SERIES IN PROGRESS

Sweet Pea Mysteries
The Baker's Guide To Risky Rituals
The Knitter's Guide to Banishing Boyfriends
The Florist's Guide to Summoning Saints (coming 2024)

Monster Smash Agency
Games with the Orc
Howl for the Gargoyle
Lessons with the Mothman (coming 2024)

Dragonkin Series
The Alpha of Bleake Isle (coming 2024)

Acknowledgments

Every acknowledgements page ought to grow longer than the last because the more I write the wider my community and support stretches. I'm so grateful to everyone who's joined me on this journey, guided me, propped me up when I wanted to wobble, and read my work! Authors are incredible people, and they make amazing friends!

Special thanks in the Howl for the Gargoyle crew includes my babe Whoop for being my brain. My beta babes, Kathryn, Ash, Jess, and Amanda! Jess and Meghan, for taking turns editing and tidying my words. Sophie for my beautiful cover, and playing along as I gushed about the Tribune Tower All of the astonishingly talented artists who provided art (shared on Patreon) and most especially my patrons who were willing to take a chance on a weekly chapter update model.

As always, thank you to my family and friends, my readers, and my little furry supervisor, Coraline.

About the Author

Kathryn Moon is a country mouse who started dictating stories to her mother at an early age. The fascination with building new worlds and discovering the lives of the characters who grew in her head never faltered, and she graduated college with a fiction writing degree. She loves writing women who are strong in their vulnerability, romances that are as affectionate as they are challenging, and worlds that a reader sinks into and never wants to leave. When her hands aren't busy typing they're probably knitting sweaters or crimping pie crust in Ohio. She definitely believes in magic.

You can reach her on Facebook and at ohkathrynmoon@gmail.com or you can sign up for her newsletter!

www.ingramcontent.com/pod-product-compliance
Ingram Content Group UK Ltd.
Pitfield, Milton Keynes, MK11 3LW, UK
UKHW040755010525
5720UKWH00013B/42

9 781959 571247